BLOOD TIDE

BLOOD TIDE

Wayne Barcomb

HotHouse PRESS

For information about permission to reproduce or transmit selections from
this book in any form or by any means, write to:

Permissions, Hot House Press
760 Cushing Highway
Cohasset, MA 02025

This is a work of fiction, names, characters, places and incidents are either
the product of the author's imagination or are used fictitiously.

Library of Congress Cataloging-in-Publication Data

Barcomb, Wayne
    Blood tide/by Wayne Barcomb
        p. cm.
    ISBN 0-9700476-2-2 (hardcover)
1. Sarasota (Fla.)—Fiction. 2. Women scientists—Fiction. 3.
Policewomen—Fiction. 4. Red tide—Fiction. 5. Tourism—Fiction. I.
Title.
    PS3602.A775B57 2003
    813'.6—dc21

                    2003007511

Printed in the United States of America

Book design by DeNee Reiton Skipper

Hot House Press
760 Cushing Highway
Cohasset, MA 02025
www.hothousepress.com

To my wife, Susan, for all she is and does.

ACKNOWLEDGEMENTS

I am indebted to many people for their help with *Blood Tide*, particularly several law enforcement people in and around Sarasota. My thanks to Chris Iorio of the Sarasota County Sheriff's office, Kevin Churchill, Greg Grodoski, and Larry Blair of the Sarasota Police Department, homicide detective Julie Massuchi of the Tampa, FL Police Department, and Lieutenant Ron Albritton of the Sarasota County Sheriff's Department. Private Investigator Roy Winkleman rounded out my education of investigative tactics and techniques.

A special thanks to Richard Pierce, Ph.D. of the justly famed Mote Marine Laboratory and Aquarium for providing me with information and insights on red tide and to Carol Thomas of Century 21 Advantage Real Estate Co. for bringing to my attention Granville Wilde's photograph used on the jacket.

My deepest thanks to four people who read the manuscript and offered enthusiastic endorsements, Robert B. Parker, multi-award winning best selling author; John Lutz, Edgar Award winner and former president of the Mystery Writers of America; Howard Kaminsky, former president, Random House, Warner Books, and William Morrow publishers, and a highly successful writer himself; and Steve Johnson, novelist and screen writer.

Wayne Barcomb
Sarasota, Florida

1

Sam Wallace knew something was up when he entered Bob Cramer's office and saw Dean Siebert Gibney sitting next to him. Departmental evaluations were only held between the faculty member and the department chairman.

"Come in, come in, Sam," Cramer said, rising to greet him. The dean remained seated, ignoring Sam.

Sam stood for a moment, observing the forced bravado coming from the normally phlegmatic Cramer. The beads of sweat lining Bob's forehead like shiny little pimples, were not a good sign either.

"Good morning, Bob," Sam said, and shook the extended hand of his chairman. What the hell is this? He thought. He'd been in his office a thousand times, and they had never shaken hands. They'd just had coffee together an hour ago.

"Come over and sit down, Sam," Cramer said, beckoning him to a chair in front of his desk. Cramer sat behind the desk next to the dean. "I've asked Dean Gibney to join us for this morning's evaluation session," he said.

Sam sat facing the two men, feeling like an applicant before the parole board. "Good morning, Siebert," he said, using the dean's first name as he always did.

Gibney looked at him for the first time, and managed a tepid smile. "Good morning."

Hmm. No good morning, Sam, huh. He knew trouble when he saw it and braced himself.

Cramer placed his hands on his desk, folded them, and leaned forward. "Let's get started, shall we?"

Sam glanced at the open pendaflex file sitting on Cramer's desk— his file. "Sounds good to me, Bob." He smiled at the dean, but got nothing back.

Cramer brushed the sweat pimples off his forehead and began. "Sam. You've been a member of the Whately faculty now for six years. We're all very much aware of what a fine teacher you are." He glanced at Dean Gibney, who nodded.

"Thank you, Bob," Sam said and smiled again at the grim faced dean.

"Your teaching is, of course, the biggest plus in our evaluation of your performance," the chairman continued. "Three years in a row the students have voted you Teacher of the Year, your classes are always oversubscribed, and your rapport with students is admirable."

Sam nodded. What was all this praise? Was he being set up? He waited for the other shoe to fall.

"And frankly, Sam, it's because of your teaching record that we have chosen to overlook the negatives in your file." Cramer tapped the folder on his desk.

"Negatives, Bob?"

"Come on, Sam." Cramer sat erect, his body language letting Sam know the gloves were off. "A less tolerant administration would have taken action long ago." Again he glanced at Gibney and received another nod of approval.

"Well," Sam drawled and ran his hand through the dark curly hair until it reached the small bald spot in back. "I guess the truth of the matter is, I'm not an easy man. I can be an entertaining one, though." He knew it was the wrong thing to say the moment he said it. But at least he stayed in character.

Cramer ignored the remark and pushed on. "Let me review some of the problems we have endured during your service here at Whately, Sam. Let's start with your working nights as a bartender at one of the most notorious strip joints in Boston. You— "

"Wait a second, Bob," Sam interrupted. "You and everyone else know that I did that for only four months to gather material for an article for the *Boston Globe*—for which I might add, I received an award for excellence in investigative journalism. I was, in fact, told that my article was instrumental in cleaning up Boston's Combat Zone. Anyway, I only worked one night a week." He nodded and smiled at the dean, who turned away.

"Goddamn it, Sam. That's not the point. How do you think it reflected on Whately College, when word began coming back that one of our professors was tending bar at the Two O'clock Lounge? Our own students saw you there."

Sam shrugged.

"And the childish stunt you pulled on Professor Sherman, completely disrupting her music class and the mood of her students as she played Debussey's *Clouds* for them."

Sam shook his head. "Bob, that was all in good fun. I saw a Frisbee land on the ledge outside my office, opened the window and went out to retrieve it. I remembered that Sherman's classroom was a few feet along the ledge, so just for fun, I strolled by and waved. No big deal."

"Sam, the ledge is on the fifth floor. You walked past flapping your arms like you were floating. The students didn't know the ledge was there. You completely disrupted the class and destroyed the mood she had created."

"The kids liked it. Anyway, that's old news, Bob."

"It's a part of your record. And your latest stunt was simply beyond the pale—depositing a dead skunk in Professor Piro's office. We'll never get the odor out of his office."

Sam looked at the dean and back to Cramer. "Bob, I came home and found Professor Piro in bed with my wife. What would you have done?"

"Piro has been reprimanded and disciplined. We live in a civilized society, Sam, but you march to your own drummer. You always have."

"Yes, I remember you telling me I was an 'independent bastard' after my first month in your department." He was getting his back up now, and fighting off the urge to tell them both to go fuck themselves.

Cramer continued. "On a more substantive issue, you have been reminded repeatedly that academic research and the publication of scholarly papers in learned journals are the criteria for performance here at Whately. You have chosen to ignore this in favor of writing articles for the popular press and books of fiction. Mystery books." He uttered the last two words as though he had just bit into a lemon.

Sam tugged at his hair and spread his palms out. "Bob, my first novel has received critical acclaim and has been nominated for an Edgar Award. My most recent article on the "Societal Significance of City Street Gangs" appeared in the *New York Times Magazine*. That's not too shabby. I like to think it reflects as well on Whately as would an arcane treatise on the *Statistical Analysis of the Kuomintang Interlude* in a journal that nobody reads."

Cramer filled his water glass from the carafe on his desk and took his time sipping the water. He exchanged looks with the dean and stroked his chin.

Oh, oh, Sam thought. They're moving in for the kill. He didn't want to leave Whately. He liked it here. He loved working with students, and he enjoyed the intellectual stimulation of his colleagues, with whom he was as popular as with the students—except for that asshole, Piro.

Even Cramer grudgingly acknowledged his value as a teacher and mentor, but he was a stickler for rules and order, and it was no secret that he found Sam—what was his favorite word for him—exasperating. And Gibney sitting over there like a sphinx, with the imagination and creativity of a slug. His favorite word was decorum.

Somehow, he'd managed to finesse them over the years and keep them out of his hair. But at the moment, he smelled blood. And more importantly, they did. "Bob, each time I come up for contract renewal, we have a discussion like this, and each time you and Siebert—Dean Gibney—receive letters of support for me from faculty and students. I think I have made substantial contributions to the college, and can only say, I want to continue to do so." That was it. He would say no more.

Cramer looked toward the dean. Gibney rose from his chair and walked to the window. He returned to Sam and cleared his throat. "Sam, Professor Cramer and I have recommended to the Board of Trustees that your contract not be renewed. The Board has accepted our recommendation." Gibney sat and nodded to Cramer, like, "The deal is done."

The chairman had the last word. "I'm sorry, Sam."

* * *

Sam stood in his apartment, sipping one of his deep dish martinis. He opened the French doors and looked down the hill to the Public Gardens. A man and woman about his age strolled hand in hand toward the Common.

He slammed the doors and finished his martini. His marriage was over, and now so was his job. What now? He went looking for Henry, hoping to find some solace, but found him sound asleep in the back bedroom.

He picked up his baseball glove and softball and paced around the apartment, throwing the ball into the glove. "Not the end of the world," he said aloud. Since the divorce, he'd begun talking to himself.

OK. He'd stashed away the advance from his book. It was selling well. He just got a nice advance for three more novels in the series, and he had a reasonable amount of money in his stock portfolio. He would get by.

Suddenly Boston had little appeal to him, and he had no idea where he was going from here. He would keep writing, but at the moment he'd have trouble concentrating on writing his name.

He threw the glove and ball onto the sofa, picked up his martini, and drained it. The phone rang as he was making another. "Hello."

"Sam. This is Jack. What the hell's going on?"

He warmed to the voice of his friend, Jack Foy. "Hello, Jack."

"Sam, I just heard the news. This is rotten, rotten. Those bastards. Everybody's in a state of shock. Even Sherman says things will never be the same around here."

Sam smiled, thinking of the ledge caper. "Thanks, buddy." He filled Jack in on the meeting and the abrupt outcome.

"What are you going to do?"

"I dunno. Have another martini, I guess, and when I get a little buzz on—have another."

"Sam, you know what you need right now, with everything that's happened?"

Sam cradled the phone against his neck and finished making his drink. "What?"

"You need to get away for a while. Chill out. Relax. Write. Get into a whole new scene, and forget all this bullshit."

"Hmm. Doesn't sound like a bad idea. But where would I go?"

"I've got just the place. You and Henry will love it."

2

Five months later—early November

Sam Wallace had never been a fan of condominiums. He was not a man to have his life regimented by people whose calling was monitoring the behavior of others.

By any standards, Paradise Towers was nondescript. Even the majestic waterfall tumbling over artificial rocks near the front entrance failed to inspire the tired looking building.

The parking lot confirmed his suspicions. Signs were posted everywhere. "Trespassing on covered space forbidden." "Trespassing vehicles will be removed at trespasser's expense." "Residents may park only in their assigned areas. No exceptions."

He pulled into a parking slot just outside what appeared to be the office, being careful to stay within the white lines. "Henry, you wait here. I'll be right back."

Henry tilted his head and cocked his ears the way he did when he wasn't sure he could believe Sam. He hopped onto the console between the two front seats, gave Sam a quick buss on the nose, and began his vigil.

Sam searched the directory outside the office. It contained a number for each resident with a buzzer next to the number. The list was alphabetical but he saw nothing for "Office." The door was locked and he tried knocking. No luck. Maybe that wasn't the office.

Better not linger too long. He'd probably already been spotted and taken for a trespasser. Trying not to look too suspicious, he headed back toward his car. Henry had taken over the driver's seat.

A few yards away an elderly man was loading his car, a Lincoln Town Car that Sam figured to be about seven or eight years old, parked in spot number 351. "Hi there," Sam said, approaching the car.

The man poked his head out from the back seat, where he was hanging clothes on a bar. He wore a Siesta Key T-shirt, khaki shorts, and one sandal. The other sat on the pavement. Perspiration rolled down his face and he looked annoyed. He eyed Sam but said nothing.

Sam pointed in the general direction of the building. "Can you tell me where the office is?"

"You're lookin' at it," the man said and resumed rummaging about the back seat.

Sam nodded toward the door he had just come from. "Yeah, I thought that was it, but how do I get in?"

The head popped out again. "What do you mean, how do you get in?"

"Well, is there a number I dial on the phone or something?"

"Course. You don't think you just walk in?" He studied Sam for a moment like it was the first time he'd really seen him.

"Is the office listed on the directory?" Sam asked.

"Sure is."

The old fart's attitude was beginning to piss him off. "Well, I couldn't find it."

"It's there."

"Yeah, well, I guess I missed it. I was looking alphabetically, you know, under O?"

"It's not under O. It's under C for condominium office." The man walked past Sam and placed himself in front of Sam's car. "That your car?"

"Yeah?"

"You're parked in Ed Turner's space."

"Sorry. Thanks for telling me. Where should I park?"

"Visitors' area out back." He pointed to an area about a hundred yards from the office.

Sam looked at all the empty spaces in front of the office door. "None of these, huh? I'm only going to be in there about five or ten minutes." He looked around the parking lot. His car and the Lincoln were the only ones in sight. "Think Ed Turner'll be back soon?"

"Nope. He's up north."

Sam started to speak but the man held up his hand. "Rules are rules. I live here, and I'm chairman of the parking committee. My job is to enforce the parking rules. No exceptions."

Sam shrugged. Now he knew who wrote the copy for the signs. He climbed into his car and nudged Henry aside. Henry licked Sam's ear and bounded into the back seat.

By the time he walked back to the office from the visitors' area, Sam was drenched. The temperature had soared to the high eighties. Couldn't leave Henry parked there more than a couple of minutes.

"My name is Sam Wallace," he said to the woman in the office. "Mr. Foy, Jack Foy in 411 gave you my name and told you I'd be oc-cupying his apartment for a while?"

The woman was about the same age as the parking lot vigilante. Her white hair was cropped close and the wrap around sunglasses she wore covered half her face. She looked Sam over, then leaned across the counter toward him as if looking for something. "Mr. Foy said that you have a dog." She spat the words out slowly, her face puckered up as if some foul odor had seeped into the room.

"Yes, I do, and Mr. Foy told me that dogs were OK here."

"Only if they're twenty pounds or under," she said with a little smile.

"Oh, well that's why he said dogs are OK. Mine's eighteen." He didn't think she did a very good job concealing her disappointment.

"We'll have to weigh him before you move in," she said.

Jack had given him a very good deal on the condo, but he was be-ginning to wonder if it was worth it. "OK, I'll bring him in."

"One other thing," the woman said. Her eyes narrowed and Sam braced himself. "You should know that we've had some problems with Mr. Foy."

"Oh?"

"Mr. Foy plays his phonograph after ten o'clock at night. There have been a number of complaints from other units." She took a step back and waited.

Phonograph? Sam thought of mild mannered Jack Foy, sitting by his CD player at night listening to his classical music. "Does he play it loudly?"

"Apparently loud enough so his neighbors have complained."

"Hmm." Sam wasn't sure where this was going. "Do you have a rule about playing music after ten?"

"Our rule says eleven, but most of our residents have retired by ten and feel that Mr. Foy has been most inconsiderate. I know there's talk of bringing him before the executive board."

He glanced at her name plate. "Well, Ms. Bunting, I'm not sure what all that has to do with me, but thank you for telling me."

"It's Mrs. Bunting. I'm telling you this so you'll be aware of the situation and be a good neighbor yourself. I just thought you should know, that's all." She returned to her post.

Fun place, Sam thought as he thanked Mrs. Bunting again and promised to be a good neighbor. "Uh, which one is Mr. Foy's park-ing space?"

Mrs. Bunting pointed out the window in the general vicinity of Ed Turner's spot. "Right out there," she said. "Four eleven."

Four eleven turned out to be two spaces away from the absent Ed Turner. Sam retrieved his car from the visitors' limbo and pulled into his space, disappointed that his friend with the Lincoln was gone.

Henry, who had spread out on the passenger seat, eyed Sam. Sam knew the look. Henry suspected something was up. They sat, staring at each other. Neither blinked. Sam was worried. Henry was off his eating schedule. They'd both been nibbling junk food all the way down from Boston. He checked the pretzel bag in the back seat. Nearly empty. Henry flattened his face on the seat and peered up at Sam.

"OK, you little shit, we're both in trouble if you've been pigging out behind my back. Pull in your stomach and let's go."

They headed for the office and the waiting Mrs. Bunting. Sam checked Henry, strutting along in the cocky way he had of walking like he owned the joint, his rear end, swaying side to side. He definitely looked bigger. "Henry, I think you have porked up since we left," he said, fearing the worst.

Mrs. Bunting was ready with the scale when they entered. Henry spotted her and wagged his tail. He stood up on his hind legs, rested his paws on her legs, and licked her hand. She recoiled and Henry tumbled to the floor. Sam tugged his leash and sat him down while Mrs. Bunting scrubbed her hand with a towel. "Can you get him on the scale?" she asked, keeping her distance.

"Sure," Sam said and guided Henry onto the scale. Henry squirmed, sniffed around the scale, and tugged on his leash in the direction of Mrs. Bunting.

Sam held him firmly. "He likes you," he said to Mrs. Bunting. "Come on, Henry. Sit." Henry settled onto the scale and began nibbling at something in his crotch.

Mrs. Bunting edged over and she and Sam watched the spinning numbers on the scale. When they stopped, the needle pointed to nineteen and a half pounds. Henry jumped off and cocked his head toward Sam.

"Nice going, buddy," Sam said and picked him up.

"He just made it," Mrs. Bunting said, graciously accepting defeat.

"I knew he would," Sam lied.

Mrs. Bunting softened and gave him a little half smile. "Welcome to Paradise Towers. Here are your keys. You get two of them. Here is a copy of our rules and regulations. Please read them carefully."

Sam took the keys and his copy of the rules and regulations. He flipped to the back—thirty-eight pages.

Riding up in the elevator, Sam felt the rigors of the grueling three day drive from Boston to Sarasota. He'd suffered through a steady diet of fast food joints with names like Denny's, Burpee's, Wendy's, Stuckey's, Hardee's, Arby's, Sonny's. Couldn't remember which, but why do they all sound like baby talk?

Henry had had a hamburger and French fries, so he was good for the night. Sam made a note to get them both on a more civilized diet starting tomorrow.

He did have a bottle of Absolut and some vermouth in his suitcase. He looked forward to sitting on the terrace and taking in the view Jack raved about.

"Let me tell you something, Sam. You sit there with the breeze off the bay caressing you, feast your eyes on that beautiful blue-green water and watch the boats cruise up and down the Intracoastal. That's pure heaven, man. Cure whatever ails you."

He wasn't sure about that. But the martini and Jack's terrace couldn't hurt.

He lugged his suitcases to 411, covering a distance worthy of a cab ride. Cooking smells filled the corridor, the pungent odor of sausage, garlic, and spaghetti sauce from behind one door, and the smoky, charred smell of hot dogs drifting out from another. Henry checked out each door. Sam let him linger long enough for a few sniffs before hustling him along.

The powder blue carpeting and shiny green wallpaper adorned with seashells and fish weren't his style, but heck, they were in Florida. "What do you think of the joint?" he asked Henry, who ignored him and waddled straight ahead like he knew where he was going.

Jack's unit was a big improvement over the corridor. Two bedrooms, two baths, tastefully furnished living room, and a decent sized dining area. He checked out the kitchen while Henry disappeared around a corner, exploring.

The kitchen was a pleasant surprise. Large by condo standards and efficiently laid out. There wasn't much in Jack's refrigerator. Two cans of beer, and some shrunken ice cubes.

He opened the sliders to check out Jack's blue-green water, stepped out onto the terrace, looked toward the bay, and stared into the concrete walls of another condo. He looked down at a small army of workers hammering, scraping, drilling, and polishing, each energetically contributing his bit to the obliteration of Jack's view. His friend was not going to be happy.

The only thing he could see other than the unfinished walls of the new building was the dust rising in thick brownish clouds. Nearly an inch had settled on the railing of the balcony.

Anyway, it didn't make a lot of difference. The sweat was already running down his face. Welcome to Florida. Jack warned him it could still be hot in November, but it was OK. Since being released from Whately at the end of the term, he'd had five months to clear up the loose ends of his career and marriage before leaving for Florida. The timing was good.

Jack was a good friend. "I can't get away this year, and I don't want to rent the place, so you might as well use it," He told Sam. "Stay as long as you want."

Back inside the apartment he turned on the air conditioning and made himself an extra dry martini on the rocks. He let the first sip linger in his mouth for a moment, before allowing it to slide smoothly down his throat. He exhaled and closed his eyes. The martini was doing its work.

He went into the master bedroom, collapsed onto the bed and sipped his drink. Henry was already curled up in the other bed. Sam had mixed feelings about the air conditioning blasting away at him. He welcomed the relief from the heat that hit him when he entered the condo, but being a New Englander, he resented having to survive on artificial air in a sealed capsule.

A gaunt looking man stared at him from across the room. He sat up quickly, nearly spilling his drink. The man in the mirror did the same.

"Jesus," he muttered. The man looking back at him was at least sixty. He was only forty-four. The man's eyes were gray and cloudy. His were blue. The figure in the mirror couldn't be Sam Wallace.

He wasn't into bragging about himself, but he knew who he was, and he sure wasn't the cadaver staring back at him. He put the drink down, closed his eyes, and flopped back on the pillow.

He thought of the stickers he used to see on cars, "Shit Happens." Nice pithy little two words that tell you when problems come up, you roll with them, and move on.

He could deal with his marriage to Lisa being over. He still belonged to that vast majority who believes that love isn't something you kid about. But the love between Lisa and him had dwindled and finally disappeared. Divorce was best for both of them. But Piro? That lard ass with the bad breath?

His career at Whately College was another matter. He would miss it, but he shouldn't have been surprised. He knew he'd been living on borrowed time ever since Cramer, who was born wearing a blue suit and a rule book in his hand, became Department Chair.

Oh well. What was it Scarlett said? Tomorrow is another day.

3

Sam opened his eyes. It took him a few minutes to realize he'd slept through the night. When was the last time that happened?

He looked over at Henry, still sacked out, flat on his back, feet up in the air. Seven o'clock. Henry would wake up any minute and want his breakfast. Sure enough he rolled over on his side and one eye opened. The other followed and landed on Sam. They watched each other for a minute and when Sam sat up, Henry rolled toward the edge of his bed, struggled to get up, and fell over the side.

Sam couldn't see him land, but he heard the whimper, really more of a squeak. "What's the matter, old buddy. still a little groggy?"

Henry came around from the far side of the bed, flattened his body, and stretched all four legs. He got up, wagged his tail, and fixed Sam with his stare.

"All right, all right. Come on, I'll take you for a walk, then we'll drive into the village, get you some food and you can eat."

He said all the magic words. Henry went into his routine, jumped in the air, spun around and landed with his nose nuzzled into Sam's leg. He looked around the apartment, then sniffed his way toward the front door, where he stopped and turned.

"I know you have to take a whiz, Henry. Let me get dressed." It took him less than a minute to throw on a pair of shorts, T-shirt and sandals. He could get used to Florida lifestyle.

When they hit the corridor, Henry put his head down and charged. Sam pulled his leash. Henry got the message and slowed down.

The elevator opened and three ladies in beach attire nodded good morning. Henry waddled over to one of them and got in a quick lick on her leg before Sam hauled him back. He kept Henry over to one corner while the ladies huddled in another.

"I can see you're going to make a lot of friends for me," Sam said as they went out the pool side door. "I don't think this crowd is going to buy your act."

He had to admit the grounds were beautiful. Lush oleander, hibiscus, and bougainvillea blended with stately palms that lined the garden paths.

The three ladies from the elevator were the only people at the pool. The tennis courts Jack promised—four of them—stood between the pool and the bay, perfectly groomed, and empty.

They had just started walking along the path, when Henry stopped, circled a hibiscus bush, raised his leg, and relieved himself. Sam glanced toward the ladies at the pool to see if they'd seen Henry pee. They had.

They continued their stroll past the marina and out to the dock and gazebo sitting on the Intracoastal Waterway. Sam settled onto a bench and Henry snuggled down next to him. They sat for a few minutes, watching the boats cruise by. Sam closed his eyes and listened to the breeze rustling through the palm fronds. He opened them in time to see a flock of pelicans skimming over the water.

He was a city guy, but this wasn't bad. He'd always put down Florida, wondering why anyone would want to come here, let alone live in the place. Florida was God's waiting room for the old geezers; strip mall plasticity, Disney World mentality, developers paving over every square foot of ground, erecting more condos, more Walgreens, more K-Marts, more Denny's.

The soft breeze coming in off the bay brought with it a smell of salt and sea, a feel of tropical decadence that somehow relaxed him. And the colors! Apricot, cerise, brilliant yellows, blues, purples. All the clichés about Florida were undoubtedly true, but he was also seeing a side of it, at least here in Sarasota, that could be very seductive.

Henry's bark interrupted his reverie. He was on his feet now, pushing his nose against Sam's leg. "OK, you tyrant, let's get you some chow."

After buying a few groceries, Sam found a car wash just off the Key and ordered the super deluxe car wash. Nothing but the best for the classy old buggy that had served them so well on the fifteen hundred mile drive.

Back in the apartment, Henry polished off some lamb and rice kibbles and a dollop of his favorite dog food, the chopped combo with chicken, beef, and liver. He'd given Sam a funny look when he saw the small portion, but Sam wasn't taking any chances with Mrs. Bunting.

Sam made himself an omelet and dug out his bathing suit. "Henry, it's a beautiful day and I'm going to the beach. No dogs allowed so you'll have to hang out here for a while. Sorry, pal." Henry trudged off to his bed. He'd had a good stroll, did his business, polished off his breakfast, and Sam knew he'd conk out again in five minutes.

He thought some more about the car and went back to the condo parking lot, where he polished its chrome and body until it gleamed in the morning sunlight, stubbornly defying its age. She was still a head turner.

After another cup of coffee, he headed for the shower, his all purpose morning place. First he set his digital radio down and turned it to the local news where he learned the temperature would be 80 degrees today with low humidity, typical for November, according to the weatherman. Next he attached his steam resistant mirror to the shower wall and turned on the shower. After shaving, showering, and brushing his teeth, he washed his hair, checking the hated bald spot to see if it had spread.

Satisfied that he looked a hell of a lot better than he did last night, he combed his hair and stepped out of the shower, ready to face the world. Toweling himself off, he thought of Lisa's comment years ago.

"If you got yourself a porta-potty, Sam, you could do *everything* in the shower."

Outside again, he walked across the street, weaved his way through a wooded pathway, and a hundred yards later, stood on the most beautiful beach he had ever seen, a two minute walk from his apartment.

He'd heard about Siesta Key and its incredible white sand. He knelt down and picked up a handful. It was like powder or flour, soft and gentle. Across the sand lay the Gulf of Mexico, the beautiful blue-green Jack had described.

Although he'd been warned about the heat and experienced it yesterday, today was pure bliss, a cool ocean breeze and low humidity. A day for lifting sagging spirits.

He walked past the volleyball nets and found a quiet spot between the lifeguard's tower and water, where he dropped his blanket and cooler, and settled in facing the water. The Gulf stood in sharp contrast to the Atlantic he'd known since he was a boy. No roaring surf, only the soft lapping of the turquoise waters.

He watched the sandpipers playing games with the water, chasing the receding waves and scurrying away as the incoming surf reached out for them. They looked like they were having fun, but maybe it was just something they did to pass the time.

The beach was uncrowded, which was fine with him. He went through the ritual of spreading the sun block over his body. The smell of it brought memories of carefree vacations. Better times.

He had his life all planned out, teach 'til maybe sixty tops, keep writing, hopefully develop a following, make some money, and he and Lisa would be free to travel. They would gracefully grow old together. Nice plans, but life isn't that orderly. Life is what happens while you're making plans.

It would be easy to blame Lisa. Finding her in bed with another man! But looking back, there were warning signs.

"Sam, let's go to an early movie and have a quiet dinner after, just the two of us."

"Lisa, I've got this damn deadline. I'm stuck at the computer for the rest of the day and evening."

"Sam, you're not teaching this Friday. Let's drive to the Berkshires and spend the weekend."

"Can't. Got a faculty meeting Friday afternoon, and my editor is coming in on Saturday, remember?"

No, you don't blame Lisa. You don't blame Cramer or the dean. You don't blame anyone but yourself. And you learn. You learn and go forward.

The breeze coming in from the Gulf carried with it the smell of salt water and tanning oil redolent of coconut and sweet jasmine. His spirits lifted. Hey, he was on vacation. Sort of.

He picked up the Ian Rankin novel he was reading, tipped his straw hat low, sprawled out on his chaise, and began his vacation. After an hour of reading, his eyes drooped to half mast. He set the book down, lowered the hat over his face, and drifted.

The relaxation felt good. After a few minutes, he sat up. Nobody loved hanging out by the sea more than him, but he'd only been here for an hour and he was already getting antsy. Could be a long six months.

He sat up and looked across the beach, which was still surprisingly uncrowded for such a great day. It had the feel of a New England beach on a fall day when summer's lease had ended, and a bitter sweet nostalgia filled the air. But even he had to concede you didn't get color like this in New England—the clarity of the sky and the Gulf, accentuated by the pristine white of the powdered sugar sand.

If he was going to go for a run, now was as good a time as any, before it got too hot. He puffed his way along the water's edge and back for about a half hour. Heading toward his base, he noticed a neighbor had arrived, a neighbor with a long curvaceous body, spectacularly put together.

He skidded to a halt. The bikini she wore did its job, leaving little even to his fertile imagination. When he finally got around to her head, all he could see were the sombrero sized straw hat and sunglasses she wore. The rest of her face was buried behind a book.

He broke out in a broad smile when he saw the title. "I admire your taste in books." He stood and waited.

The book was slowly lowered, revealing a face to match the body he had already rated a ten and a half. She held up her hand to shield the sun, removed her sunglasses, and studied him for a moment. "Oh? Are you a Sam Wallace fan?" she said without smiling.

"His biggest."

She sat up, hugged her legs, put her glasses back on, and studied him.

Sam felt his smile fading and shifted from one leg to the other.

"I've never read anything by him before" she said. "In fact I've never heard of him. A friend recommended it and loaned it to me."

He got the smile back. "Your friend is a good judge of literature. How do you like it?"

"I like it, but I'm not sure I'd call it literature. It's a good mystery, good beach reading."

He walked into that one. "Yeah, I guess you're right," he said, deciding not to fish anymore.

"I do like it though. Actually, he's a good writer. I'd like to read more of him. What else has he written?"

She said all this with a kind of friendly, wide-eyed enthusiasm. Unless his first impressions were wrong, which they usually were, this was a woman to die for. Kill for? Whatever, interesting observations, especially since he'd barely noticed a woman for the past six months.

Long hair, the color of a sunset, framed an angular face with lips that parted easily when she smiled, revealing perfect white teeth, the kind you see in milk commercials. It was her lips with the slight curl that gave her face a hint of danger that he found very sexy.

"That's his first book," he said and kneeled down next to her. Too early to sit yet, he thought. "He's just finished another that will be out in the spring."

"You are a fan," she said, her eyes taking note of his not so subtle effort to settle in. She closed the book and set it down on the blanket, revealing Sam's smiling face on the back of the jacket. "What's the new one about? Do you know that, too?"

When she put the book down he took it as license to sit, which he did. "Uh, yeah. It's about an upscale couple in Boston. The husband becomes infatuated with a dancer in New York and bad things happen." The game was getting uncomfortable and he was about to change the subject when she glanced down at the face on the jacket.

She looked back at him, about to reply. Her head snapped back down to the book. She picked it up, looked at the face, and back to Sam. He grinned.

"Oh, my God." Even with her slight sunburn the blush came through. She checked the face on the book again and back to Sam. "Are you..."

He nodded before she could finish.

She gave him a smile that eclipsed the sun, threw her head back, and laughed. "I don't believe it. I do not believe this," she said, slowly emphasizing each word. She stopped laughing and put her hand over her mouth, her eyes widening, like she'd just remembered something. "When I said your book wasn't literature, what I meant was—"

He held up his hand and stopped her. "Hey, you're right. My book is just what you said." He grinned again and popped up on his haunches. "In fact I liked what you said about it."

"I think you're a wonderful writer. I really like your detective, Dirk Flanders. He's very direct. I like that."

Was she laying it on a little thick now? He definitely needed to change the subject. "What do you do when you're not reading books?"

She took one last glance at the book and slid it out of the way, ready to move on. "I'm a marine biologist."

He nodded, like, of course, and sat back down. "Where do you work?"

"Here in Sarasota. The Galt Marine Laboratory. Do you know it?"

"No. Should I?"

"If you live here, yes. If you don't, not necessarily. Where do you live?"

"Here."

She gave him another lip curl and took a swig from her water bottle.

"Before you condemn me, let me add that I've lived here now for about," he checked his watch, "eighteen hours. What do you do at the Galt Marine Laboratory?"

"My thing is red tide. Know what that is?"

"Isn't that a whole bunch of those creepy little dinoflagellates?" He liked the way she raised her eyebrows. "Didn't expect that, did you?"

"To be honest, no. What else do you know about it?'

"Not much. I've done a lot of fishing, and I've seen what red tide can do to fish. I remember back in the early seventies they had to close the shellfish flats from the Canadian border to Massachusetts. Some people got real sick before word got around."

She wrapped her arms around her legs and leaned forward. "How do you know about dinoflagellates?"

"I like words, and I always remember that one. Sounds like Dean Martin doing something he shouldn't be doing. They're algae, aren't they?"

"Yes. They're microscopic algae, and when the number of cells increase from only a few cells per liter of salt water to thousands and millions of cells per liter, a red tide bloom occurs. The toxins cause massive fish kills, contamination of shellfish and severe respiratory irritation to people along the shore. It's bad stuff."

He stared at her, wondering how a dissertation on red tide could get him horny. "Is it a serious problem down here?"

"Very, particularly since this is a resort area. Anyway, enough about red tide. Are you a full time writer?"

"No, I'm a—" He caught himself and bumbled his way out of it.

"Oops, forgot. I was a teacher, but recently decided to write full time."

"Are you always that forgetful?"

She had a little edge to her. He liked that, too. "Not always—just sometimes. I thought it would be fun to come down here and write. How about you? How long have you been here?"

"Well, like most people, I'm a transplant. After I got my degree, I got the offer from Galt. Been here ever since."

"How long is that?"

"Are you trying to figure out how old I am?"

"Maybe."

"I've been here for nine years, and I'll save you the arithmetic. I'm thirty-four."

"You must like it here."

"Love it. The Galt is a great place to work. It's one of the top marine science centers in the country. You said you just got here. How long are you staying?"

"Uh, I don't know."

She gave him a sidelong glance. "You don't know?"

"Well, I live in Boston, and there are a lot of distractions for me there. So, when I decided to write full time, I thought I'd come here and focus on my writing." He wondered how all of this was coming out. Maybe easier to just tell her he got fired and slinked down here.

"Boston's a great city. Have you always lived there?"

He watched her pushing the sand in front of her into a small mound. "Pretty much. I was brought up in Massachusetts, went to college there, and I've always lived there. Pretty provincial when you think of it."

"You're full of coincidences, Mr. Wallace. So did I. Well, not quite, but close. I took my Ph.D. at the University of Rhode Island."

The mound was getting bigger, and she began to shape it. He eyed it, wondering what she had in mind. "One of the two or three best doctoral programs in marine biology in the nation. It's Sam, by the way."

When she smiled he decided he was going to spend the rest of his life sitting here on the beach with her.

"You're right, it is," she said. "Shall we look for more coincidences? Where do you live in Boston and where did you grow up?"

The mound was turning into a little castle. Very creative. "I live on Beacon Street on Beacon Hill, and I grew up in Cohasset on the South Shore."

She shook her head and he watched her red hair flare out like a silken scarf and flutter gently back to rest on her shoulders. "We have to stop right now. This is getting too weird."

He continued watching her, amazed at the impact she was having on him. "What do you mean?"

"I was an undergraduate in Boston, and I had an apartment near Beacon Hill. And I grew up in Scituate, next town to Cohasset."

He paused, waiting as she put the finishing touches on her castle. "And here we are in Sarasota. All seems pretty fatalistic to me. Shall we just give in to it?" He grinned and nodded toward the castle. "Nice job, by the way."

Her eyes flicked down to his hands for the second time. The first time he noticed was when he kneeled next to her. It was the instinctive act of an unattached woman, checking the status of a new male acquaintance. When she does it a second time she's probably getting ready to make a move on him. Right!

She responded to his question with that musical laughter and looked at her watch. "I'm afraid I do have to give in but not to fate. Gotta go."

"Wait a minute. You can't go. We're still exploring coincidences."

She smiled, but began stashing things in her beach bag: sunscreen, water bottle, book, beach towel, sandals, and cell phone.

Sam winced when he saw the cell phone. He refused to own one and considered them instruments of the devil.

When she got up, he noticed for the first time that she wasn't much shorter than his six feet, maybe five-ten or eleven, most of that, those magnificent legs. He tried to think of something clever like, "Can I buy you lunch?"

She wrinkled her nose and shook her head. "I can't. I just don't have the time. I took the morning off from work, and have to get back. I've got a million things to do, including trying to get an appointment with my hair stylist for tomorrow, which, unlike most women, I hate."

"You're right. Very unusual. I doubt your stylist hates it, though. With your hair you must make her look like an artist." He nodded toward her beach bag. "Why don't you just call her on your cell phone?"

"She's a he, and my cell phone isn't working. Anyway, I do have to go. I got myself roped into going to a fancy black tie fundraiser tomorrow night. It's really not my thing and I'm not looking forward to it."

"Then why are you going?"

She sighed and looked toward the Gulf. "I'm going because it's one of those obligations that goes with the territory. I'm a senior scientist at the Galt. The man giving the gala evening is a big financial supporter of our work. He actually sent the invitation to my boss, the associate director. He can't make it but conned me into going to suck up to this zillionaire, so he'll slip us a few million. An organization like ours always has to raise money. We have a fundraising staff but it's also part of every scientist's job, buried somewhere in the job description." She reached inside her bag, withdrew the water bottle, and took a quick hit on it.

"Your boss can't make it, but he's sending you. Nice guy. You're not going alone?"

"Unfortunately I am. My dear sweet boss just informed me yesterday of his change in plans."

He tried to think of a subtle way to suggest that maybe she shouldn't have to go alone. Something not too obvious or too pushy. "I'll go with you."

Her eyes arched, and she looked as if she'd seen a cockroach crawl along her foot. "You?"

Why did she have to make it sound like he just told her he killed JFK? "Sure. I'm safe and harmless. When I'm washed and cleaned up I can be presentable. I won't throw food or write on the walls, and you already know I can talk about dinoflagellates. I can be your lab assistant." He put his hand out and grinned. "Deal?"

She started to protest but nothing intelligible came out. Instead she gave him an "I don't believe you" little smile and shook her head. "You're crazy, you know that? I don't even know you."

"Good way to get to know me, and if I turn out to be a bore, you'll have all those rich people to talk to. You know, buffer zones."

She was still shaking her head. "It's formal. You need a tuxedo. It's—"

"I have a tux. Goes everywhere I go. I never know when a beautiful woman is going to invite me to a black tie fundraiser."

"I'm not inviting you, and you don't even know my name."

"What's your name?"

"Jennifer Belding."

"OK, what else?"

"What would I tell people?"

"Do you care?"

"No."

"Deal?"

She studied him.

His hand went up to the bald spot on the back of his head.

"Hmm." She stroked her chin. "You do look harmless in a safe middle-aged kind of way."

Ouch.

"You probably wouldn't look bad in a tuxedo. I could tell people you're my uncle, works for the phone company in Toledo."

"I'll be from Cleveland. I hate Toledo."

She threw her head back, her hair floated for a moment with the sun behind it, creating a color no painter could match. He hoped she wouldn't do something dumb, like let the stylist cut it.

"This is insane," she said. "It makes no sense."

"That's right, one of those spontaneous things that makes life interesting. What time shall I pick you up?"

4

After Jennifer Belding left, Sam lost interest in the beach. Anyway, he was hungry. The interlude with Jennifer had revved up his appetite.

The red hair. He'd never known a woman with hair like that. Had to be real. No way you could get that color out of a bottle.

He frowned, thinking how instinctively his hand shot up to that damn little bald spot. Acting like a school kid. Six months, showing no interest in women, and he's suddenly gaga over a marine biologist, after a thirty minute conversation. About time.

He got up and walked along the beach which had gotten crowded while he was absorbed with Jennifer Belding. But then, UFO's could have landed with little green creatures playing volleyball, and he wouldn't have noticed.

Dozens of colorful umbrellas now dotted the sand, like a giant box of gumdrops had spilled out of the sky. The snatches of conversation he picked up were largely European, German, French, British, Italian. Why not? Made sense for Europeans to come over here for their holidays. Air fare was about the same as flying down to the South of France, and they could frolic about the West Coast of Florida for no more than they'd spend in Europe.

Even in bathing suits Europeans somehow looked different from Americans. He could read the differences in their faces, their bearing, the way they held themselves. He was good at it. Didn't know why, but he was.

The earlier pleasant weather had been replaced by increased Florida heat and humidity. After a quick swim, he returned to base camp and gathered up his gear, his thoughts back to Jennifer Belding.

Henry greeted him at the door and went into his pirouette routine. He ran back to the bedroom and returned, carrying his leash. Sam hooked him up and took him for a quick spin around the grounds. Henry sniffed around, exploring, until he found his favorite hibiscus bush.

When they returned, he took a shower and changed, left Henry a few milk bones and told him he was leaving again. Henry showed no interest in going with him. He'd had enough Florida weather in his stroll. He liked his air-conditioned condo.

Sam was glad he'd brought his car down with him. A 1969 Mercedes 280 SE convertible, it was his most cherished possession, not that he had a lot of possessions to cherish. Long and sleek, the five passenger silver beauty, its chrome glistening in the sun, was a head turner. If some evil spirit told him he would have to take the car away from him or cut off his arm, he would hold out the arm and say, "Cut."

He'd bought the car ten years earlier from an elderly man in New Hampshire, who only parted with it because he could no longer drive. Over the years he had gradually restored it to its present showroom condition. He rarely drove it in Boston and felt guilty keeping the beautiful machine stashed away in storage, yearning to be free. Now it would be his everyday car for as long as he was here.

He put the top down, fastened the boot over it, and was off to explore Siesta Key. He headed down Ocean Boulevard and drove along parallel to the beach, inhaling the salt air, wearing his straw hat, sunglasses, T-shirt, and shorts.

After about a mile, he rounded a corner and was in Siesta Village. He drove slowly past little beach shops and restaurants with outdoor decks, filled with people sipping tropical looking drinks. A group of young men and women sitting on the rickety patio of a place called the Daiquiri Deck hooted and whistled at him. "Nice car," one of them yelled. He nodded and continued along the main drag, chuckling over the name Ocean Boulevard, a misnomer for a street barely wide enough to allow two cars abreast.

The rustic funkiness of the small, brightly colored wooden buildings lining both sides of the street like a movie set of old Florida,
oozed a laid back charm in sharp contrast to the soulless architecture
of the towering concrete condos. After little more than a hundred
yards he was out of the village, heading toward the North Bridge.

The drive through Siesta Key was a treat in itself. The thin bar-
rier island was a tropical wonderland stretching for eight miles along
the coast of Sarasota. His condo was just about in the middle.

He drove along the northern half of the Key, admiring the palm trees,
sea grapes, Australian pines, and olive trees that lined the narrow two
lane road. Little shell roads snaked off and disappeared into thick foliage,
making their way out to the bay on one side or the Gulf on the other.

Driving the few miles to the North Bridge he recalled Jack Foy's
words. "Be careful, Sam. The Key is seductive. You may never want
to leave."

The drawbridge was up when he reached the north end of the
Key. He sat in line with the other cars, enjoying the fresh sea air,
waiting as a high masted sailboat cruised gracefully under the bridge.

Off to his right the Intracoastal Waterway meandered through
mangrove islands, twisting its way south. To his left, wide open Sarasota Bay and the skyline of the city glistened jewel-like in the sun-
shine. The sleek, new-looking office and condominium buildings
appeared to be sitting on top of the Bay.

On the mainland, he headed north toward the city, driving along
Bayfront Drive and a tree lined park perched along the water. At the
end of the park was a marina and restaurant called Marina Jack's,
which looked interesting. He pulled into the lot and parked.

"That's a beautiful car you got there, friend."

Sam turned and saw a man about his own age walking toward
him. He had a gold earring hanging from his right ear and a tattoo of
some kind of dragon on his left arm, giving him a kind of balance. He
also wore a broad smile. "Thanks," he said simply, accustomed to
people complimenting his car.

"Yes sir, she's a beauty," the man said, caressing the side of the car the way you might pat a horse. "Sixty-nine 280 SE, 3.5. Beautiful machine, friend."

"You know old cars?"

"Yeah, you could say that." He offered his hand and stretched out the smile. "I'm Mike Rossi. You want to sell that baby, I'll give you a check right now. Take you across the street to my bank and get you a cashier's check. What do you say?"

"Slow down," Sam said and took Rossi's hand. "I'm Sam Wallace, and the car's not for sale."

"You sure?"

"Positive."

"Name your price."

"A hundred thousand."

"Hey, I like you. You got a sense of humor. You live here, Sam?"

"For a while."

"Where you from?"

Sam wasn't used to this business of where you from? Nobody ever asked that in Massachusetts. They either didn't care or assumed you always lived there. "Boston."

"Great town. Used to go there a lot. I'm from Philly, but I did a lot of business in Boston. Cars. I bought and sold exotic cars." He pointed to Sam's. "Like yours. Lot of car buffs in Boston, Sam. You a car buff? You like to talk cars?"

Sam started to answer but Mike looked at his watch and interrupted him. "I gotta run, Sam. Got an appointment." He made a fist and pumped his arm back and forth. "Know what I mean?"

Sam shrugged. The guy was a little crude, but he liked his friendliness. "Anyway, the answer is yes, I do like to talk cars," he said.

"Here's my card. My place is out on 41, not far from here. Where do you live?"

"Paradise Towers on the Key."

"Hey, you're only fifteen minutes from me. Drop in anytime. I'll buy you a coffee or maybe we'll go have a beer. Wait'll you see my cars. Gotta go."

Sam watched him climb into a Mercedes SL 600, a real hundred thousand dollar car. The window slid down and Mike popped his head out. "Hey, Sam, you know how many of your 280 SE convertibles they made in '69 and '70?"

Sam shook his head.

"Nine hundred and thirty-two total, both years." He gunned the car and was gone.

Sam stood for a moment looking at Mike's card. It was jumbled and disorganized. In one corner was a drawing of a car that looked like Sam's. Another corner held a '57 Thunderbird. Big, bold letters proclaimed, Mike's Classic Cars with the words "For that rare car you've always dreamed of. If we don't have it and we can't get it, it doesn't exist." Somehow the address, phone and fax numbers were squeezed into the mess, while in another corner, the smiling face of Mike Rossi beamed.

The card and the guy he had just met seemed to fit together. He smiled and made a mental note to drop by and talk cars with Mike Rossi.

Marina Jack's was about what Sam expected. Nothing fancy, but it had some style, the kind of waterfront funkiness that made you feel like taking off your shoes and having a few cold ones. He left his shoes on, but he knocked down two iced mugs of Red Dog before his seat was warm. Hell, it was Friday afternoon. And then he caught himself. Friday, Monday, what difference does it make now?

He sat at the end of the bar with his back against the wall and looked out across the bay. Water seemed to be everywhere in Sarasota.

A big guy walked in, grabbed a waitress, hugged her, and picked her three feet off the floor. Another waitress walked by, yelled, "Jimbo, honey," and got the same treatment. She giggled and hugged him back. He made the rounds of the tables, slapping people on the back, shaking hands, ordering rounds of drinks.

Sam sipped his beer, marveling at the impact the guy had on the place. Before he walked in, the bar was almost sedate, people talking quietly over lunch, others simply enjoying the view. No interaction between tables.

Jimbo was like an incendiary bomb dropped in their midst. Everybody except Sam seemed to know him, and he wasn't sure he wanted to. Gotta be from Texas, he thought.

Some guy got up from a table to high five him and Jimbo gave him a chest bump, like some of those clowns in the NBA do, and sent him sprawling across the room. "Man, I gotta get me a drink," he announced to no one and everyone and plowed his way toward the bar. Sam watched him, trying not to make eye contact. The guy was huge, at least six-four and pushing three hundred pounds. If he didn't know everybody, Sam would have figured him for a tourist just in from Hicksville in his plaid Bermuda shorts, striped shirt, black socks, and black high top sneakers. The big fella was not a fashion plate.

He moved across the bar, shoving empty stools aside until he reached Sam and plopped into the seat next to him. "Hi, name's Jimbo Conlin," he said.

Sam eyed the king-sized paw waiting to mangle his hand and re-luctantly offered it to him. "Sam Wallace."

"Aren't you the fella I saw talking to that scum-bag Rossi in the parking lot?" Jimbo asked.

"Yeah, but I didn't know he was a scum-bag."

The bartender brought Jimbo a Jimbo-sized mug of beer. He drained it and signaled for another. "Well, he is. Screwed me over on a deal once. Old Jimbo don't forget."

Sam watched the man's eyes narrow, fascinated at how abruptly his demeanor changed. The Jolly Green Giant now looked like a guy you wouldn't want to meet in an alley. "Sorry to hear that. I just met him. He wanted to buy my car."

Jimbo erupted with a laugh so hard he hacked and wheezed for two minutes before he could speak. "Sounds like the sumbitch," he said when he finally caught his breath. "Hope you kept the keys in your pocket and your hands on your wallet. You live here or just visitin'?"

"I'm kind of house sitting a friend's condo for a few months. How about you?" He gestured toward the dining area. "I take it you live here."

"Yep. Twenty-eight years been building things in this town. Sheeit, I built half of Siesta Key. Here's my card. You ever want to move here and need a good builder, you just call old Jimbo. Billy, bring me and my friend a couple more."

The two he'd already had were plenty for the middle of the day, and he put his hand up to decline but Jimbo ignored it. He stuck around for another beer and a hamburger with Jimbo and learned that he was more than just a builder of things. He was the biggest developer in Sarasota. He also had a thing about Mike Rossi.

"I'd still like to crunch that little worm. Every time I think of how he screwed me I want to wring his greasy neck." He squeezed his beer mug until Sam thought it would pop.

"Well, life goes on, Jimbo." He looked at his watch. "Speaking of going on, that's what I have to do. Good talking with you." He signaled the bartender for his check but Jimbo waved him off.

"Man drinks with Jimbo, he don't touch his money. It's on me, and don't give me any shit about it." He grinned and grabbed Sam in one of his bear hugs. "Nice meetin' you, Sam. Maybe I'll see you again. I come in here a lot."

Sam thanked him and started to leave. He stopped and turned. "Hey, Jimbo, where you from?"

"Texas."

He drove slowly along Bayfront Drive, enjoying the late afternoon and puzzling over his chance encounters with Mike and Jimbo. He was amused by them both, each a character in his own way. He wondered what happened between them that made Jimbo so bitter. He could still see the look in his eye when he squeezed the beer mug and decided he wouldn't want to get on the wrong side of Jimbo.

Without warning the sun disappeared, and the temperature dropped. He looked up, and the blue sky of moments ago was replaced by dense, gray clouds. For a moment an eerie silence fell, as all sound seemed swallowed into a black hole.

And then the wind picked up, bending the palm fronds, transforming them into graceful, swaying ballet dancers. The clouds darkened. He watched the tree leaves turn inside out, and heard the distant rumbling of thunder. He scanned the roadside for a place to turn off and raise the top.

The sky was now black, and an ominous darkness settled over everything. The air turned heavy with moisture and the thunder rolled just overhead. Bolts of lightning crackled through the darkness, followed by more thunder, louder, angry.

Sam knew he was about to get very wet, but he was fascinated by the abrupt change in the weather. The heavy, tropical, sensuous feeling in the air was not at all unpleasant. Actually, rather sexy, he thought.

Another explosive burst of thunder snarled across the sky, and he braced himself for the rain. He spotted a place to pull over and cursed the primitive technology of his car's top. He hopped out, removed the boot, and threw it in the back seat. Next he manually lifted the top forward and fastened it into the connectors over the windshield. He scurried back into the car just as the deluge came. He winced, thinking of his freshly cleaned car.

The road quickly filled with massive puddles, and his windshield wipers were no match for the ferocity of the rain. He inched onto Route 41 peering helplessly through a river of water sloshing across the windshield. The lights of the gridlocked cars blinked like swarms of fireflies in the afternoon darkness.

After a torturous quarter mile, he spotted a large sign, Mike's Classic Cars. "Any port in a storm," he muttered and pulled in.

Huddled in the haven of his car, he waited for the rain to let up. He had heard about Florida's sudden late afternoon rains, how quickly they come and stop, and hoped he could wait this one out. After ten minutes, the rain softened, and he scrambled inside.

The place was a candy store. He strolled between a 1971 Rolls Corniche and a sleek '68 Aston Martin Volante and climbed inside a fire engine red 1954 Corvette that looked like it just rolled off the assembly line. An early rare six cylinder, there couldn't be more than a few hundred around today.

He rubbed his hand along the burled walnut wood on the dashboard and doors, gripped the leather steering wheel and let his imagination take him away. Tooling along in his Corvette, he spotted a car he'd never seen in person, a 1959 Ferrari 250GT. He leaped out of the Corvette and slid into the car he thought defined the word "classic." Sam roared the Ferrari past the checkered flag and into the winner's circle and got out to see the smiling face of Mike Rossi.

"Like it?" Mike asked.

"Yeah, I just took first at Le Mans. Hey, I thought you had an appointment." He winked at Mike and imitated Mike's fist pumping.

"Aw, I, uh, decided I'd rather come play with my cars." He grabbed Sam and gave him a hug. "Good to see you. Come on over here, and let me show you the beauty we just got in."

5

Sam smiled. He'd met one beautiful woman and two guys today. And he gets hugged by the guys.

Mike's outfit was ghetto cool. Black linen pants, black sandals, black mesh shirt open halfway down his chest, showing strands of gold chain. Armani shades. Al Pacino in that awful movie, *Scarface*. He also noticed the Cartier watch and diamond ring. Business must be good. "I like your cars."

"No shit. Who wouldn't?"

They walked around the showroom displaying nine cars that Sam figured to have a total value of between five and six million. Rare cars that people only read or dreamed about. Mike led him to a far corner and stepped back.

Sam stood in front of a car that took his breath away. He looked at Mike who had a cat-who-caught-the-canary grin on his face. "You know the car?" Mike asked.

Sam slid his hand over the car's body. "Jaguar XK 120. Either a '51 or '52. Very little difference. Twin overhead cam 3.4 liter. Won its first race at Siverstone and went on to win five Grand Prix. Also a great cruising car."

"Not bad, Sam. You know your cars. Want to buy it?"

"Yes. But I can't afford it, and I don't even want to *know* how much it is."

"OK come on in the office and I'll buy you a coffee."

Mike's office was like his card. Cluttered. Sam tripped on a basketball on his way toward a beat-up beige leather sofa.

"Just throw that over in a corner," Mike said. "I got a backboard and rim out back. He simulated a jump shot. "Nothin' but net. I never miss. Sit down, relax, Sam."

Sam settled into the sofa and sank out of sight.

"Oh yeah, I should have warned you. The springs are kind of shot. Got to get a new couch one of these days." He prowled around the office, straightening pictures, playing with replicas of classic cars, eyes moving everywhere.

"Yes, or you could have a rope handy to haul people out when they need to get up."

Mike poured them each a cup of coffee and stood in the doorway, watching the showroom. "Charlie," he barked.

A man hurried out of another office. Mike motioned toward the customer who had just walked in, and Charlie headed over to greet him.

Mike finally landed on a wicker chair that had also seen better days. "So what's up, Sam? You live here or just visiting or what? I notice your car's got Massachusetts plates. Long way to drive that jewel. Hope you shipped it. Man doesn't want to drive a car like that fifteen hundred miles. You get shit kicked up from trucks and stuff, and you never know when some asshole's gonna do something crazy out there. No sir, no way you wanna drive that car from Boston to Florida.

"You look like a smart guy, Sam. I mean one of the things I'm good at is spottin' a guy with class and style. You know what I mean, Sam?"

Sam started to reply, but Mike just kept talking. He was off his chair and prowling about the office.

"I can tell as soon as a guy walks into my showroom if he's for real or just a tire kicker still paying on a three year old VW. Don't get me wrong. I'm always polite and courteous to people. I mean you never know. I find out if they know anything about cars and if they don't, I tell 'em I have to go take a dump or somethin' and thank them for coming in.

"Now, a guy like you, Sam, I see you in the parking lot and I say, there's a guy with some style. Belongs in a car like the 280 SE. I figure you're the kinda guy probably buys a car off me some day. And I can tell you know how to take care of a car just by lookin' at yours.

No sir, no way is a smart guy like you going to drive that baby down here. You shipped it right?"

"I drove it."

"Well, you know the problem with a car like that, a lotta people just keep it in the garage and go look at it and pet it every once in a while. Bad for a car, just sit there. Car needs to be driven, put through its paces, you know? Sheeit, that SE's just gettin' broken in at two hundred thousand miles. So once in a while, nice long work out's good for it. Get the kinks out. Took the drive beautifully, didn't it?"

Sam nodded, not sure he'd get a sentence out.

"Have the top down?"

"Part of the way."

"Course. That's what it's for. So you're visiting, right?"

"In a way. I'll be here for at least six months, maybe longer. Met a friend of yours today, by the way. Guy named Jimbo Conlin."

Mike snorted. "Old Jimbo. He still pissed at me?"

Sam shrugged.

"Aw, Jimbo's all right. He gets a little testy sometime, but he's a good ol' boy. Jimbo's bark's worse than his bite. He tell you why he's ticked off at me?"

Sam was sorry he brought it up. "No, not really."

"Well, we were going in on a gambling boat and the deal fell through. No big deal, but Jimbo thinks I let him down." He drained the last of his coffee and arched the cup into the wastebasket. "Two points. Yeah, Jimbo doesn't like it when deals don't go the way he wants. So you think you like Sarasota, huh Sam?"

Sam leaned back on the sofa, draped one leg over the arm, and ran his hand through his thinning but still curly hair. "Well, I only arrived here yesterday, but yes, I like it OK. It's not Boston, but then, it's not supposed to be."

"Maybe so, but I like it here. Sure beats Philly where I come from. It's a good place for a business like mine. There's a lot of money down here, and a lot of people who like classic cars. Good way to make a statement that you got more than money. You got style. Any shitbird can drive around in a new Caddie or nice conservative Midwestern Lincoln. New Mercedes, Lexus? Fugedduhboddit. Man wants to set himself apart from the rest of the crowd, he tools around town in one of Mike Rossi's cars." He moved to the doorway and watched Charlie and the customer. "I like being around money. Always try to rub up against money, because if you rub up against it long enough, some of it's going to rub off on you."

"Well said, Mike, but you know, don't you, that last line's not original with you."

"How'd you know?"

"Because I've read Damon Runyon."

Mike shrugged. "Hey, I borrow from a lot of people. I'm not proud. Here's another one for you. 'I'm tired of love, still more tired of rhyme, but money gives me pleasure all the time.' "

"Hilaire Belloc."

"Ooh, you are good. What're you, an intellectual?"

"Are you?"

"Shit no. I just like poetry and all kinds of literature. I got a million like the Belloc. But I gotta say, you floored me, knowing it."

Sam smiled. "I read a lot."

"Hey, you and I are going to get along just great, even if you don't sell me your car. Give you thirty grand."

Sam shook his head and hauled himself out of the sofa. "Forget it. Where's your john?"

Mike pointed to the other side of the showroom. "It's over there in that corner."

In the showroom Sam nodded at Charlie who was heading back to his office. Customer must've been a tire kicker.

He found the men's room just the other side of a canary yellow 1937 Bentley convertible. He came out of the bathroom and drooled some more over the Bentley. Guy could get in a lot of trouble hanging around this place.

But he felt like he'd found a second home. Mike was an engaging guy, a little wacky, but that's what he liked about him. And these cars.

He was about to tear himself away from the Bentley when he heard shouting. "You are an unscrupulous, unprincipled, perfidious, wicked person."

He couldn't tell if the squeaky voice was a child or a woman. He peered over the Bentley, and saw a man who couldn't have been four feet tall standing just inside Mike's office, pounding his little cane on the floor, screaming at Mike.

"You lied to me about the Gullwing, which is unforgivable, and now I learn that you have been having an affair with my fiancée. I want my money back on that car, and I want an apology and your word that you will never see my fiancée again." He hopped up and down and thumped his cane some more.

Even from where he stood, Sam could see the little fellow's face all puffed and red, ready to pop with the prick of a pin. He was acting pretty tough, but when Sam spotted the large black man at his side, he figured the little guy could afford to.

Mike, who had been out of Sam's line of vision, came into view. "All right, Francis, I've taken enough shit from you. Now either leave or I'm calling the cops. You're on private property, and I'm ordering you to leave."

The giant took a half step toward Mike, but Francis blocked him with his cane. "No, Cecil. Not now." He turned back at Mike. "We're leaving, but before we do, I want to know when you are going to refund my money."

Mike snickered. "Never. Is that soon enough for you? Now get the hell out of here you little gnome before somebody steps on you."

Cecil looked at Francis for a signal. Francis shook his head and regained his composure. "Very well, but I warn you, you have not heard the last of this. Francis J. Wilson is not a man to be trifled with. Good day, sir."

Cecil gave Mike one more of his looks and the two of them marched out. Mike flipped them the bird and went back out of sight.

Sam moved across the showroom, reflecting on the tender scene he'd just witnessed. Francis was a tough cookie. And Mike isn't the most sensitive guy in town.

"Did you hear that little asshole?" Mike asked when Sam returned.

"Uh, yes. It was kind of hard not to." He shrugged. "But it's none of my business, so it went in one ear and out the other."

Mike was in his chair with his feet up on the desk. He lit a cigar and offered one to Sam. Sam shook his head.

"There's just no pleasing some people, you know, Sam? I sold him a beautiful Gullwing Mercedes. A hundred grand. Gullwings, if you can find one, *start* at a hundred and a half. But I wanted to move it, and he seemed like an OK guy. So I gave him a deal. Now he's all worked up because he saw another one in town. Says I told him his was the only one. Says the guy told him there's another one around, too. How am I supposed to control who cruises in and out of Sarasota, right?"

Sam said nothing, but couldn't help wondering about Francis' other beef. Mike read his mind.

"As far as that other crap goes, I did pop his broad once, but so's every other guy in town. She walks around with a mattress on her back. Probably got pissed at him and told him about me. Big deal. You want another cup of coffee, Sam?"

"No thanks, Mike. I have to go, but I'll drop in later this week. Take care."

He drove home, still thinking about the little man's confrontation with Mike. Mike seemed totally unconcerned. Sam wasn't so sure he'd be.

6

Mike sat back in his chair, rubbed his eyes, yawned and checked his watch: 9:30! It had been a long day, and that ugly business with the midget didn't help. The little fuck barges in and humiliates him in front of Sam. And that stupid broad, Melody. Only way the midget's gonna know about him and Melody is she tells him. Only way.

He should have known better, get mixed up with a loose cannon like her. She's a lush, and you never know what she's gonna say—or do. Probably got drunk and spilled her guts to lover boy. Now he's got the big bastard riding shotgun with him, trying to give me a hard time. Mean lookin' dude.

He opened his desk drawer, pulled out a bottle of scotch, and poured himself a hit. Seemed like he never got out of his office before nine any more. But he liked being around his cars, making deals, tracking down new finds like the 1961 300 D Mercedes convertible he found in Durham, North Carolina. When the restoration is complete he'll get two hundred and fifty grand for it. Lucked out finding that one. Guy didn't know what he had. Like he couldn't believe how dumb old Mike was to pay him seventy-five grand. Another fifty or sixty in the restoration and he's got a nice profit of better than a hundred grand. He poured another finger of scotch and put the bottle away.

But his private life sucked. Picking up with bimbos like Melody would get him nothing but trouble. But even the hookers could be a hassle, like the night he caught Big Carole going through his wallet when she thought he was asleep. Then she turns nasty as a waterfront rat on him and roughs him up before he can get her out of his house.

He finished his drink and put out the office light. The night light in the showroom was barely enough to let him navigate to the front door. He'd have to put in another.

He set the building alarm and made sure all of the cars in the lot were locked before driving away. Traffic on Route 41, or the Tamiami Trail, as the natives still called it, was heavy. Seemed like it always was these days. Sarasota was growing too fast.

He drove South on 41 and turned onto Stickney Point Road and over the South Bridge onto Siesta Key. He'd thought about stopping at Coasters for a nightcap and a bite to eat before heading over the bridge and home. But he was tired and not the least bit hungry. All he wanted now was to climb into the sack and maybe read for a while.

He crossed the bridge, turned left on Midnight Pass Road and cruised along the South Key toward home. His car lights sliced through the black, moonless night, barely illuminating the narrow road. His was the only car, and all the hustle and bustle of Route 41 and the busy world of Sarasota seemed far behind. The South Key was his refuge, and his home was his sanctuary, where he didn't have to impress or hustle anybody.

He continued down Midnight Pass Road past replicas of the Taj Mahal and Snow White's castle and snickered. Builders were always after him to sell his house, so they could tear it down and build another palace. Fuck 'em. He didn't need the money and he liked his little place just the way it was. Anyway, people were putting up too many mega-mansions on postage stamp lots.

After a little over two miles, he turned left onto a dirt lane hidden between tall sea grapes. Palm fronds reached out of the shadows and caressed the side of his car. Two hundred yards later he reached his house, shrouded in darkness at the edge of Sarasota Bay. He could barely see the water, but he heard it, gently lapping against his sea wall.

He pulled into the garage and went through the laundry room into the house. Only the night light was on, and he left it like that, with the house in semi-darkness, the way he liked it.

Crossing the living room, he opened the sliders and stepped outside. The clouds had parted, and he watched the waters of the bay rippling in the moonlight. He sat down and settled into the peace and solitude of the deck, listening to the soft splash of a fish jumping, the distant buzz of a boat's motor, and the wind rustling softly through the palm trees. He closed his eyes and drifted, letting the scotch do its work.

Another sound, this one different. He opened his eyes and sat up straight, listening. There it was again. Someone or something was moving along the shell walkway. He hoped he'd remembered to snap the cover shut on his trash can. Two raccoons had taken up residence in his yard. He remained still. Nothing. The noise had stopped.

He went inside to the laundry room to check the trash barrel just outside. The laundry door was ajar and the garage door was open. He'd forgotten to push the remote and close it, but he thought he shut the door into the laundry room. After closing both doors, he checked the trash can outside. The top was on nice and secure. No goodies for the raccoons tonight.

Back in the kitchen, he grabbed a beer from the refrigerator. The pop of the can shattered the stillness. He smiled, took a long pull on the beer, and stood listening to the gentle groans of the old house that never stopped settling, the dim hum of the refrigerator, and the monotonous ticking of the old clock on the counter.

He finished his beer, walked to the laundry room, and threw the can in the recycle bin. He started to turn inside, then stopped and stared at the door. He gave it a puzzled look, then stood holding the doorknob for a moment. He snapped his fingers. "Goddamn it, I shut that door when I came in." He remembered now because it squeaked when he shut it, and he reminded himself to oil it in the morning.

Maybe he hadn't shut it tight and it popped open. It was old, like everything else in the house. He shrugged and went back into the kitchen.

The business with the laundry door still bothered him. He closed and locked the sliders leading to the deck. He was getting jumpy in his old age. Maybe another beer would relax him.

He started back toward the kitchen, when he heard something in the hallway leading to the bedrooms. As he turned his head, he thought he saw movement between the living room and the hall. His tired eyes were playing tricks on him in the darkness. He snapped on a light. Nothing.

Did he really see something move or was it only shadows? He remained still, his head cocked, listening. A sluggish fly limped its way through the air. All the night sounds seemed to stop and a heavy silence fell over the house. The only sound now was his own raspy breathing echoing across the room.

He left the light on in the living room and moved toward his bedroom at the far end of the hallway. As he reached for the light switch, he heard quick footsteps behind him. He turned, and for an instant, saw the outline of a figure, before a searing pain tore through his head and into his brain.

He sank to the floor, struggling to stay conscious. Something was very wrong inside his head. He was conscious but drifting, unable to move, sliding away, helpless to control what was happening to him.

He felt something tighten around his neck, and he could no longer breathe. Enough of his brain still functioned to tell him that he was about to die.

7

Sam looked up from his computer long enough to glance outside at another beautiful Sarasota morning. He'd already had a swim, fed Henry and taken him for a walk, had breakfast, and written four pages on his new book. And it was only nine o'clock.

He'd never been a morning person, but he had a pretty good handle on today's burst of energy. It must have something to do with Jennifer Belding and his date with her tonight. The word sounded strange. It hadn't been in his vocabulary in years.

* * *

Jennifer left the hair salon and picked up her dress from the cleaners. She wasn't into clothes and saw no point in spending good money on a new outfit for the stupid fundraiser. The black sheath would serve her well, as it had many times.

She still couldn't believe she let herself get talked into going to this affair with the writer, a guy she just met and spent a grand total of a half hour with. But he was sort of fun, and he could turn out to be the most interesting man there. By default.

Maybe she should have had him meet her somewhere. Picking her up at home is too much like a real date. She shrugged. It is a real date.

Today, Saturday, was her day off, but she was running ahead of schedule. She could get in an hour or two at the lab to clean up a few things and have her deck cleared for Monday.

She drove across the Ringling Bridge toward St. Armand's Circle. The breeze coming off the water blew through the open Jeep, sending her freshly coiffured hair flying behind her. No big deal. She could comb it out when she got home.

The guy on the beach came back to her. Sam Wallace. What a coincidence, reading his novel and he sauntered by. He really was a good writer. And not bad looking.

She angled the Jeep around St. Armand's Circle with its fashionable shops and restaurants. She liked the upscale feel of the circle in spite of the traffic that clogged it during the season. But the season hadn't started yet, and it was delightfully empty.

St. Armand's was a unique place, a perfect circle. She thought of it as a round, ersatz Fifth Avenue. In the center of it all was a rather formal park with perfectly groomed gardens, statuaries and symmetrical walkways. John Ringling, the fabulously wealthy circus man, created St. Armand's in an effort to duplicate the posh ambiance of Worth Avenue in Palm Beach. He missed the mark, but the Circle did have a flavor of its own.

It was quiet now in Sarasota with few tourists around, and the slow, languid pace of life suited her. November was hot. No question about it, but the humidity was down and she turned off the hated air conditioning and let fresh air into her house. She started to feel the same sense of coming alive again, as the transition from winter to spring in New England.

She checked her watch. Time to spend a couple of hours in the office. Make up for taking off yesterday morning. Going in on her day off made her smile and think of her mother.

"You're married to that job of yours. Jennifer," her mother often scolded. "How are you ever going to meet and marry a nice man when you're always working?"

She knew she was a workaholic, but she loved her job at the Galt. It was one of the most prestigious marine research centers in the United States, and she took pride in being a part of it. She also enjoyed her reputation as one of the country's leading authorities on red tide. Her work was important, and she didn't need to marry a nice man to complete her life.

She didn't always feel that way. Throughout her twenties there were always plenty of admirers, and she never wanted for dates. She even had two proposals from a couple of terrific guys, but she wasn't "ready." She would wait for Mr. "Absolute Perfect," and there was no question he would come along.

But by the time she hit thirty, he hadn't, and for the first time she began to question if he ever would. When he finally did show up, shortly after her thirty-second birthday, they got engaged. Three months later, when he broke it off, saying he wasn't ready for marriage, she immersed herself in her work, vowing never to be hurt by a man again.

She settled into her small windowless office, catching up on her mail and reading research reports that she'd been putting off.

"When do you rest?"

The papers fell out of her hand, and her head snapped up. "Cliff. My God, you scared me. I didn't think anyone was here."

"Sorry, Jennifer, I didn't mean to frighten you." He came in and sat down. "Maybe I should pull rank on you and order you to go to the beach and relax. You're working too hard."

She flicked him a little smile, knowing he was only half kidding. Cliff was her boss, the director of research and associate director of the Galt. And he did like to pull rank.

She knew he didn't care if she worked a hundred hours a week, as long as he knew what she was up to. Cliff was a brilliant marine biologist, and his main goal now was to become director of the Galt Marine Lab. Everyone knew it. He kept a sharp eye on his staff to make sure no one rocked the boat.

"I just came from the beach," she said. "I wanted to clean up a few things before getting ready for the big soiree you sucked me into attending. Too bad you can't make it." She was not about to let him off the hook. Anyway, she liked to tweak him.

"Come on, Jennifer. I told you something came up."

"Yeah, like an aversion to fundraisers."

"What's the latest with your research on predicting?"

She put the mail and research reports aside, her hopes of catching up dashed. Cliff wasn't about to go away, and his question was not casual banter. "It's coming."

"Yes, so I understand. Give me a quick update."

She wasn't ready for this, not on a Saturday afternoon, a few hours before she was going out with a man she didn't know. "Well, in a very brief nutshell, we've made some progress in developing re-mote sensor capabilities to monitor red tides and possibly predict outbreak."

Cliff nodded but said nothing.

She leaned back and put her feet on the desk. "As you know my year long study on prediction is nearly finished. I think we've made some encouraging breakthroughs." She was into it now and standing. "Cliff, we've developed a chemical fingerprint to distinguish the red tide blooms from other harmless phytoplankton blooms for use in re-mote sensing. Do you know what that means?"

Cliff settled into a chair and rested his face on his hand. "I believe so, but tell me."

"We've been able to monitor the progress and direction of the G. Breve algae out in the Gulf."

"But you can't monitor it with any degree of accuracy."

"Yes, yes we can," she nearly shouted and pulled a chair up next to him. "We've been studying the circulation of the water for nearly a year now, the biology of the organism and the chemistry that drives it. We started monitoring the physical circulation of the organism in early April. It was a hundred miles off shore. It's sixty miles off shore now and moving this way."

"We've never been able to track the movements of G. Breve."

"That's because we've never been able to isolate it or distinguish it from the other harmless blooms that move up and down and for-ward in the water. This is a big breakthrough, Cliff."

"What are your results?"

"Scary."

"What do you mean?"

"Well, as you know, the G. Breve organism in its normal state measures about one hundred in a quart of water. When a bloom occurs, it goes up dramatically and you can get three or four million in a quart."

"I know all that, Jennifer." He got up and leafed through notes she had on her bulletin board.

She followed him. "OK, but what you don't know is that the bloom we tested eighty miles out measured forty million to the quart, and in the test we just did the other day at sixty miles out, it's up to over a hundred million."

"Jesus Christ."

"Cliff, if these things keep multiplying at this rate, we are going to have the most noxious, virulent strain of red tide in our waters in all its ugly history."

They stood in silence for a moment. She watched Cliff's eyes and knew what he was thinking. "Anyway, it'll all be in my report, which you should have in a couple of weeks. I've got to go now." She got up to leave. Cliff stayed put. "Lock my door when you leave, OK?"

"Jennifer?"

She turned. "Yes?

"What's your data show for arrival time here?"

"Late December to early March."

8

Sam pulled into the narrow shell driveway, nearly hidden by the thick growth of palms and schifelera flanking either side. The small cottage sat behind a white picket fence. If it were not for the tropical foliage, he would have thought he was looking at a summer house on Cape Cod.

Bougainvillea clung to the fence and trailed over the top. Impatiens neatly lined the fieldstone path leading to the front porch, where an old verandah swing sat. Everything looked immaculate.

Sam smiled. It all fit his image of Jennifer.

He walked onto the porch and looked for a doorbell. There was none. He opened the screen door to knock and saw one of those old fashioned key-like turners in the middle of the door. He turned it and heard a thick sounding *brring*.

He checked his tux out in the opaque glass door. A little wrinkled but not bad. Anyway, who cares?

He'd let himself get into a bit of a funk a while ago, thinking about Whately. He hoped it wouldn't show tonight, but black tie, fundraising affairs were not his thing. Then again, they weren't Jennifer's either. Should be an interesting night.

"Hi." The musical voice interrupted his reverie.

He turned around and she was standing in the driveway. He wasn't sure if he actually staggered backward. Later, she would tell him he did.

If she wasn't the most stunning woman he had ever seen, she was right up there. Her shoulder length hair gleamed with a luster that lit up her face, highlighting the soft green eyes she'd kept hidden behind the glasses on the beach. Those wonderful lips looked even more sensuous with a little lipstick emphasizing the natural curl. He smiled when he noticed she was carrying her water bottle.

The black dress she wore followed every curve in her long body. The dress, in its own way, revealed as much as her bikini—maybe more, depending on your imagination. This was one good looking marine biologist.

"Hi. Where'd you come from?"

"I was next door and I saw you drive in."

He stood for a moment, staring. "You-look-terrific," he said, drawing each word out. She smiled and all that Whately College bullshit was history.

"Thanks, but we have to get going. It'll take us twenty minutes to get there. It's over on the mainland. You were right, by the way," she said, giving him the once over. "You are presentable when you're all cleaned up."

"I like your house," he said. "I thought I was back home for a minute."

"Thanks. It is like an old New England cottage, isn't it? That's why I bought it. Reminds me of my roots."

She admired his car and even guessed the year, which endeared her to him all the more. Most women paid no attention or simply dismissed it as an old car.

They drove along the Gulf. The sun hung over it, a big yellow ball inching its way toward the water, promising a beautiful sunset.

"Nice area. Lido Beach is it?"

"Yes," she said. "This is Lido Key. It's a very special place. I love it here." She took the cap off her water bottle and took a quick pull on it.

With the top and windows up, he felt a coziness with her inside the car. He wondered how she'd feel about bagging the party and making out on the beach. "Is everything a key down here?"

"No, but the keys are the most beautiful. There are four of them. Siesta Key where we met, my Key, Lido, Longboat Key which is just over another bridge beyond Lido, and down about ten miles south of Siesta is Casey Key. Have you been there yet?"

"Nope."

"It's wonderful. Like Gilligan's Island, totally tropical and—"
She interrupted herself. "Actually, as I think of it, it's not really like
Gilligan's Island any more. It's still pretty, nestled between the Gulf
and the bay, but now it's one multi-million dollar mansion after another, cheek to jowl. But anyway, you should see it."

"Maybe you'll give me a tour."

"Maybe."

"So what's the deal on this party? You want to brief me?"

"Oh, God. First of all you have to know Sarasota to appreciate
how deadly these things can be."

"What do you mean?"

"Well, there are a lot of people here who have made a great deal
of money in places like Cleveland, Columbus, Sheboygan, Wichita,
Des Moines, and they've come down here to Sarasota to enjoy it and
become patrons of the arts. It's kind of a contest to see who can display the most money and be the most artistic, vicariously. What little
bit I know of you, you're going to love them."

"I hope you're being sarcastic."

"I am, but to be fair, these fundraisers play an important role in
raising badly needed money for some very worthy causes. There just
aren't enough tax dollars. Anyway, a lot of the people you'll see
tonight think Sarasota is the artistic capital of the world, and if it's
not, their goal is to get it there eventually."

"Doesn't sound like a bad goal to me."

"Oh, it's not, and Sarasota has some wonderful cultural activities.
It has an opera house, ballet company, symphony, loads of theater, an
active concert schedule, a performing arts center, a—"

"Is that that purple thing I saw driving over here?"

She made a face. "Yes, but it's really rather impressive inside.
Anyway, there's also the Ringling Art Museum, which had gotten a
little tired for several years, but has come back strongly."

"Well, every place needs its patrons. What would Venice and
Florence and even Paris look like today if it hadn't been for patrons?"

"Yes, but they're a little pretentious about it here. All these people vying to outdo one another to see who can be art patrons of the year and get their names in the paper most often."

"Sarasota sounds like a city on the make, and when it gets there, everyone will relax and simply take for granted what they have and enjoy. Those places you mentioned where people came from aren't exactly bastions of culture, so they want to create their own here. It looks to me like they've done a pretty good job. Frankly, from what little bit I've seen so far, Sarasota seems like a wonderful place."

"Maybe I'm just frustrated, because having said all of that, the Galt needs some of this money, too. It's the fundraising part I hate, but it's a necessary fact of life for a non-profit organization. Which gets me back to this thing tonight. I feel like a hypocrite even coming."

"Just stay close to me and drink lots of champagne. What's the fundraiser for tonight?"

"A new cultural center. It's something the city has wanted for years, so this is a big event. Normally, this is not the best time to hold an affair like this, because a lot of the wealthy fat cats are away. But most of them have flown in for this one. Oh, turn left here."

He jammed on the brakes and turned. "Thanks for the warning. Now what? This is a shopping mall. The fundraising, black tie affair of the year is being held in a shopping mall?"

"This is Florida, Sam, not Boston. The restaurant and ballroom are on the other side of the mall. It's really quite lovely. There. Park there and we'll walk around the corner."

9

Francis J. Wilson inspected the ballroom of Mickey's On West. Everything seemed to be in order, but Francis was not a man to take things for granted.

The room did look beautiful. The floral arrangements at each table were breathtaking. Place settings of Herend china, Christophe silver, and Baccarrat crystal sat elegantly awaiting the important guests.

The fountain in the middle of the huge ballroom was a special touch. Francis had never seen such a fountain. He stood for a moment, listening to the melodious rippling of the water and became so overcome with joy, he did a little dance and clapped his hands.

Francis was glad he'd allowed ample time to check each of the place settings at all forty tables. He found a wilted hibiscus at one table, a knife with a fingerprint on it at another, and a napkin, improperly folded at yet another.

With the discovery of each offense, Francis pounded his cane on the floor and tongue lashed Cecil, who was helping out at Mickey's for Francis' gala.

Cecil, a former NFL player, stood six feet five and weighed three hundred and fifty pounds. He was terrified of Francis.

Francis glanced over at Melody, sitting at one of the tables waiting while he conducted his inspection. She looked especially lovely tonight. He had insisted on her wearing the plain white evening dress with one strand of pearls. The outfit gave her a sophisticated look, although the dress was a little lower cut than he would have liked.

Francis had worked hard with Melody and his efforts were beginning to pay off. No one in Sarasota knew that she was once a Roller Derby queen. He'd found her in Zanesville, Ohio where he'd gone for the dedication of the Annabelle Redding Zoo.

It had been six months since Francis inherited nearly one hundred million dollars of the sizable fortune left by Mrs. Redding. He felt he had earned that money many times over. Two decades of caring for the Grande Dame had not been easy. Twenty long years he had endured her vile temper, the insults, occasional beatings, and the dreadful incontinence in her final years.

His years with the circus, being the object of curiosity and belittlement, especially by all those nasty little brats had not been pleasant, but they paled in comparison with his servitude to Mrs. Redding. With the closing of the circus, he had nowhere to turn, and when Mrs. Redding offered him the position, he grabbed it. He was paid well, with the promise that when she passed on, Francis would be handsomely provided for. How was he to know she would live to be 95 years old?

Melody was at first put off by his appearance, but she quickly warmed up when he presented her with a diamond bracelet ten minutes after they met outside her locker room. Francis stayed in Zanesville for a week. When he left, Melody left with him, her new Gucci luggage filled with treasures.

During the past six months Francis had been slowly achieving recognition through his financial contributions. Choice seats at the opera, patrons parties for the ballet, his nameplate on the back of one of the seats at the Grande Theater, recognition in the programs of the Florida Main Theater and the Henzle Performing Arts Center. His name began appearing in Cynthia Mayfair's column, and twice his picture was in the *Sarasota Herald*.

Tonight would be the culmination of all his dreams. And Melody would be there to share it with him.

She was still at the table, filing her nails over the damask tablecloth. Cecil came over, retrieved the champagne flute in front of her, and replaced it with another.

Francis frowned and hobbled off to the ballroom for one last check. He reviewed the place cards at the head table, admiring the names. The president of the First National Trust Bank, president of the Sarasota Opera, the leading society columnist of Sarasota, the board chairmen of the Radford Museum and the Grande Theater brought both culture and power to the table. The president of Sarasota University and his wife were considered to be catches at any party.

The courtyard was soon filled with the town's movers and shakers, sipping champagne or whatever they wanted. It was all provided by Francis J. Wilson.

Francis mingled, greeting his guests, introducing himself to those who didn't know him, which was most of them. The problem was that Francis could barely see through the crush of people milling around him.

"Come over here, Senator Gilson," he heard Leona Cavendish say. "I want you to meet Francis J. Wilson."

Francis straightened his tie and buttoned his jacket. State Senator Janet Gilson was at the top of everyone's guest list, and arguably one of the most powerful politicians in all of Florida. Francis had heard from several knowledgeable people that Gilson would one day be Governor of Florida.

"Ah, here he is, Senator," Leona said.

"Where? I don't see him," Francis heard the Senator's voice.

"I'm down here."

"Oh yes," the Senator said, bending over to see Francis thumping his cane. She found his hand.

Francis turned hers over and kissed it. "An honor to meet you, Senator."

The Senator told Francis how thrilled she was with the good things he was doing for the community. "We Sarasotans are fortunate to have a man like you, Francis."

It was getting too risky for him to remain any longer in the courtyard, which was now wall to wall people. Twice he had been stepped on. His patent leather shoes were no longer shiny and his feet hurt.

He wondered where Melody was and hoped she wasn't drinking too much champagne.

Francis found Melody standing by the fountain talking with an alarmingly handsome man. The man appeared to be looking down Melody's cleavage.

"Good evening," Francis said.

"Francis." Melody bent over and kissed him on the top of his head. He hated it when she did that.

"Francis, this is Dexter Kingman. He's the president of the University of Sarasota."

"Sarasota University," the man corrected her with a smile.

Francis wasn't sure, but he thought Melody's voice was a little slurred. He wondered how much champagne she'd had.

As if in response she set her empty glass down and plucked another from a passing waiter.

"A pleasure to meet you, Mr. Wilson." Kingman was bent over nearly in half, shaking Francis' hand.

"My honor, Mr. Kingman," Francis said. "And, may I ask, where is your lovely wife? From what I hear, you're a lucky man, sir," Francis said, glancing at Melody.

"Ah, here comes Susan now," Kingman said, gesturing toward a stocky woman heading their way.

"A pleasure to meet you, Mr. Wilson." She turned her attention to Melody, who continued to watch her husband the way a mackerel eyes a minnow.

"My fiancée," Francis said, sensing Mrs. Kingman's puzzlement as to who Melody might be.

"Oh, how nice," Mrs. Kingman said. She scrutinized Melody as she might an applicant for a domestic's position and extended her hand.

"I'm not exactly Francis' fiancée," Melody said. She winked at Kingman and gulped more champagne.

At the head table Francis had strategically placed himself

between the Chairman of the Board of the Grande Theatre, Joshua Fishman and Cynthia Mayfair, columnist for *Evening Out*, Sarasota's flashy society magazine.

Melody was seated between Leonard Braunfeld and Dexter King-man, a selection Francis now regretted. If she put her hands on King-man again, Francis would find a way to discreetly reprimand her.

Joshua Fishman inherited his fortune from his father, who was the nation's largest manufacturer of suppositories. Joshua enjoyed the prestige that his endowments to the arts purchased, and was an active part of the Sarasota social scene.

Francis envied Joshua and hoped to one day follow in his foot-steps. "You're doing some wonderful things at the Grande, Joshua," he said.

"Well, thank you, Francis. As you know, our next production will be *The Matchmaker*."

"I'm going to be a co-producer of that show," Francis said proudly.

"Yes, I know. And don't think we're not grateful."

"Well, I've always liked Neil Simon," Francis said.

Joshua winced and nodded.

Francis wanted to talk with Cynthia Mayfair, but she was talking with Finley Spaulding with her back turned to him. He tried to catch Finley Spaulding's eye, hoping Finley would include him in his con-versation with Cynthia, but had no luck. Spaulding said something that brought a giggle from Cynthia. Francis leaned forward and laughed loudly, although he'd not heard the comment. They contin-ued to ignore him.

He did manage a brief eye contact with Susan Kingman, but she was too busy watching Melody to pay any attention to him.

Melody was acting like a slut, a common trollop, throwing her-self at Dexter Kingman. And she was getting very loud. He could tell the wait staff not to give her any more, but that could cause serious trouble.

The band began to play.

"Francis, what a marvelous orchestra."

He turned and acknowledged Cynthia Mayfair's compliment. "Thank you, my dear. I had the musicians flown in from New York for the occasion. I'm so glad you like them." Perfect way to get the conversation going, he thought.

"That's impressive. You don't do things halfway, do you?"

"No madam. When Francis J. Wilson gives a party you may be certain it will be done with style and class." He liked those words and he hoped Cynthia would quote him correctly. "After all, this is an affair for the people who make things happen in Sarasota." His voice squeaked to a crescendo with this pronouncement.

"Yes, yes," Cynthia agreed. Her pad remained on her lap.

Francis straightened his back under his custom designed chair. Now that he had Cynthia's attention he intended to take full advantage of his opportunity. "I plan to host several evenings such as this over the course of this next year, each one more lavish than its predecessor. I am a fortunate man, and I shall be pleased to share my largesse with my community and friends." His little arms flailed about, encompassing the room and its occupants.

Cynthia finally retrieved the pad and pencil and began writing. "Largesse with community and friends," she mouthed. "Wonderful, Francis, wonderful. You're a credit to Sarasota."

Francis smiled. That would make an excellent quote for Cynthia's column. But there would be more, much more, when he gave his speech later in the evening.

10

Sam was having a good time observing Sarasota's high society in action. But mostly he enjoyed Jennifer.

He had to admit, Mickey's on West wasn't bad. He liked wandering around the courtyard, admiring all the tropical plants and flowers and the wide range of art on the walls.

The place was jammed. He got off to a bad start by stepping on Francis. He didn't realize it until he heard a scream, and someone or something kicked him in the shins.

"Please be careful, sir," a squeaky voice from somewhere below admonished.

Sam looked down and saw a little man, glaring up at him. "I'm sorry. I didn't see you. Are you OK?"

The man wiggled his way through the forest of legs and emerged next to Sam. "I'm all right," he said.

Sam blinked and realized he was talking to the little guy who had savaged Rossi. He still had the same pugnacious look on his face.

"I am your host, Francis J. Wilson. And you are?"

"Sam Wallace, but I'm nobody important, Francis. Just passing through, you might say. I'm with Jennifer Belding."

"Who's that?"

Francis was qualifying his guests and Sam didn't seem to be passing muster. "Uh, she's a marine biologist with the Galt."

"Oh," Francis made a face that told Sam he wasn't impressed. That was the extent of Sam's conversation with his host before he and Jennifer wound up at their table in the boonies.

It didn't take Sam long to figure out that he and Jennifer and their dinner companions were not simpatico. They were a mixed bag, a mid-fiftyish southern belle, still playing the ingenue and a nondescript man she kept referring to as her date.

Rounding out the table were two octogenarian couples who knew each other and a couple from Longboat Key, whose contribution to the conversation was to regale everyone about The Forum.

"It's simply the most elegant condominium residence in all of Sarasota," the woman gushed. "It's so Italian. We've been to Italy, and I can tell you they have done a wonderful job of recreating the splendor of an Italian palazzo." She lowered her voice. "It's very exclusive. We feel fortunate to have landed one."

Her husband broke in with a hearty laugh. "Yeah. Their advertising tells you they begin at two million, but that's a joke. They do have one at that price, but you wouldn't want to live in it. You only get a side view of the Gulf, and there's no pizzazz, you know what I mean?" He poked Sam.

"I certainly do. You don't get much for two million these days," Sam said.

The two elderly couples said little to Sam and Jennifer, except to complain about the location of the table and how there must have been a mistake. Sam got the feeling that their being seated with him and Jennifer was part of the mistake.

Jennifer nudged him, "Having a good time?"

"Is this my punishment for forcing myself on you?"

"I warned you," she whispered.

"Actually, this is kind of an interesting evening," he said. "I've been watching Francis over there. Nobody's talking to him. His girlfriend's falling all over that guy next to her, and Francis is just sitting there in his highchair looking lost. I kind of feel sorry for the little guy. Oops. The one you said is the society columnist just started talking to him. She's taking notes."

"Keep your eyes and ears open, Sam. Francis is a little jerk, but he's a very rich one. Hell, I might even dance with him."

Sam gave her a look.

"The Galt needs a new aquarium," she said.

The band began playing again. Sam ordered some more wine and sat back to watch Francis and the rest of the action. "Oh, oh, look what's happening," he whispered to Jennifer.

* * *

Francis hopped off his chair to dance with Melody. He would lead her to a quiet corner and lay the law down to her.

Too late. Melody had Dexter Kingman in tow, hauling him off to the dance floor. It wasn't long before the great ballroom was filled with couples dancing to the big band sounds of Leslie Tremain.

Francis returned to his chair, watching Melody. She was dry humping Kingman! Her long legs were wrapped around one of his, holding it hostage while her pelvis ground into him.

Dexter Kingman seemed not to know where he was. His eyes rolled crazily and then shut. His head came to rest on Melody's bosom. Francis fidgeted in his chair. He wondered how much champagne Kingman had drunk. And then he remembered Melody ordering brandy stingers for them at the table.

Susan Kingman stood at the bar watching the display. She finished her drink in two hefty gulps and grabbed another. Francis smelled trouble.

Francis tried to focus on his upcoming speech, which he knew would electrify the crowd and forever enshrine him in Sarasota Society. But he needed to act quickly. The situation on the dance floor had deteriorated.

Susan Kingman had retrieved her husband from Melody. Francis spotted them talking in a corner of the room, partially hidden by a large potted palm. Melody was headed toward them. Francis groaned and scuttled across the room.

He was too late to intercept Melody. She was already in Susan Kingman's face when Francis joined the group.

Dexter Kingman had distanced himself from Melody and was standing behind his wife. Melody pointed her finger at Mrs. Kingman and weaved precariously.

"You think you're the Queen of Sheba or somethin'? Think

you're better than other people, you uppity bitch? The fuck, you afraid to let your prissy little husband have some fun? You——"

"That's enough, Melody." Francis thrust his cane between Melody and Susan. Melody lurched backward and fell onto a chair.

"I'm sorry, Mrs. Kingman. I'm afraid the glass or two of champagne and Miss Griggs' medication have not been compatible. I'll take care of her. Again, my apologies, madam." His eyes darted about the room. No one seemed to notice what was going on.

The Kingmans turned and headed for the exit.

Francis went over to Melody, who was sprawled across the chair, her eyes closed. "You pull yourself together, you strumpet. You are a disgrace to Sarasota and all these fine people. And you can forget the surprise I had for you."

Melody rolled her head in Francis' direction and opened her eyes. "Fuck you, Francis." Her eyes closed again.

Francis circled her chair twice, pondering what to do when he spotted Cecil. He waved his cane and beckoned him over.

"Cecil, I need your assistance," Francis said, pointing to the inert form of Melody about to slide off the chair. The band broke into "Jail House Rock" turning the dance floor into a frenzy of hurtling bodies. Francis was grateful for the distraction while he dealt with Melody.

"Miss Griggs is ill, Cecil. Please take her into Mr. Kendrick's private lounge where she can sleep comfortably. And be discreet about it."

The band changed moods and slid into a silky version of "Stardust." Cecil lifted Melody into position and danced her limp body out of the ballroom, into the courtyard and out of sight. Francis spotted Mayor Cudworth and hurried toward her. "I'm ready for my introduction, Madam Mayor."

When the music ended, Mayor Cudworth stepped to the small stage and grasped the microphone. Her politician's smile lit up the room. "May I have your attention, ladies and gentlemen?"

The guests formed a ring about the glittering ballroom. The fountain, illuminated with soft pastel lighting, sounded like a gentle mountain stream. The light from the two gleaming crystal chandeliers dimmed ever so slightly.

Francis gazed across the room and thought he had never seen so many beautiful people gathered in one place, and all of them so important. His friends. In spite of everything, Francis wished that Melody could be with him to be a part of this.

The room was still. "Thank you, folks," Mayor Cudworth began. "I'd like to take a moment to interrupt the festivities if I may to pay tribute to a man in whom all Sarasotans can take pride. Now, we all know that Sarasota is the cultural center of Florida—if not the universe."

Everyone nodded and applauded.

"But it takes money and a lot of work to stay in front of the pack, and we can't rest on our laurels. Into our midst has come a man, a true patron of the arts whose generosity and vision will carry us into the next century, beginning with the building of our long needed, long sought after, Sarasota Cultural Center. Our dream will become a reality because of the dynamic, energetic, creative," she paused for a moment, turned and looked down warmly at Francis. "Charming Mr. Francis J. Wilson."

Francis climbed up onto the small platform that had been provided for him and let the applause sink into his every pore. "My friends," he began. "I hope you are enjoying this evening as much as I am enjoying bringing it to you.

"Mayor Cudworth spoke graciously of my vision and generosity. I intend to share these qualities with you, and I will not stop with the Cultural Center. And now, I have an announcement to make." Francis paused. His years performing in the circus had taught him the value of timing.

Cynthia Mayfair's pen hovered over her notebook. Joshua Fishman flashed him a thumbs up. The room was silent. Francis wished he could preserve the moment forever.

It was time. "Ladies and gentleman, my dear friends. As you know, this evening is the kick off fundraiser for the Sarasota Cultural Center. I believe that when all the proceeds are tabulated, we will have raised over two hundred thousand dollars. The two hundred thousand will help a great deal, and I shall be presenting you with additional comparably lavish evenings to raise even more. But, in order to get us off and running in dramatic fashion, I, Francis J. Wilson will get the ball rolling with my personal donation of . . ." Here he paused again and raised his voice to a squeaky crescendo. "Five million dollars." Francis shook with excitement and pride as he squeezed out the words that would enshrine him in Sarasota lore forever.

The crowd erupted. The band broke out in "He's a Jolly Good Fellow," and under the direction of Mayor Mildred Cudworth, the four hundred most important people of Sarasota serenaded Francis.

Francis basked in his moment of triumph, his outstretched arms embracing the adoring crowd. When they finished paying homage, Francis thanked them. "This has been a splendid evening. My fiancée and I wish to thank all of you, and we look forward to our continuing friendship with each of you."

"I'm not your fiancée, you little asshole."

A single collective gasp rose from the audience. Francis dropped his cane and it fell, clattering across the ballroom floor. In that moment it was the only sound in the room. All eyes turned toward the courtyard.

Melody stood weaving in the doorway. Her hair and dress looked like she had just gotten out of bed. Francis knew she had and cursed Cecil.

She lurched into the ballroom and began wobbling across the room. Francis gazed in horror as he watched Melody limp toward him, wearing one spike heel shoe. The room remained deathly silent as Melody continued her unsteady journey.

Melody broke the silence. "You son-of-a-bitch. You stash me back there with that big ape. Well, I've had it with you, you little twerp."

By the time she finished delivering her speech, Francis had scrambled off his platform and met her at the bandstand. "Melody, you are humiliating me," he whispered. "Come. We are leaving at once." He retrieved his cane and courageously faced the crowd. "My friends, Melody is ill. I'm afraid I must get her to a doctor. Please excuse us."

No one said a word. Mouths remained open.

As Francis attempted to maneuver Melody toward the door, she reacted. "I'm not ill, I'm drunk. You're the one who's ill, you pompous little fuck," she screamed.

Francis started to move her forward with his cane, when she turned, reached behind him, slid her hand under his waist, and picked him up. Francis flailed his arms and legs, looking like a large crab, as she carried him across the ballroom floor.

"Let me go. Put me down." He raised his head and saw himself moving past a smirking Finley Spaulding. Other familiar faces flashed by.

Francis was still squirming and screaming when Melody dropped him in the fountain. He thrashed about and managed to clutch one of the gargoyles spitting water. Even Francis' weight was too much for it. The gargoyle collapsed and the water, no longer directed, shot straight out and into the crowd.

Francis hauled himself out of the fountain and sat on the edge, rubbing the water from his eyes. He opened them and watched the orderly movement of the crowd sloshing toward the exits.

11

Sam and Jennifer returned from the courtyard, from where they had watched Francis' speech. They stood in horror as the disastrous events unfolded. Along with everyone else, they scrambled for dry ground when the fountain let go.

They made their way back into the ballroom where the flood waters had receded. Francis was out of the fountain being dried off and ministered to by Cecil, and a man in a chauffeur's uniform. Satisfied that Francis was OK and in good hands, they left.

"Crazy night," Sam said as they drove along Bayfront Drive with the top down. It was Jennifer who suggested they put it down.

"I felt so sorry for that poor man," she said. "Even though he's a shameless social climber, you still hate to see something like that happen."

Sam agreed. "Yeah. Francis J. does have an edge to him, though. I'll bet he can be a nasty little fella when he really puts his mind to it. I told you how he climbed all over Mike Rossi. Anyway, there goes your aquarium."

"Be serious, will you?"

"Kind of interesting, wasn't it, watching Francis' so called friends stampeding out of there while he's going under for the third time. I think they were more worried about their Guccis than Francis J. Anyway, it was quite an evening for our first date. It was a date, wasn't it?"

"I suppose, but I don't know if first date is necessarily accurate."

He turned and looked at her. The glorious red hair fluttered and snapped in the breeze like fine silk. Her lips were parted and her eyes closed. "Oh?"

"Well, first date implies more to come," she teased.

"That strikes me as a good idea. Left here?"

"Yes, and then your next left. Does that mean you're going to ask me for another date?"

"Yep. This one didn't really count except for our half hour alone in the courtyard. I want some quality time when I'm not sharing you with four hundred people."

"You just went past my house."

"Oops." He put on the brakes and backed up. "Sorry, almost gave in to my fantasy."

"What fantasy?"

"Running off with you. Now about that second date."

"Tonight really was fun, Sam, in spite of the bizarre ending." Her hand groped for the door handle. "I enjoyed our talk in the courtyard, too, and I would like to get to know you better."

"Well, then?"

"But I can't make any commitments right this minute. Call me in a day or two if you'd like."

"What time do you get up in the morning?"

She gave him her sideways glance. "I get up the same time every morning. Seven o'clock."

"Call you at 7:01."

She shook her head. "No. Call me at the office during the week. It's in the book. I really have to run. Good night."

She was out of the car and at her front door, while he was still trying to think of a reply. He sat and watched her unlock the door, wondering if she would turn around and wave before she went in. She did.

Henry was asleep on his bed when Sam arrived home. He opened one eye, acknowledged Sam's presence with a smile and a little wag of his tail, and went back to sleep.

Henry's smile was one of the things Sam loved most about him. It was a real one, delivered for the same reasons humans do. The smile was always accompanied by a wag or two of his tail. Henry was not a big wagger, just enough to let you know he was happy.

He made himself a drink, slipped in a Dave Matthews CD and went out to the balcony. Even in the shadow of the encroaching condo, he found it pleasant sitting there. A cool breeze off the Bay managed to find him, and he settled back to reflect on his second full day in Sarasota.

Time for a reality check. His life at Whately was over. In all likelihood, so was his academic career. OK, he could live with that. He loved that phrase. Of course he could live with that. What choice do you have? Die?

He sipped his drink and forced the bad thoughts away. His two days in Sarasota hadn't exactly been dull. And that fundraising dinner! He could understand now why Jennifer wasn't looking forward to going.

He had the impression from Jack Foy that Sarasota was a laid back, low key little spot, full of artists and writers. There is obviously more to it.

And Jennifer Belding was an interesting woman. He did manage to get to know her a little when they slipped out to the courtyard for a while.

Never been married, no comment on male relationships. Sort of a none of your business attitude about that. Jogger, tennis player, loves her work but sounds like she works too hard. Very smart lady. A little hard to reach and definitely not easy to read.

Actually, he wasn't that forthcoming himself. She tried to get him talking about Lisa, when she asked him if he'd been married, but he changed the subject. He also stiff-armed her when she started asking about his teaching.

Some people get a kind of catharsis talking about their problems with friends they like and trust. He envied them, but he just wasn't built that way. He wished he were. He stood up, stretched, and leaned over the balcony, catching a glimpse of water.

Yes, Sarasota had promise. And the town sure is beautiful. The drive from Mickey's across the bridge to Lido, with the moon shining on that fabulous bay! And cruising along Lido Beach to Jennifer's, he felt like a kid again. Who knows? Maybe everything does happen for the best.

And he had a feeling there were more characters around like Jimbo and Mike Rossi. He hoped so.

12

Sam awoke early. He looked at the clock and smiled: 7:01. Coincidence? Should he call her? No. She said to call her at the office, and that's what he would do. Anyway, he should probably play it cool and not make it too obvious that he was sort of interested. Sort of. Like he can't wait to see her again.

No rush. He still wasn't totally awake and he had nothing scheduled. He let himself drift back to sleep.

A movement on the bed awoke him and he opened his eyes. Henry was sitting on the bed, his face a foot from Sam's.

Sam wiggled around in the bed and stretched, enough to convince Henry it was time to make his move. He pounced and went into his licking routine. Ears, nose, eyes, lips. He got them all. Sam burrowed his head under the sheet, but Henry squeezed under and found him.

"OK, OK. I get the message." He gave Henry a few tummy rubs, got up, got dressed in shorts, T-shirt, sandals, and a Red Sox cap, and took Henry for his morning whiz.

Back in the kitchen, Henry cocked his head and held his ground next to his bowl until Sam opened the refrigerator and pulled out a can of dog food, causing Henry to jump up and hit his head on the counter. He let out a yelp and crept under the table.

"Serves you right, you little heathen," Sam said, doling out his breakfast.

Henry crawled out from under the table and sat until Sam set the bowl in front of him. He smiled and dug in.

After their morning walk, Sam made some coffee and sat on the terrace for a while, enjoying the sunny morning.

Sarasota was shaping up nicely. He'd met some people that he liked, one in particular, and he felt like he was beginning to settle in and become a Floridian. Get himself a new white belt, some white shoes, and pick up a nice powder blue polyester sport coat. Naw, that wasn't Sarasota.

A few more days and he'd get back on a regular writing schedule. No more procrastinating. He was finding it too easy to blame his troubles for not being able to focus on writing, and that had to stop.

He went back inside for more coffee. Against his better judgment, he switched on the TV. He'd once read somewhere that people who live alone have the tube on constantly whether they're watching it or not. Companionship. Not for him. He was getting back in the game.

Nancy Wilson, Channel Seven's news anchor looked serious. She was speaking, but Sam couldn't hear until the sound kicked in.

". . . here in Sarasota. The victim was found early this morning, about forty-five minutes ago by his cleaning lady.

"The exact cause of death does not appear to be known at this time, but we are told that he was hit on the head with a blunt instrument, and he had apparently been dead for twenty-four hours or more. That's all the information we have at this time.

"Police arrived about a half hour ago and are still at the murder scene, the victim's home. Channel 7's Charles Butler is at the murder scene now, and as soon as we have further information to report we'll be hearing from him."

"Murder in Sarasota?" Sam said aloud and sat down to watch more.

"The victim, Mike Rossi, was a well known figure in Sarasota. He—"

"Oh, Jesus Christ." Sam flew off his chair.

"He was the owner of Mike's Classic Cars, a landmark in Sarasota for fifteen years. Rossi was unmarried, and it's not known at this time if he has any family in the Sarasota area. He moved here from Philadelphia and has lived on the south end of Siesta Key for the past ten years."

Sam prowled around the apartment, muttering to himself. "Mike Rossi murdered. I just saw him day before yesterday. My God! That's probably when he was killed. Oh, Jesus, Francis J." He had to get over there. See what he could do. He shook his head, as if trying to clear it. "Mike Rossi. Murdered."

The Siesta Key phone book had no listing for a Mike Rossi. He tried information. Unpublished number. The south end of the Key. His place shouldn't be hard to find this morning.

Sam slipped into some sandals and started out the door. Henry let out a yap, and when Sam turned, he stood with his nose in his empty water bowl.

"Sorry, buddy." He filled the bowl with water. Henry drained it, and they went downstairs for a quick whiz. After depositing Henry back in the condo, he was on his way.

It took him less than five minutes to reach Mike's street. There were already a number of cars parked along Midnight Pass Road, with small groups of people gathered, waiting for whatever. A Sarasota police cruiser with two cops in it blocked the dirt road that Sam assumed led to Mike's house.

Even though he'd probably get a ticket for his troubles, he parked on Midnight Pass Road and approached the officers. One of them came out of the cruiser as Sam approached.

"Can I help you, sir?" he asked in a voice that conveyed something more than an offer of help. What he was really saying was, "Get lost, Buster."

Sam kept his cool and replied in the polished voice of a Whately College professor. "I would like to speak with the officer in charge. I have some information that may be of help in your investigation."

The cop measured him, trying to figure how to deal with this curve ball to his authority. But he was not about to cave in. "Like what kind of information, and who are you?"

"My name is Sam Wallace, officer, and my information is for the person conducting the investigation. I'm a friend of the victim, and I believe what I have to say is important." In all honesty, he hadn't known Mike long enough to call him a friend, but strangely, he felt this need to involve himself.

The cop continued to eye him, like he was waiting for Sam to pull a gun. Sam read the indecision in the man's eyes. His job was to keep people away, a responsibility he considered important. And yet, if he turned this guy away, and what he had to say turned out to be important, he could get his ass in a sling. "Wait here," he said.

Sam watched him exchange a few words with his partner in the car. They both nodded and the young officer headed up the road toward the house. A few minutes later he returned and motioned to Sam. "Follow me."

Sam kept a respectful distance behind the cop, admiring the shrubs and palms framing the narrow dirt lane. He thought what a lovely place to live, and a wave of sadness swept over him.

The small house came into view about the same time the open bay spread before him. The beautiful setting was now a crime scene. Yellow tape surrounded the house and police cars clogged the road and lawn. An ambulance that stood near the front door told him Mike's body was still inside.

The officer stopped near the ambulance, turned, and put his hand on Sam's chest. "Wait here," he said again. Sam smiled and nodded. It was the cop's parting shot before surrendering his authority over him.

He should cut him some slack. He was just doing his job. But he was never big on authority figures. That's probably what made it easy for Bob Cramer to let him twist in the wind when the trouble started. He thought back to Cramer's comment about him being an independent bastard. His response was to compliment the Chairman on his perceptiveness.

The front door opened and he looked up at the house to see a striking looking black woman in the doorway. She studied him for a moment, and he shifted from one foot to the other. The woman had presence. There was no question she was in charge.

"Mr. Wallace?" she said and walked over to him. She didn't offer to shake hands, so neither did he.

She was as tall as Jennifer, but that's where the similarity ended. Her eyes were hard and cold where Jennifer's were soft and luminous. But then, this wasn't exactly a friendly encounter at the beach. "Yes, I'm Sam Wallace."

"I understand you have some information for me," she said. No introduction. No name.

"Yes, Mike Rossi was a friend, briefly. And I want to help in any way I can."

She nodded, her raised eyebrows asking, "And?"

"Well, I was with him at his car place the day before yesterday around three-thirty, and he had a visitor." He went on to describe Mike's encounter with Francis J. and Cecil. "It may be nothing but I thought you should know."

She made a few notes and said simply, "Thank you." No expression. No questions. No nothing.

Sam shrugged and said. "Well, that's it. You want to ask me any questions?"

She looked over her shoulder, back toward the house. "Yes, but not now." She handed him a pad. "Here, write down your name, address, and a phone where we can reach you."

He began writing, aware that she never took her eyes off him the whole time. He handed the pad and pen back to her. "And your name is?"

She smiled.

My God, the woman is human, after all.

"Sorry, I'm Detective Lewis, Diane Lewis." Still no handshake.

"Detective Lewis, I was very fond of Mike." He laid it on a little. "Can you tell me how he died?"

She frowned and opened her mouth, no doubt to tell him to take off. He braced himself. She hesitated for a moment and her face softened. "Mr. Rossi was hit very hard on the head. We're not sure what he was hit with, but it was obviously a hard, heavy object.

There are also marks around his throat, the kind that would be caused by a garrote. He was either killed by the blow or by strangulation. It's too early to say for certain."

"Uh, the news report said he had been dead for twenty-four hours or more. When do you think he was killed?" He waited, not sure how far he would get with that one.

Her expression told him. "Mr. Wallace, I can't tell you anything more than what you heard on TV."

"Do you have any leads at this point?" He knew it was a stupid question the minute he asked it. He, of all people, should know better.

The hardness returned. "What I've told you, sir, is nothing more than what I told the media." She gestured toward the crowd of reporters and camera people milling around the yard. "And that's all I'm going to tell you. We'll call you later today to come in and give us a statement. Please be available." She nodded to the young officer who had stayed within arm's reach of Sam and headed back into the house.

"OK, let's go, sir," he said, in charge again. He escorted Sam down the lane to his car. Sam removed the ticket from his windshield and drove off.

13

Back in the condo, Sam, fixed himself a breakfast of coffee and an English muffin. He spread butter on the muffin and watched as it melted and slid into the muffin's little crevices. Next came his coup d'grace, the peanut butter.

Henry came over and sat at his feet. He eyed the muffin, but Sam knew it was the peanut butter he was really after. Sam polished off the last of the muffin, but Henry hung in there.

He put a dollop of the peanut butter on a spoon and held it down to Henry, who scarfed it up and gummed it for several minutes before getting it all down. He waited for more, but Sam thought of Mrs. Bunting's scale and put the jar away. Henry reclaimed his spot at Sam's feet.

Mike's murder was still on his mind as he poured himself another cup of coffee and sat at the small kitchen table. He turned on the TV, but the news of the moment was of a dog that had been snatched and eaten by an alligator. They must have already aired the latest on Mike's murder.

Nice quiet little place, Sarasota. He'd already met two people who had it in for Mike. How many others were there?

He saw how Mike dealt with Francis J. Not exactly a diplomat. Probably gave Jimbo the same treatment. He thought about Jimbo squeezing the beer mug.

He doodled on a piece of paper, jotting down names of people he'd met. And then he got an idea. With all the commotion and upheaval in his life, he was having trouble getting back into his writing. Why not do some real research? Life imitates art. He would step into the shoes of the character he'd created. Be a cop again. What would Dirk Flanders do now? He remembered Jennifer saying how much she liked Dirk.

"Dr. Belding's office," the perky voice announced.

"Dr. Belding, please."

"May I ask who's calling?"

"Sam Wallace." He wondered if she'd be in a meeting or peeking at dinoflagellates.

"Hi there," the familiar musical voice.

"Hi. Did I get you at a bad time?"

"Hmm—"

It was a dumb question, like asking a busy person if she's busy. He was out of practice calling a woman. "OK, I probably did, but you can't stay cooped up there all day. Don't you have to come up for air and eat? How about meeting me for lunch?" She's probably brown bagging it. "Put your lunch bag in the refrigerator. It'll keep 'til tomorrow."

"I was just about to tell you no, because I brought my lunch."

"I know."

"I can't really take a lot of time, Sam. I'm in the middle of a research report which I need to finish this week. It's going to be tight."

"That's OK. I'll come up there and we can eat close by. Have you back in an hour."

Another pause. "I'll meet you at 12:30 at Crab and Fin on St. Armand's. Just drive around the Circle and you'll see it with the tables outside. See you then," she said and hung up.

Minutes later he was in his car, glad for the excuse to drive over the causeway to St. Armand's and doubted he would ever tire of driving over that beautiful bay. When he neared the bridge, he stopped behind a long line of cars. The bridge was up, and a sleek sailboat cruised under it with two more not far behind. He glanced down at the long fishing pier jutting into the water and smiled as a guy hauled in what looked like a good sized redfish. Pelicans glided low over the water, looking for their share.

On the other side of the Ringling Bridge, a man and woman skimmed along the bay on wind surfers. They were good. He'd tried it a few times on Cape Cod, but couldn't get up on the board.

The bridge remained up long after the boats passed, and the horns began honking. Must be stuck, he thought, continuing to admire the view.

He was ten minutes late when he found a parking space in front of Crab and Fin. The restaurant was on a corner, and comfortable looking tables and chairs ran along both streets, sharing the sidewalks with blooming shrubs. A grand piano sat where the streets intersected, and a pianist played Gershwin. Perfect spot to have lunch with Jennifer Belding.

He spotted her standing by a table, waving. He let his eyes linger, making sure to get the whole picture. She had on a knee length pale green, cotton dress, held up by thin shoulder straps—spaghetti straps Lisa had called them. Beneath the dress, he could see bikini panty lines. She wore no make-up, no nail polish, no jewelry, no earrings, and the red hair was pulled back in a ponytail. And she looked spectacular.

"Sorry I'm late, but the bridge was up, and it got stuck."

She laughed. "I figured that. You live out here, and you get used to it. That's why they're building a fixed bridge."

They sat, and she studied him for a moment. "You look very serious. What are you thinking about?"

He couldn't get Mike out of his mind, but he didn't know it showed. Did Jennifer know him? It was a small town and their paths might have crossed. Should he tell her what happened? Not exactly a light note to start on. The waiter came by and saved him.

After they ordered he decided to forget about Rossi and enjoy Jennifer. "Nice to see you again. Let's not wait so long next time."

"Right," she said. "It's been a whole day."

"Seems like a month."

She shrugged. "Seems like a day to me."

"Ooh." He had a way of walking into things with her.

"To tell you the truth, I'm glad you called, Sam. I've been working on this damn report almost non-stop for a week." She gave him one of her sly smiles. "I need a break, and you're a good buffer zone."

"Yes, I remember. That's me, old B.Z. Wallace. What's the re-search report on, red tide?"

"Yes, I recently completed a year long study and I'm writing it up along with my recommendations. My boss is pressing me for it."

"The same boss who ducked out on the fundraiser and sent you?"

"Yes."

"I don't know him, but I feel like I owe him. Have you been working on predicting red tide?"

Her head snapped up. "My God, yes. How did you know?"

He smiled. "I told you, I'm a fisherman, and I've read about red tide up north. I've read that the hardest thing in dealing with red tide is predicting it. I figured anything important enough for you to spend a year on must have to do with predicting."

She raised her eyebrows and nodded. "Well, aren't you smart. Anyway, that's what I'm involved in. I've developed a computer model of red tide bloom dynamics for prediction and for testing control hypothesis. With this we can develop an environmentally sound method for control and management of red tide by understanding the meteorological and hydrological factors controlling the offshore development and transport of red tide. And then we can—My God, listen to me run off. Sorry, Sam, I get carried away. I forget, I came over here to relax. I even gave up my little carton of cottage cheese and carrots to see you."

"Hey, that's OK. I'm interested." He was, but then, she could read the yellow pages and he'd be interested.

"No, that's enough. How about you? Are you getting acclimated to Sarasota? I guess you got total immersion Saturday night on Sara-sota's social scene, didn't you?" She giggled. "Excuse the pun."

"Speaking of which, I saw the little social lion before yesterday."
"Oh? Where?"

The piano player slid into a dreamy "Embraceable You" and Sam paused for a moment before answering. He knew where the conversation was going to lead now, and he wished he hadn't opened it up. "I love Gershwin. Must be the safe middle age in me."

"Not at all. I love his music, too. It's ageless. But tell me about Francis."

Sam sneaked a look at his watch. They were only halfway through their lunch and he still had thirty minutes to enjoy her. He wanted to talk about good stuff, but Mike's murder was still too much on his mind to drop it. "Jennifer, did you watch the news this morning?"

"No, why?"

"Does the name Mike Rossi mean anything to you?"

"Yes, I know who he is. He's that car dealer. What'd he do now?"

"It's not what he did. It's what somebody did to him. He was found murdered this morning."

She slammed down her iced tea glass. "Oh, my God!"

"Sorry to spoil our lunch, but I was with him two days ago, probably only a matter of hours before he was killed. I kind of liked the guy. Just wondered if you knew him."

She turned her chair around and looked off across the circle. "Yes, I knew him. Not well, but I knew him. What's Francis J. got to do with it?"

He told her about Francis' and Cecil's confrontation with Mike. "I was in the showroom. They didn't see me, but I saw and heard the whole thing."

"Have you told the police?"

"I went to his house this morning after I heard it on the news. That's where he was killed, and the place was crawling with cops. I told a detective what I saw and left."

Jennifer let out a long breath. "Whew! You're having quite a stay in Sarasota. How'd you get to know Rossi?"

"I bumped into him at Marina Jack's parking lot the day I met you on the beach. He admired my car, and we got talking. Invited me to stop by his place, which I did. I got a kick out of him, thought he was a character and a bright guy."

"Yes, well speaking of character, I not sure that's something you're a very good judge of. You liked him?"

"Yes, I liked him." What, was he going to lie? "I take it you didn't."

"He was a jerk. Sorry to speak ill of the dead, but you asked me."

He nodded. Naturally she would pull no punches. "How did you know him?"

"He hit on me at a party a couple of years ago. I told him politely to get lost. A few weeks later, I was eating lunch alone—here as a matter of fact. He walked by and sat down, and no matter how many hints I threw at him, he stayed until I finished. Kept making suggestive remarks. I'm getting indigestion again thinking of it." She checked her watch. "I have to get back, Sam."

"OK, sorry about the indigestion. I didn't mean to bring up Rossi's name, but his murder has been on my mind, and I've been a little bummed out since going over to his house. I tried to think of something nice to focus on, so naturally you came to mind."

"Thanks, Sam. You're sweet. Don't worry about the conversation. Actually, I'm kind of intrigued myself. The cops have their work cut out for them. You may be the only person in town who liked him. You're probably the only non-suspect."

"Gee, that's a relief." He paid the check, and stuffed a few bills in the piano player's jar. Cheap enough for an hour of Gershwin.

They stepped onto the street. Sam looked around the circle, which was nearly empty. "Off season in Sarasota, right?"

She smiled. "Right, and I love it."

"I'll walk you to your car," he said.

"I don't have a car. I rode over with a colleague. Figured I could hitch a ride back with you."

Neither of them said much on the drive back. Sam puzzled over her comments about everyone being a suspect, and wasn't sure whether to pursue that or drop it. Why not?

"Jennifer, would you care to mention any of those legions of people who disliked Rossi?"

"I knew you were dying to ask me that," she said. "Turn left here."

They pulled up to her building and parked next to the big sign saying Galt Marine Laboratories. Off to his right he saw a line of people waiting to enter another building.

"That's the aquarium," she said. "It's very popular."

"You're right," he said. "I have been wanting to ask you that question."

She opened the door and got out. Must have pressed her too hard. He wished he had Dirk's savoir-faire.

She poked her head back into the car. "You might try Alexis Helfrich. She runs an escort agency called Partners. Also runs a 'spa' called Hedonism out on the trail. I know there was something going on there between her and Rossi, some kind of bad blood between them from what I hear."

He started to speak, but she held up her hands. "That's all I know, Sam, and all I've got time for. I really do have to run." She pulled her head out of the car, then popped it back in. "Come on in for a minute, and I'll give you a quick tour."

The first thing he noticed in her office were the dozens of compact discs piled next to her computer. He commented on them.

She waved her hand in their direction. "That's all my research right there. Thousands of hours of work wrapped up in those little babies." She looked at her watch and took him by the arm. "Oh God! I'm already late for a meeting. Sorry, but I'll have to show you around another time." She ushered him to the door. "Call me?"

"How about this weekend?" he asked.

"Hmm. Sunday might be good. Do you like canoeing?"

"Sure."

"OK, I'll show you a beautiful river. Talk to you this week."

He drove back toward the mainland, thoughts of Jennifer and Mike competing for his attention. Canoeing on Sunday. He hadn't been on a canoe since Camp Ashmere when he was ten. He stood up and tipped it over, and his brother punched him in the stomach when they got back to shore.

But the thought of having Jennifer all to himself on a river sounded appealing. A beautiful river, she said.

Her comments about Mike rattled around his head. Jimbo and Francis J. must have had a lot of company in their lack of affection for Mike.

He spotted a sign, Gulfside Drive, and slammed on the brakes. The car in back of him careened around his. The driver barked something at Sam and gave him the finger.

He pulled onto Gulfside, the street where Jennifer told him Francis lived. "He lives right around the corner from the Galt. He's our neighbor. Calls his place Shangri-La."

Sure enough, halfway along Gulfside he came to a house the size of a palace, sitting behind a wall with a crest-like sign that read Shangri-La. In quotes. He pulled up in front of the wrought iron gates, and to his surprise, Francis J. stood twenty yards away.

He actually heard Francis before he saw him. He was chewing out a gardener for something. The poor man must have committed a dreadful offense, as Francis was really lacing into him.

He spotted Sam and waved his cane at him. "Go away," he yelled.

Sam got out of the car. "Mr. Wilson, I'm Sam Wallace. We met at your fundraiser at Mickey's Saturday night. I wonder if I might see you for a minute."

Francis left the cringing gardener and hobbled over. He reached the gate and studied Sam for a moment. "Yes, I remember you. You stepped on my foot in the courtyard. You were with that pretty lady from the Galt."

Sam was not only impressed, he was flabbergasted. "Yes, that's right. May I come in?"

Francis buzzed the gate open and Sam hopped in his car and drove through. He wasn't sure why he was there or what he would say to Francis.

14

Opulent was the only word Sam could think of when he entered Francis' house. All marble and tapestries, the entry hall looked more like the entrance to a museum than a home. Beyond the cavernous foyer and sitting room, behind twenty foot high windows, the Gulf of Mexico gleamed. The sun bounced off it and exploded through the house. Sam groped for his sunglasses.

Francis noticed and pushed a button. Blinds slid down, shutting out the sun and the Gulf. "The afternoon sun can be quite brutal here," he chirped. "May I get you a cooling beverage, Mr. Wallace? A soft drink, a cocktail?"

Francis was being very gracious to a guy he only knew because he stepped on him. Never would have known this was the same Francis who savaged the gardener only minutes ago.

He didn't feel like having anything, but he knew that accepting the offer and sitting down with a drink was buying time. "Thanks, I'll have a Coke."

Francis pressed another button and Cecil appeared. He was pushing the buttons from a remote he carried with him. Push a button, the gate opens, push a button, blinds go down, push a button, Cecil pops up. Did he have a button for Melody, or had she been banished?

"Cecil, bring Mr. Wallace a Coca-Cola, and I will have a Perrier," Francis barked. Cecil gave a little bow and lumbered off.

Sam pondered the power of money as he watched Cecil react like a trained seal. The big man could crunch Francis like a bug, but he endured the little tyrant's abuse. MONEY.

"What can I do for you, sir," Francis asked as they settled into the spacious sitting room. That's what Francis called it. Sam wasn't sure what you call the rooms in a house this big.

He watched Francis fidget on the couch, getting comfortable, his stubby legs dangling over the side. He wore white cotton slacks and a blue blazer, covering a beige silk shirt with a crimson ascot tucked in at the neck. Dapper little dude.

He would have to be careful with what he said. He'd heard that Francis was mercurial and you never know what might set him off. "Well, Mr. Wilson, I don't know if you saw on TV today or heard the news that Mike Rossi, the car dealer, was found murdered this morning."

Francis frowned and Sam was afraid he'd launched into it too fast. Should have maybe had a little foreplay, talked about the cultural center, compliment him on his house, his ascot.

"Yes, I did see it on the news," Francis said. He seemed cool but his expression turned puzzled. He waited.

"I had just gotten to know Mr. Rossi," Sam said. "And well, it sort of threw me for a loop. I've never known anyone who was murdered, and to be honest, I guess I'm just curious. Actually, I'm a writer, and I write novels about this kind of stuff. I thought I'd talk with people who knew him, maybe learn more about him and why anyone would kill him."

"I see. And that's why you came to see me?"

"Yes," Sam said simply. He couldn't think of anything else to say.

"Who told you I knew Rossi?"

Sam didn't like the belligerent look that came over Francis' face. For a little fella, he could be intimidating. Best not to beat around the bush, though. Slice through the bullshit. "You did know him, didn't you Mr. Wilson?"

Francis rearranged himself on the sofa and looked toward the foyer. "If I did, what business is it of yours, sir?"

A good question that Francis had a right to ask. "Probably none, except I happened to be inside Rossi's showroom on the day you and Cecil came in to see him. You didn't notice me, but I heard the exchange between you and him. I'd say you were a little upset."

Francis' face puckered and puffed and turned the color of his ascot. "You were eavesdropping? I find that reprehensible, sir."

Not too bad considering the bombshell he'd just dropped. He expected worse. "I wasn't eavesdropping. I just happened to be there, and I couldn't help overhearing. You weren't exactly whispering."

"So you felt an obligation to come here and tell me something we both already knew." He took the remote from his pocket. "I believe you have overstayed your welcome, Mr. Wallace, and it's time for you to make your departure."

Sam moved into his best imitation of his novel's detective, Dirk Flanders. "You threatened him, Francis, and he was killed only hours later. I'm harmless, but I suspect the police will take a dim view of the coincidence."

Francis fondled the remote, his finger poised over what had to be the Cecil button. Sam stayed put.

Francis sighed and put the remote back in his pocket. From his other pocket he fished out a gold pill dispenser, took out two tablets, and popped them into his mouth. His face unpuffed and the redness disappeared.

"Mr. Wallace, this Rossi was a wicked, abominable person. He was a liar and a thief, a man with no scruples. He was a man who would not hesitate to cheat a person and then cuckold him by seducing his fiancée. He was a man, who, frankly deserved to die. But it was not by my hand."

Francis J. had himself worked up. The pucker and redness were back, and Sam was afraid he would burst like an over-inflated balloon. He waited a moment until Francis calmed down. "I heard what you charged him with at his car place, and I don't blame you for disliking him. I'd have felt the same way. But then, a few hours later—"

"I am not a man of violence, sir. Not that it is any of your concern, but Cecil and I returned home after the distasteful scene with that wretched man, where we remained for the duration of the evening. It was only upon awakening this morning that I learned of his demise. And by the way, I am hardly the only person who despised that unprincipled scoundrel."

"Oh?"

"Instead of wasting your time badgering Francis J. Wilson, a man of culture and refinement, a man of integrity, a benefactor of Sarasota, you would do well to explore the seamy side of Mr. Rossi's world."

"Like Alexis Helfrich?"

Francis blinked. It was enough to tell Sam he'd rung a bell.

The little guy popped off the sofa and walked across the room into the foyer. He stood gazing toward a part of the house behind Sam. His body slumped and it appeared to Sam that his cane was the only thing holding him up. The size of the vast marbled foyer dominated by the biggest crystal chandelier Sam had ever seen, made Francis look even smaller. The oversized house and the undersized Francis were a whimsical mismatch.

Sam wondered if Francis was looking for Melody. Was she still housed in this mausoleum or was she gone, dispatched by Francis? He doubted she could have survived the debacle at Mickey's. In a way, he hoped Melody hadn't left. Francis obviously needed her, and Sam couldn't help feeling compassion for this odd little man. But then, he could be a murderer.

Francis came out of his trance and looked at Sam. "Mr. Wallace, you are a very inquisitive man." The high pitched voice echoed about the foyer and squeaked its way to Sam in the sitting room. "You seem to have taken on the task of injecting yourself into other people's affairs. And now you mention a woman of unsavory reputation, obviously implying that I would know such a person or help you make a connection between her and the deceased. Well, you are sadly mistaken, sir."

"How do you know she has an unsavory reputation?"

"Everyone in Sarasota knows that." He was back in the sitting room but remained standing, facing the foyer. The double-breasted blazer stretched taut against his pudgy torso.

Francis moved in closer to Sam. "Why don't you leave all of this alone, mind your own business, sir, and let the police handle the matter of Mr. Rossi's death instead of pestering decent people? Or, have you already bothered them with the scene you witnessed while eavesdropping?"

Sam smiled. He'd been wondering why Francis hadn't booted him out long ago. Now he knew. He set his glass on the coffee table, and when he looked up, Cecil stood in the foyer. Francis skittered over to him.

"Cecil, Mr. Wallace has the misguided notion that I threatened that scurrilous car salesman the day we visited him. Our visitor strikes me as a trouble maker, Cecil. What is that colorful phrase you use?"

Cecil glowered at Sam. "Shit stirrer."

"Yes, that's it. Vulgar, but descriptive." With Cecil at his side, Francis no longer leaned on his cane. He stood tall, pointed at Sam and said, "You sir, are a shit stirrer."

He could handle being insulted by Francis, but he didn't want him to get Cecil worked up. If they did kill Rossi, who knows what the little jerk might do now? "To answer your question, Francis, of course I told the police what I saw. Funny though, they didn't look on it as eavesdropping. In fact they were very interested." He got up and walked toward them, show them his tough side the way Dirk would. "Just thought you might like to know that."

Cecil assumed the stance Sam had seen with Rossi. He looked toward Francis for a signal. Sam wondered what it would be like to be leveled by a three hundred and fifty pound giant. He eyed the front door, a few feet away.

Cecil stepped between Sam and the door. Francis remained still, both hands leaning on his cane.

Sam assessed the situation. Francis looked pensive. Was he trying to decide whether to sic Cecil on him, break a bone or two? Squash his skull and bury him in the cellar? The silence unnerved him so he broke it. "Well, Mr. Wilson, thank you for letting me visit, and also, by the way for your hospitality last night at Mickey's. Ms. Belding and I enjoyed the evening. In fact I just had lunch with her on the circle and told her I was going to drop by and see you. She said to give you her regards." He waited to see if his clever ploy would dissuade Francis.

"Good afternoon, Mr. Wallace." Francis nodded. Cecil moved away from the door and disappeared into the bowels of the house.

"Again, let me assure you, I had nothing to do with the death of Mr. Rossi," Francis said. "However, the person who committed the act has done the community a service. As for you, sir, I would suggest that you leave the matter alone and tend to your own affairs."

Was Francis threatening him?

Francis opened the door and with a courtly sweep of his hand, told Sam to get lost.

Sam stepped to the doorway and turned. "I liked your speech the other night, Francis. How's the Cultural Center coming?"

Francis' expression brightened, the way a person's might when you ask about his family. "Very well, thank you. My friends are behind the Center and me one hundred percent. They fully understand the nature of Melody's illness which caused the unfortunate incident."

Sam moved onto the driveway. He hadn't expected Francis to bring up the embarrassing end to his evening and didn't really want to hear about it.

Francis followed him out, running along now to keep up with Sam. "I will see that Melody's illness is properly treated. Cecil put her on a plane to her home in Zanesville where she will receive the best of medical care for her condition. I will spare no expense. Francis J. Wilson is a man of compassion. I am not a vindictive person."

Sam drove away, pondering Francis' last statement.

15

Jimbo Conlin paced the floor of the penthouse living room in his brand new Gulf front resort. He liked the feel of the plush carpeting under his bare feet. Something about the smell and feel of new carpeting made a man feel good. He walked out to the terrace, inhaled the rich smells of the sea, and surveyed his kingdom below. He admired his two swimming pools nestled among the acres of flowering trees and palms. His pride and joy was the Olympic-sized pool, but the kidney shaped one, the one old Jimbo himself designed, wasn't exactly chopped liver.

He went over to his Gitzo tripod, where his 503 C-W Hasselblad camera was mounted, and trained the Carl Zeiss lens out on the whole shebang. Jimbo liked nice things. The camera was the best money could buy.

He made sure to get in the six clay tennis courts and the Gulf beyond. None of that concrete shit for Jimbo. Clay was the way to go. Expensive and a pain in the ass to maintain, but he would have the only real clay courts resort on the Key. In fact, the only clay courts in all of Sarasota. All these old duffers with their bad knees, bad backs and weak ankles come down here to play tennis. Soft courts, that's what they want, and that's what Jimbo's gonna give 'em.

If his tennis players got thirsty they wouldn't have to go far. The thatched roof bar perched in the center of the tennis area provided just the right "island" flavor. If a cold beer or mai tai didn't do the trick, they could slip into one of the cabanas, put on a bathing suit, and stroll over to the Gulf for a dip. Old Jimbo had it all in this baby. He took a dozen or so shots at different angles and went back inside.

Five years of hard work, kissing asses, greasing palms, fighting for permits, but he'd prevailed over all them sumbitches. The worst ones were the environmental weirdos, worrying about bullshit like beach erosion, pollution, birds and wetlands. The wackos even gave him a hard time about fucking turtle nests.

But Jimbo, he got too much savvy to let that shit sidetrack him. "Polluting the aesthetics of the environment," he said aloud. How could anybody look at all this and say it's not aesthetic. No satisfying some people.

Now he had another problem and this one could be big time. He checked his watch: nine o'clock. Cliff would be in his office by now.

He went to a corner of the room, lowered himself to a sitting position on the floor, and leaned his back against the wall. The furniture and stuff wouldn't be coming for a few days. That was his strong suit, his furniture.

He liked to work with the decorators, piss 'em off when he picked out all the furniture. But he knew what he liked and he was never wrong.

Use the cheap wicker shit for the cookie cutter crap he put up on the mainland. Upscale place like this, you give it class, put in the Baker, Henredon, plantation shutters, the whole bit.

He liked it when the big shot decorators with their degrees and fancy A.S.I.D. initials after their names would whine about his butting in and then finally admit that he was pretty good when it all came together. They had trouble dealing with the idea that a good old boy from West Texas knew anything about decorating.

He pulled out his cellular phone and punched in the numbers.

"Cliff Bracken here."

It was Jimbo who insisted that Cliff get a direct line into his office, so he wouldn't have to go through the same bullshit every time he called, like:

"Hello. Galt Marine Laboratories."

"Cliff Bracken, please."

"Who shall I say is calling?"

"Jimbo Conlin."

"Hello. Mr. Bracken's office."

"Let me speak to Cliff, please."

"Who shall I say is calling?"

"Winston fucking Churchill!"

He thought Cliff sounded a little wary when he announced himself. He always did whenever Jimbo called. They had a kind of understanding that Jimbo would only call when it was something very important. They even played it cool about being seen together in public.

"Jimbo, just a minute."

Goin' over to close the door. Same old chickenshit routine.

"Hi, what's up, buddy?"

"We got a problem." Jimbo didn't believe in beating around the bush.

"Oh?"

"Yeah, I understand you got a scientist there doing some heavy duty research project on red tide."

"Jimbo, we have several scientists who study red tide. It's one of the things we do here. You know that."

The Ph.D. in him coming out. Sounding official. Important. "Hey, buddy-boy. This old Jimbo here. I'm talkin' about the stuff that Belding broad is doing. You know, the one with the boobs and the nice tight little ass."

"Yes, Jimbo, I'm familiar with Dr. Belding's work. What about it?"

"What about it? This about it. I understand she's been working on predicting red tide, got it all figured out. Says a real bad red tide's gonna hit here right smack in the middle of the tourist season. Comin' on like a freight train. And you know the worst part of what I understand? She's getting ready to go public with it all. That right, buddy-boy?"

Jimbo waited. Cliff was most probably wiping the sweat off his face. It's what he did when he got stressed out. Sweat.

"How do you know all this, Jimbo. Where are you getting such information?"

"That ain't important, Cliff. What is important is that it's true, and you know it. Don't bullshit me."

"Yes, Dr. Belding has recently completed a year long research study on predicting red tide. Her report is due to me in a couple of weeks as a matter of fact."

Jimbo sighed. Cliff had been good to him, and they'd developed a friendship over the years.

Jimbo was a young builder, trying to make a few bucks when Cliff gave him the break he needed to get over the hump. Cliff was chairman of the biology department at Sarasota University and chairman of the building committee. The college owned a large piece of bay front where they had hoped to either expand or build a new campus.

The school fell on hard times financially and needed to sell off the land quickly to survive. Cliff told Jimbo about it and helped him work a deal to acquire the land before anyone else got wind of it. Jimbo put up a big condo, and five minutes after the last nail went in, condo prices in Sarasota skyrocketed. Jimbo made a fortune and he never forgot.

But sometimes Cliff could be a stuffy, evasive bastard. "Cliff, I know what's gonna be in that report. She's gonna tell you what I just told you. She's also gonna tell the whole fucking world. Thinks people need to be warned. You know, that moral obligation shit. You get people talkin' like that and that's when they stop bein' sensible."

Jimbo was getting uncomfortable, sitting on the floor of his new penthouse. Time to slice through the crap, get off the phone. "I don't need to remind you, Cliffie boy, what this moral obligation thing would do to me. Nothin' big. Just bankrupt me, that's all."

"Look, Jimbo—"

"No, you look. She gets that news out before the season starts and I'm finished. I got two big conventions booked. I got the whole place sold out for January, February, March, and April. Everybody cancels out, and ol' Jimbo is left holdin' his dick and nothing else. I'm history."

"Jimbo, I'll handle it," Cliff said.

"You better, Buddy-Boy. You can't afford to get me mad at you guys. Worse yet, you can't afford for me to go broke."

"I get the message, Jimbo. I'll take care of it."

Jimbo hung up and put the phone in his pocket. He glanced around the room and noticed that one of the window shutters had a slat a tad narrower than the others and made a note to have it replaced.

He struggled to his knees and hauled himself upright with a groan. One last look around reminded him that there was more than money at stake here. He loved the place. It was his crowning achievement. He'd be goddamned if he would lose it now after all he'd been through.

* * *

Cliff hung up the phone and wiped the sweat off his face, drenching his handkerchief. He stuffed it in the drawer and took out a clean one.

The conversation with Jimbo reinforced how much he hated the Galt's dependency on contributions and fundraising. He was a distinguished scientist, and so were all of his colleagues. It wasn't right that they should have to toady up to people like Jimbo for their existence.

Jennifer's work on red tide was important, and he, of all people, should be encouraging it, not listening to imbeciles like Conlin who would suppress it for their own selfish financial gain. What was the world coming to? Money. Money. Money. Well, he would be damned if he would let money compromise the integrity of his people.

But he was kidding himself if he thought that research was still his thing. He was an administrator, and he was good at that, too. In fact when Dr. Stringer retires next year, it's no secret who the new director will be. Maybe he was a masochist, but he wanted that directorship badly. It was a plum position in the scientific community and he deserved it.

The fiscal year would be over in a month. Nearly all the major financial commitments were in, and they were running behind goal. His career was on the line if they didn't make it. He wished he had never let himself be talked into being an administrator. He would still be a functioning scientist doing the kind of important work he loved. Like Jennifer.

He dabbed at his face with the fresh handkerchief and got up to turn on his small fan. The director's office had its own AC thermostat. A small perk but one that would be nice to have.

There was a knock on the door.

"Who's there?"

"It's Donald."

"Come in."

Donald Frazier entered. He looked upset, and Cliff wasn't sure he was up to dealing with Donald right now.

Donald was Director of Development, which was a euphemism for fundraising. It was Donald's job to see that the money flowed in, and he was very good at it. He was also the only person at the Galt as ambitious as Cliff. Maybe more so. Donald was pushy and abrasive. He was also an ass kisser. It sickened him the way Donald sucked up to Conlin and his ilk. But he tolerated him, because he was a genius at raising money. He didn't like Donald, but he respected and needed him. Every worthy scientific institution has its Donald Frazier.

Donald wore his uniform when he expected to be in the office all day, the Galt Marine T-shirt, khaki shorts and sandals. After twenty-five years in the fundraising world of New York City, wearing three piece suits and commuting three hours a day, Donald had quickly adapted to the Sarasota lifestyle. His personality had not. It was still three piece and button-down.

"Cliff, I'm very concerned about something," he stated before he even closed the door.

Cliff groaned and didn't really care if Donald heard him or not. He went back to his desk and sat down. "What's the matter?"

Donald remained standing. "Well, I called Jimbo Conlin last night about his annual pledge. As you know we're coming down to the wire and Jimbo hasn't yet sent us his check. He was very evasive with me, not like him. What's going on?"

Cliff loved Donald's style. He barges into his office with his jaw jutting out, no "how are you today?" No chit-chat, just charge ahead. Presents his problem, then makes it sound like it's your fault. It also annoyed him to have Donald standing at his desk, hovering over him.

"All right, Donald, sit down. Relax and we'll talk about it." He spun his chair and faced the other way, his back to Donald. He would stay like that until Donald stopped leaning over him.

Donald got the message and sat down. Cliff turned back to him. He would have to level with Donald. He'd eventually find out through Jimbo anyway. "I just got off the phone with Jimbo. He's upset about the research results of one of our scientists."

"What do you mean?"

Cliff had to smile. Donald was a great fundraiser, but he could care less about the nature or quality of scientific work being done at the Galt. He had to be kept abreast to properly represent the importance of Galt's work, but he retained only as much as he needed to do his job. He had no intrinsic interest. Money was his God, and raising it, his mission. The Galt could be developing nerve gas for all he cared. He had his job to do.

"It seems that one of our people has made a major breakthrough regarding red tide, like finding a way to predict it. The research shows that a bad strain—maybe the worst ever—is scheduled to hit around late December, early January. Jimbo is concerned about our publicizing this and destroying the first season for his new resort."

Donald shot off his chair. "My God! I don't blame him. That would ruin him." He stopped and pondered for a moment, then walked slowly over to Cliff's desk and pointed his finger at Cliff. "That's why he was evasive with me. If we let this out, he's not going to honor his commitment."

Cliff watched him drag the last words out like he was announcing an execution. He nodded. "You got it."

"How can you just sit there and say, 'You got it?' Jimbo Conlin is our biggest contributor. Need I remind you how important his money is to the Galt?"

"You don't need to remind me of anything, Donald." Cliff got up from his chair and walked toward the door. Not very subtle, but he wanted Donald the hell out of his office.

"Two million dollars," Donald said. "That's what Jimbo's commitment is this year. We don't have a prayer of making our goal if he backs out, and you know it." He moved between Cliff and the door. "You *are* going to talk to that scientist of yours, Cliff?"

Cliff walked around him and opened the door. "Donald, I'm perfectly capable of dealing with my scientists without your advice. Now, I have an appointment. Thank you for dropping in."

16

Sam entered his apartment, flicked on his message machine and listened to Detective Diane Lewis ask him to call her. She would like to take his statement in the morning.

Henry waddled out from the bedroom. Sam asked him if he would like to go outside, a word Henry knew well. He responded by hopping onto the sofa and burying his nose under the pillow. Sam shooed him off and he wandered back into the bedroom.

Only a few days, and he was already becoming an apartment dog. Henry needed to get outside, get some exercise. He was getting pudgy. If Mrs. Bunting notices, she'll haul him back on her scale, and it'll be all over for him.

After calling Lewis and making a date for 9:30 in the morning he made himself a drink, put on a Sarah Brightman CD, and went out to the terrace. It was quiet. He leaned over the railing and was relieved to see that the workmen had left for the day.

The gentle breeze drifting in from the water and the haunting sounds of Brightman's voice seduced him. He sprawled out on the chaise with his thoughts. It had been an interesting day. The lunch with Jennifer, brief though it was, only whet his appetite for more.

Mike Rossi. Sounds like whoever killed him will probably get a civic award. Even Jennifer badmouthed him.

So? He met Rossi twice and got a kick out of him. Actually liked him. What he didn't like was the idea of somebody bashing his head in. Nobody deserves that.

Still, he was pushing the envelope knocking on people's doors, giving them the third degree, playing Sherlock Holmes. He was lucky Francis didn't let Cecil have his way with him.

Good way to get inside Dirk Flander's head, though. It looked like he and Dirk were going to be together for a while. No better way

to see what makes him tick. And he had to admit he did like the challenge of snooping around Mike's murder. Anyway, it's not as if he
didn't have some experience

Maybe that's why he started writing books about this stuff. Playing out his own fantasies. Getting vicariously back into the police
work he once liked. Now that his teaching career seemed all but over,
maybe it was good for him to get his nose back into a little investigative work. Couldn't hurt his writing, either.

Henry came out and joined him. He flattened himself at Sam's
feet, his front legs splayed out in front of him. Sam smiled and
scratched his ear. When Henry lay like that, it was like he had no
bones. Just fur and muscle. "Come on, buddy," Sam said. "Let's go
for a walk. Get your leash."

Henry raised his head, cocked it, and studied Sam before letting
his head fall back on the floor. He closed his eyes and burrowed his
head into his body.

"Henry!"

Henry bolted up, scurried into the kitchen, and returned with
the leash in his mouth. Sam attached it and they left.

Ten minutes later they were back in the apartment. The walk
had not gone well. Henry got into a tiff with a cocker spaniel who
nipped him on the nose. Sam washed the red abrasion on his nose,
and Henry skulked off to the bedroom.

Still early and it was a beautiful night. Too late to do anything
very productive and too early to go to bed. He thought of the convertible cooped up under its car cover. Terrible waste on a night like
tonight. He threw on a light wind breaker, grabbed an apple, and left.

Munching on his apple, tooling along the Key with the top down,
he felt loose and relaxed. Contented? Whatever, it was something he
hadn't felt in a while. Even the bad dreams were fading.

But some things would take longer. Time was not the great
healer he'd been promised but now, at least for the moment, the
bleeding was in remission, and he was moving forward.

He drove along Bayfront Drive, past Marina Jack's. It seemed like months since he'd met Mike and Jimbo there. Was it really only a few days ago?

A breeze came in from the Bay, filling the car with the seductive smells of the sea. Millions of stars twinkled overhead, harbingers of another beautiful day to come. He turned left toward Lido and Longboat Key and was soon at St. Armand's Circle, resisting the temptation to angle onto Lido and cruise over to Jennifer's.

Instead, he drove north, across the bridge toward Longboat Key. He continued driving north along Gulf of Mexico Drive, past condominiums set back in perfect symmetry between majestic gates, lush landscaping, and the Gulf of Mexico.

He found himself in a different world from laid back, unpretentious Siesta Key. Most of these babies looked like they had been built by Donald Trump. He wouldn't have been surprised to see The Donald's limousine come cruising out from one of them. He passed The Forum and nodded. "Yeah, they do have one for a couple million, but you wouldn't want to live in it."

Longboat Key had to be where most of that crowd from Francis J.'s party lived. Had to be. The place is a world unto itself, he thought. Very elegant, very impressive, but not for him. He preferred Siesta Key.

Things turned a little more commonplace at the north end of Longboat. Not exactly "down home," but a bit more relaxed. He spotted a Hilton Resort on the left. Attracted by the "Poolside Bar" sign, he pulled into the driveway.

The bar was very tropical and very empty. A lone customer sat at the far end chatting with the bartender, a young man who looked like he spent his days surfing in the sun and working out in the gym.

His eyes didn't stay on the barkeep for long. It was his customer, leaning over the bar, exposing the dark areolas around her nipples that grabbed his attention. The blouse she wore was stretched to its limits and looked ready to burst at any moment. He also noticed her fingernail polish. Purple with yellow flowers.

The woman laughed at something the bartender said. She threw her head back, sending the bleached blonde hair in all directions, turned, and looked Sam's way. He blinked his eyes and looked again. It was Melody.

What was Melody doing here? She's supposed to be in Ohio. At least that's what Francis thinks. Anyway, here she is, working on the young bartender. Move in, talk to her, and find out what she knows. Problem is how to snag her away from the stud behind the bar.

Three couples came in and sat down, chattering away in German. Sam waited until the bartender went over to wait on them and made his move. He moved to the stool next to Melody and with his best Dirk Flanders smile said, "Hello, you're Melody, aren't you?"

Her head snapped around like she hadn't noticed him slide in next to her. He held his smile in place while she eyeballed him with an expression that told him he was a poor substitute for the bartender. "Do I know you?" she asked.

"No, not really, but I know who you are," he said, not sure where he was going with this.

"Oh?" She took a hit from a pale looking drink in a long stem cocktail glass. Looked like a stinger, but he wasn't sure. "How do you know me?" she asked after another quick sip.

"Well. I, uh . . ." He shrugged. Might as well get to it. "I was at the fundraiser the other night, the one at Mickey's?" He heard his voice trail off. To his relief she laughed.

"Oh yeah. So you saw all the fun."

He nodded.

"Guess I got a little carried away. Poor Francis. I really felt bad the next day. But he's pissed at me now. Tried to send me back to Ohio."

"I thought he did."

"Who told you that?"

"Francis. I talked with him today."

She squinted, tilted her head, and stared at him. "Who the hell are you?"

He was waiting for that. Better be careful. He wasn't sure how many stingers she'd had, but having seen her in action, he didn't want to get her worked up. "I'm a writer, Melody. I write mystery novels and I'm doing some research for my next book. I thought maybe you could help."

She softened. "You're a writer?"

"Yes, and since there's been a real life murder here in Sarasota, I'm sort of using that as a laboratory for my work."

She frowned and drained her drink. "You wanna buy me another?"

"Sure," Sam said.

"You're talking about that asshole, Rossi, I take it," she said.

Another affectionate ode to Mike. He waited until the bartender set their drinks down before continuing. "How'd you get out of going back to Ohio?" he asked, changing the subject.

She set the drink down after another hefty gulp. "You kiddin'? Who the hell was he to send me back to Ohio, have that big gorilla, Cecil drive me to the airport, check me in like I'm some little kid." She snickered. "Soon's he left I took a cab here. Anyway, I'll call Francis in a few days. He'll be horny by then, and he'll be OK."

Sam nodded. She was probably right, although he had trouble picturing Francis in the saddle with the zaftig Melody. But then, it wasn't something he wanted to spend much time thinking about. "Getting back to Mike Rossi, Melody, I dropped in to see him at his car place the day he was killed. I have a vintage car, and I'm interested in them."

"So?"

"Well, while I was in back of the showroom, looking at cars, Francis and Cecil came in."

"Oh, Jesus." She finished off her drink and looked around the bar. "What'd Francis want? Yoo-hoo," she yelled to the bartender. He turned and she held up her glass.

Sam winced. He would have to get through this fast. Cut to the chase. "He was upset. Said that Rossi had sex with you. They had an ugly scene, Francis warned Rossi that he hadn't heard the last of him, and he and Cecil stormed out. Sort of makes Francis a suspect. At least that's what the police think. By the way, they never saw me standing in the showroom." He didn't have to wait long for her reaction.

"Bullshit," she screamed.

Sam smiled at the other patrons, now looking their way. "It's all right, folks. Just having a little discussion." They went back to their business and Sam went back to Melody. "Calm down, Melody. I'm just trying to bring you up to date, that's all."

She reached inside her blouse and pulled one of her bra straps back on her shoulder. "Yeah, well Francis may be a lotta things, but he's no killer. You tell your friends, the cops they should be looking at Alexis Helfrich and that big bimbo Carole, who works for her."

"Alexis, who runs the escort service?"

"You're goddamn right. They both hated Rossi. And for good reason."

"How do you know this, Melody?"

"How do I know it? Because that muscle bound Carole used to be a friend of mine, that's how. I know all about the shit that went down between all of 'em." She grabbed her fresh drink, downed half its contents and hiccupped.

He watched Melody's features seeming to change with each gulp of her drink. Her mascara had smudged and settled under one eye like the stuff football players wear. Her face began to sag, and he noticed the beginnings of jowls trying to crowd their way in. She couldn't be more than early thirties, but the drinking was already taking its toll. "What kind of shit went down between them, Melody?"

Melody looked at him like he was demented. "He was blackmailing them." She paused and studied Sam as if seeing him for the first time. "You know, you're kinda cute. What's your name, anyway."

"Oh, sorry. It's Sam. What was he blackmailing them for?"

She continued eyeing him. "Aw come on, Sam. I'm sick of talking about that slimeball, Rossi." She set the glass down and put her hand over his. "You married?"

"Yes, I am," he lied. "Can you tell me what he was blackmailing them for?"

"I told you I don't want to talk about it anymore." Another hiccup slipped out. "Fuck you anyway." She waved her glass. "Bartender."

It was time to leave.

17

At exactly 9:29, Sam entered the reception area of the Criminal Investigation Division of the Sarasota County Sheriff's Department. Punctuality was not one of his strong suits, but he had the feeling that Detective Diane Lewis was not a lady to be kept waiting.

The receptionist buzzed her office and invited Sam to sit down. He thumbed through a copy of *People* magazine, and his name popped out at him. There it was, a brief, two paragraph review of his book.

". . . And Mr. Wallace, a professor at Whately College, writes with subtlety and insight. Dirk Flanders is a character we will want to meet again. Dirk has style, charisma, and he's interesting."

"All right," Sam said aloud

"Excuse me?" the receptionist asked.

"Nothing. Just talking to myself." He remembered now, his editor telling him that *People* was going to do something on his book. She wasn't sure if it was going to be a review or maybe a short article. He would take the review.

"Mr. Wallace?"

He looked up and Diane Lewis stood in the doorway. Dressed all in black, slacks, black cotton T-shirt, she looked even more formidable than he remembered at Rossi's house. She barked his name the way his fifth grade teacher used to when he got frisky. Lewis had the same annoyed expression on her face.

Even with the expression and the shoulder holster stretched across her chest, she was very good looking. He wondered if the holster and the thirty-eight sitting in it were for his benefit. "Hi, nice to see you again, Detective."

They shook hands, and he was totally unprepared for the crunch he felt. He extricated his hand and grinned at her, as if to say, "If you're trying to bust my balls, you're doing a pretty good job."

"Follow me," she said and led him down a narrow corridor. He was still appraising her. Late 30's, beautiful skin, hair tied back, but soft, nicely styled. Hard to tell if she had any make-up on. Probably not. He wrapped it all up with the conclusion that she was tough, but very much a woman.

They went into a windowless room with a small conference table and several chairs. A tape recorder sat in the middle of the table.

"Please sit down, Mr. Wallace," Lewis directed. "Do you have any objection to the tape recorder?"

Sam shook his head, "No."

She flicked on the recorder. "Please tell us in detail exactly what you observed on November 8, of this year at the auto dealership of the murder victim, Michael Rossi."

Sam provided an extensive account of his visit to Rossi on that day and concluded with a smile. "That's it, Detective. Any questions?"

"No, you've been quite thorough. Thank you."

He thought the same about her. When he was on the force in Boston, he'd gotten to know many of the female cops and two of the detectives. Most of them were damn good, actually better than many of the men. Part of it was that they worked a lot harder at their jobs, because, being female, they had at least one strike against them. Hard to believe, even back then, but that's the way it was. Lewis probably had to work even harder, being black, in a small southern city. He got up. "That it?"

Lewis remained seated and began writing on her pad.

Sam, still standing, waited for an answer. The room was hot and he was being ignored. He felt his good humor slipping away.

She put her pen down and looked up. "That's all for the statement, but there's something else we need to talk about. Sit down."

He suspected what might be on her mind and braced himself as he sat. "Sure, what would you like to talk about?"

"You went to see Francis J. Wilson yesterday."

Yep, he was right. Only why did she have to make it sound like he was seen selling heroine in the school yard? "Yes, I did, didn't I?"

"Why did you do that?"

"I was in the neighborhood, heard about his nice house, and wanted to see what it looked like. A little garish, but not bad."

She got to her feet so abruptly the chair fell over. "Don't be flip with me, or I'll have your ass in jail for obstructing justice. Now let's try again. Why did you go to see Wilson?"

She is a ball breaker—with a very short fuse. "OK, I went to see Wilson, because we had met at a fundraiser Saturday night, and I thought maybe I could learn something further from him. I had just met Rossi and I liked him. When I heard about his murder on TV, I of course thought about Wilson's threat. That's why I went immediately to tell you about it. To be honest, you didn't seem all that interested, so when I happened to drive by his street, I decided to stop in and talk to him.

"That's all. Sorry if I butted in. I thought I could help." He didn't like groveling, but she was probably right and being a wise-ass wasn't going to help matters.

In any event, his change in attitude seemed to calm her down. "Look," she said. "I'm a pragmatic police officer. I'm also smart enough not to turn down any legitimate help I can get."

Sounds good so far.

"But what you did was not helpful. You alerted Wilson to the fact that we would obviously want to talk with him. You gave him time to think about it, and if he did kill Rossi, to perfect whatever alibi he planned to use. It wasn't very smart of you, going to see him like that, and I don't want you to do it again."

He watched her body language, hands on hips, legs spread apart and noticed a harshness come back into her voice. In spite of the situation, he was impressed with the way she handled herself and decided she was probably a very good cop.

He also couldn't help watching her as a woman, and it made him feel a little sexist. But she was a sexy lady. He wondered if she knew that. "You're right, it wasn't smart. I apologize." He stood and put his hand out. "Friends?"

She hesitated for a moment before extending hers. Even let a little smile slip.

Oh, oh, he thought, remembering the first time they shook hands. This grip, however, was warm and gentle—or at least it seemed that way after the first one. Maybe his contrition softened her.

"Friends? I don't know about that, Mr. Wallace, but we can at least be civil. As a writer you probably have good instincts, and your book shows exceptional insights into criminal investigation—for a layman. You have obviously done some homework. But other than that, I can think of no good reason to allow you to poke your nose into police business."

"You've read my book?"

"I read a lot of mystery books. You might say it's my hobby. I also have a good memory. I read your book a few weeks ago and recognized your name and face. As I recall you are or were a college professor. I read your book jacket, too."

It was the first time he'd ever talked to anyone who actually recognized his name from his book. Maybe he was beginning his fifteen minutes of fame. He thought about offering to autograph her copy but decided not to press his luck. "I promise I won't meddle or cause you a problem, but given the fact that I am a writer, am incurably nosy, and I knew Mike Rossi, I'm very curious to see if I can learn anything further. Also, I'm not exactly a layman, when it comes to police work."

"What do you mean by that?"

"I was a police officer with the Boston Police Department for almost four years."

She gave him a quizzical look, which turned into a frown, and the hands were back on her hips. Very threatening. She was good.

"The book jacket says you're a college professor."

"Yes. I was on the police force when I was much younger. I left to finish college."

"Why didn't you mention this before?"

"Sorry, I guess I should have, but when I first talked with you, I didn't think it was particularly relevant. I thought I was just being a good citizen reporting information to you. Now that I seem to be 'poking my nose into police business,' I'm telling you, so maybe you won't be so hard on me." He grinned. "Maybe I can help and I promise not to be a nuisance."

She started to speak, but he went on. "Anything I learn, I'll share with you immediately. Before I talk with anyone who could be connected in any way, I'll check with you first. Maybe I can help, and I'll cooperate in every way." Not bad, he thought. At least the frown was gone.

She took a step forward and stood eyeball to eyeball facing him. He detected a slight smell of jasmine that he hadn't noticed before. Being female in a rough man's world she might have had trouble being taken seriously, maybe overcompensated by sublimating her femininity. He didn't think she was doing a very good job of it. And it wasn't just the jasmine.

"Maybe some time you'd like to tell me how you went from being a police officer to college professor to playing detective in Sarasota."

He nodded and started to speak, but she waved him away. "I don't have the time right now. I'm late for an appointment, but we'll talk again. In the meantime, I'll give you an opportunity to cooperate with us, provided you don't become meddlesome and don't preempt our work."

"Thank you, Detective Lewis. I hope I can help." He looked toward the door. "I take it I'm dismissed now?"

She nodded and he started to leave.

"Mr. Wallace."

Oh, oh, what now? He turned and stood outside the door, facing her, relieved to see a smile on her face. "Yes?"

"I do want to hear more about how you wound up here—trying to be a cop again."

He returned her smile and left.

* * *

Cliff Bracken was not having a good morning. Jimbo's phone call was bad enough, but he had to listen to that sniveling ass, Frazier. Sometimes he wished Donald wasn't so good at his job. Then he could get rid of him and not have to put up with his whining.

It won't take Donald long to find out which scientist is causing the trouble. Time to nip this thing in the bud.

He picked up the phone and punched a couple of numbers. "Jennifer, can you come over to my office?"

He liked Jennifer. She was probably the brightest scientist on his staff. A little headstrong and independent, but that hadn't ever really been a serious problem. Still, he couldn't help feeling uneasy when the knock came on his door. "Come in," he called.

She walked in and stood for a moment. "You want this open or closed?" she asked, without saying hello.

After all these years of working together, he never felt comfortable around her. He considered himself at least her intellectual equal—probably superior. But she always seemed to act like she simply didn't like him. He was a professional and couldn't care less. But still.

"Yes, close it if you would, Jennifer and come sit down."

She closed it and settled into the chair in front of his desk. "Closed door session, huh Cliff?"

"No, it's just hectic out there. I've had it closed all morning. How's your report coming?" He slid his chair back and leaned his foot on one of his open desk drawers.

"It's coming."

He waited for her to continue, but her expression said, "Next question." "Well, Jennifer, I thought you could give me a brief executive summary. I have a meeting later today where I might want to talk a little bit about it."

"I'll have the written report to you by the end of the week. It's not like I've been doing this in a vacuum, Cliff. I've tried to keep you apprised on a fairly regular basis. But, yes, I could give you a brief summary of my conclusions now, if you'd like."

"That would be fine."

"Well, as you know, we've developed a scientific design for predicting red tide outbreaks based on cyclical physical parameters measured as far as ninety miles out in the Gulf and as close in as Egremont Key at the mouth of Tampa Bay."

She was out of her chair now, pacing about his office. He knew she wouldn't sit for very long.

"As I believe I told you, we have been patiently tracking the circulation of the water for a year as well as the chemistry that makes up and drives the organism. By finally isolating G. Breve from the other harmless blooms, we've been able to study it and follow its movements."

"And?"

She returned to his desk, placed her hands on it and leaned toward him. "Cliff, we're getting close to identifying the point of origin for a given tide. Do you know what that means?"

"Tell me."

"It means we could mitigate the intensity of the neurotoxins and reduce the impact of airborne neurotoxins. We're not quite there yet, but we will be. This is a huge breakthrough, Cliff. It'll put us in the forefront of red tide research."

He smiled and wanted to say that the Galt has been there for some time. Instead, he said, "That's fabulous. Very exciting." Red tide was not Cliff's field, but he fully understood the enormous implications of what she was saying. That was more long term, however than his concern at the moment. "Tell me more about your prediction research regarding this winter."

She sat down. "That's the bad news."

"Tell me."

"Well, the increase in global warming has enhanced conditions for growth of the type of organism that produces the toxins. As I told you the other day, tests we've done show that the bloom moving this way contains over seventy million of the G. Breve organism to a quart of water. Normal state is a hundred to a quart. Last year's red tide, which as you remember, was very noxious and a lot of people got sick, measured between three and four million."

He swiveled his chair around, facing away from her, as he spoke. "Well, you say a lot of people got sick. I'm not sure what a lot is, but it really wasn't any big deal, a few runny noses, maybe a little coughing and sneezing. I live on the water, and I didn't have any problems."

She bolted off the chair. "Goddamn it, Cliff, you're a scientist. How can you talk like that? There were over twenty-two hundred cases reported of people treated for respiratory problems directly related to red tide. You didn't have any problems," she said, mocking him. "You also don't suffer from emphysema or heart problems. Red tide can cause serious bronchial constricting. Its threat to people who are vulnerable is very real.

"Did you hear my description of the tide coming this winter?" She waited, but he said nothing. "Cliff, it's going to be twenty times more virulent than last year and fifteen times more potent than the worst strain we've ever recorded."

"And your conclusions?"

She studied him for a moment, and in a flat, unemotional voice stated, "The strain of red tide I've just described will hit this area sometime in early January, and there is nothing we can do to prevent it."

Cliff nodded, waiting to see if there was more.

"But there is one thing we can do," she said.

"What's that?"

"Warn people."

"Yes, well I want to talk with you about that, Jennifer."

18

When Sam entered the condo, Henry pounced on him, bounced off, pulled himself up, and leaped again. Sam rubbed his ears and Henry rolled over a couple of times before assuming his vigil in front of the door.

"I hear you, Henry, and I've got just the place for you. Get your leash."

Henry disappeared into the bedroom and emerged with the leash in his mouth. He dropped it at Sam's feet and nudged Sam's leg with his nose.

"All right. Come on, we're going for a ride and then I've got a surprise for you. Oops, wait a minute." He went over to his machine and checked for messages. Nothing. On the way out, he grabbed an apple from the refrigerator, and they left.

Sam drove into the village and along Beach Road, pulled onto a side street and parked. They walked two short blocks to a small beach on the Gulf. "Henry, old boy, this is called Dog Beach. It's a little spot of heaven, reserved for guys like you." He unhooked the leash and gestured toward the beach. "Go for it, Henry." Henry looked up and down the beach at a half dozen dogs romping and chasing one another. He didn't budge.

A Doberman came over and sniffed around Henry. Henry backed in between Sam's legs, warily eyeing the big dog. After a few more sniffs, the Doberman took off, answering the whistle of a large man at the other end of the beach.

Henry edged out from behind Sam and picked up the leash. "I get the message, pal. We'll have to ease you into this." He hooked the leash and they began their stroll across the beach.

The big guy coming toward them with the Doberman looked familiar. He wore a flowered bathing suit that hung below the knees and a tent sized T-shirt with the words Sarasota Brewing Company on it. A straw sombrero sat atop his head.

As they drew closer the man pointed at Sam. "Hey, I know you," he said.

"Hello Jimbo. Sam Wallace. We had a couple of beers together at Marina Jack's the other day."

Henry began yapping at the Doberman, who was now ignoring him. Being ignored seemed to piss Henry off, and he lunged forward, straining at the leash.

"You want a piece of him, Henry?" Sam asked and dropped the leash. Henry stopped, glanced down at the leash, and scuttled around behind Sam.

"Thought so," Sam said and retrieved the leash.

Jimbo chuckled. "That's a tough lookin' little critter you got there, Sam. He wouldn't make no more'n a snack for Thunder here. Good thing Thunder ain't hungry." He looked at his watch. "Hey, you got time for a beer?" Without waiting for Sam to answer he started across the beach. "Come on. Follow me."

Sam nodded and fell in behind him. Perfect. He was planning to look up Jimbo, and he bumps into him.

They walked a half block up the street and turned right onto a small lane lined with beach type cottages. Jimbo stopped in front of one and beckoned to Sam. "Come on, we'll have a beer here."

Sam eyed the house and smiled. It was freshly painted in pinks and yellows and pale greens. A picket fence with each picket the silhouette of a flamingo. A wooden deck ran the width of the house. Sam shook his head. Perfect. Pure Florida.

Sarasota was so many different things, ranging from the pristine sterility of Longboat Key and its glittering wealth to the tacky little strip malls and trailer parks. This cottage and the comfortable, laid back feel of the beach neighborhood, represented for Sam, the best of Florida—of Sarasota.

Jimbo opened the gate and went onto the deck. "Sit down,

Buddy-Boy. I'll get us a coupla beers." He and Thunder disappeared into the house. When the door closed, Henry growled in Thunder's direction, looked up at Sam, and settled down next to him.

Sam sat at the umbrella table and put his feet on the railing. Great little spot, but not exactly what he would have expected from a guy who claims to have built half of Siesta Key. Then again, maybe it was. Maybe that's what he liked about Jimbo.

Jimbo came out and plopped two Coronas on the table. He sat down and laid his feet next to Sam's on the railing. Henry peeked around him, looking toward the house. "It's OK, little feller," Jimbo said. "Thunder's inside."

"You live here?" Sam asked.

"Naw, I live down the South end of the Key."

Sam nodded.

"This here's my house, though. It's one of my rentals. Not much demand for it right now so I keep it stored with stuff for me and Thunder. We come here and hang out after we've done our beach thing. It's my hideaway, and I love it. Whatcha doin' with yourself, Sam? Havin' fun here in Sarasota?"

Sam took a swig of his beer and peered out at the Gulf. Was he having fun? Good question. The place was looking better every day. "Yeah, I'd say I'm having some fun. Sarasota's an interesting place. Been here less than a week and one of the first guys I meet gets murdered." He looked up at Jimbo and watched his eyes narrow under the sombrero.

"You mean that fuckhead, Rossi?" Jimbo asked, the merriment gone from his voice.

"Yes, that's right. I remember you told me he was not one of your favorite people."

"Sheeit, he wasn't anybody's favorite people. Ain't nobody liked that sumbitch." He downed the last of his beer and nodded toward Sam's. "You finish that up, Buddy-Boy and I'll getcha another."

Sam finished his beer and watched a small dog chasing a kid on

a bike. The street was an odd mixture of year round, family bunga-
lows and vacation beach cottages like Jimbo's. He liked the street. Being less than a block from the beach, it had a simplicity that he found
appealing. Yes, Jimbo definitely fit the whole scene. But mentioning
Rossi didn't bring out the best in him.

They were on their third beer when Sam got around to asking
Jimbo if he had any idea who might have killed Mike Rossi.

"Sheeit," Jimbo roared. "Just look in the phone book and pick
out a name."

Sam smiled. Jimbo was being cagey. "Come on, Jimbo. You know
everybody in this town. You know what's going on."

Jimbo sat, staring, looking like Hoss Cartwright under the sombrero. Just kept staring at Sam, like maybe trying to figure him out.
Sam remembered Jimbo squeezing the beer mug at Marina Jack's.

"Who the hell are you anyway, Sam? How come you ask so
many questions?"

Sam laughed and nodded his head up and down, like yeah, good
question. "I guess I'm just nosy, Jimbo. I write mystery books and
this kind of thing fascinates me."

"You write mystery books?"

"Sure do," Sam said, relieved at the change in Jimbo's tone. "I
have to make them up, and now all of a sudden I'm privy to the real
thing. Guess it's too tempting not to nose around a little."

"No shit. You really write books? You published and all?"

Sam had a feeling he'd bought some time from Jimbo. "Yep, you
can go down to Barnes and Noble and buy a copy of my book right
now. It's called "Jeopardy" Get a copy and I'll inscribe and sign it for
you."

"You hot shit, you," Jimbo said, looking at Sam like he just dis-
covered him. "I'll do it."

"So what do you think, Jimbo? Any ideas?"

Jimbo was still looking at him, shaking his head, smiling. "You'n
me's gotta have us another beer, Sam." He went inside and came out

with two more Coronas and a handful of dog cookies for Henry. Henry, who'd been flattened out under Sam's chair, came to life and scarfed down the cookies.

Jimbo settled back in and took off his hat. "Like I said, anybody in town could have killed Rossi, but if I had to pick somebody, I'd look at that German broad Helfrich and the big hooker that works for her."

Sam nodded. Alexis Helfrich rears her head again. "Why do you say that, Jimbo?"

"Hey Buddy-Boy. Ol' Jimbo knows what he's talkin' 'bout." He took another hefty slug of his beer and farted. Sam slid his chair away.

"I known that old broad for a dozen years. I own the building she's in on the Trail. She rents it from me. Dumpy little place, but I get good money for it, 'cause of it's location." He snickered. "Used to take it out in trade with her once in a while if she was havin' a bad month, but I stopped that shit years ago."

Sam waited. He had Jimbo talking. Now his problem was to keep him on track. "So you think Alexis Helfrich is capable of murder, Jimbo?"

"Sheeit, ain't nothin' that bimbo wouldn't do if she got pissed enough."

"And how did Rossi get her pissed?"

Jimbo's laugh bubbled up from somewhere around his groin and rolled on until it got him coughing. When the coughing stopped, he hocked a lunger across the jasmine bush. "That's the fun part, Buddy-Boy. Allow me to e-luc-I-date.

"Rossi was a regular customer of Helfrich. He had a thing for Big Carole. Used to have her over his place two-three times a week. Seems that Mikey was a real pervert and had Carole doing some pretty disgusting things, which we won't go into if you know what I mean."

Sam didn't and he didn't really want to. If Jimbo thought they were disgusting, he could do without the details.

"Anyway, one night he's got Carole doing some pretty degrading stuff, until she finally draws the line and tells him she's takin' a hike.

Rossi gets pissed and refuses to pay her. So, Carole loses it and beats the livin' shit out of him."

"Why would Helfrich kill him? Sounds like it should have been the other way around."

"Right. But Rossi does the next best thing. He starts black-mailing Helfrich. See, he's big buddies with one of our City Commissioners. They go way back to Philly days. He can have Helfrich shut down just like that." He snapped his fingers.

Sam watched Jimbo line his empty bottle up alongside the other six all in a neat row. Sam's would soon join them to make eight.

Jimbo was on a roll now. "So anyway, he's been bleedin' Alexis dry and part of his deal includes a free weekly session with Carole. The broad told me herself she gags every time she has to look at the asshole. You should pardon the expression."

"Who's the City Commissioner, Jimbo?"

Jimbo shook his head. "Sorry, Sam. That's where I have to draw the line. I know the individual in question and see no reason to draw that person into anything. You press hard enough, you can find out, but it ain't gonna be from me." He looked at his watch and bounded from the chair. "Shit, I'm supposed to be at a closing now at the bank. Gotta get over there."

Sam got up and helped Jimbo put the bottles into his recycling bin. He watched Jimbo tie on a pair of high top black sneakers, tuck the now beer stained T-shirt into his bathing suit, gather up Thunder, squeeze himself into a '74 Cadillac convertible, and head off to the bank for his closing.

19

Sam pulled into the parking lot of Hedonism and drove to the back of the building. Can't have the good folk of Sarasota see Sam Wallace in front of a joint like this. Right. Like, who cares? Jennifer? Nope. Jimbo? Maybe. Francis J.? What if he spots him and blows his little whistle for Cecil? Detective Lewis? Have to tell her anyway. He shrugged and pulled in between a rusty pickup and a late model Jaguar sedan.

The guy in the pickup doesn't want his wife to see him spending the grocery money. The Jag? A pillar of the community, slipping in for a little down and dirty poontang.

He approached the door of the small, one story building—Jimbo's building, and stood for a moment, trying to focus on how Dirk would handle this without getting thrown out on his ass.

The building fronted onto Route 41, but the entrance was on the side, discreetly out of view from passing motorists. The red neon sign, Hedonism, offered the only light.

He opened the door and walked into a small reception area. The smell of incense pierced his nasal passage, forcing a sneeze. He sat on the vinyl sofa, blowing his nose and sneezing when a young woman wearing a knee length robe and spike heels appeared from behind a curtain.

"Hi there," she said. He stood and watched her, looking him up and down, getting a fix on him. Eighteen, nineteen at most. Christ! She's eyeing him like she can't wait to ravage him. At least that's what he's supposed to believe. The heavy makeup didn't do much to hide a bad complexion. The kid looked tired.

"Hi," he said. "I'm looking for Alexis Helfrich"

Her expression changed. The predatory look disappeared and she was all business. "And you are?"

"I'm Sam Wallace, and I have something I'd like to discuss with Ms. Helfrich if she's in." He sniffed and squeezed his nose with the handkerchief, trying to ward off another sneeze.

"She's gonna want to know what it's about."

"Well, it's of a rather personal nature." He barely got the words out before the sneeze let go.

She backed away and stood her ground in her wrinkled robe, looking at him, frowning.

He looked at his watch. Whatever, he had to get away from the goddamn incense. "I don't have a lot of time. It's important that I see her."

"Wait here," she said and disappeared through the curtain.

Another sneeze exploded before he could get the handkerchief out. Two more followed, leaving his eyes and nose running and red. He slumped back onto the couch. Dirk was a tough act to follow, and he was beginning to wonder if he was up to it. Dirk would have charmed the young hooker, not let himself be treated like he was looking for a hand-out.

The kid returned, tottering on her five inch heels. "Follow me," she said and led him through the curtain. They walked along a corridor lined with rooms on either side. At least that's what he assumed were behind the closed doors. He expected to hear muffled moans and groans coming from within, but heard nothing.

At the end of the corridor they reached another door and stopped. The young woman knocked and entered. Sam followed. "This is Mr. Wallace," she said to a woman sitting at a desk, and left.

Sam stood facing the woman behind the desk. She looked to be in her forties, maybe fifties. Hard to tell with all the make-up and the cigarette smoke surrounding her. She took a puff from the long, thin spangled gizmo that held her cigarette. Her hair, a reddish orange, did her a disservice. She'd have been better off with it natural, no matter what color.

He looked around the room and nodded to an attractive younger woman sitting on an expensive looking sofa to the right of the desk. She ignored him. He walked over to the desk and the older one motioned him to a chair. "Sit down, Mr. Wallace," she said, in a cultured sounding accent, overlaid with the raspy voice of a woman who smokes too much. "Now, what's this about a personal matter?"

He glanced around the office again, impressed with the décor. Silk drapes covered the two windows, twin marble top tables held expensive figurines, and the art work on the walls were definitely not prints. Soft piano music came from a sound system.

"I'm sorry to intrude upon you Ms. Helfrich. My name is Sam Wallace, and I'm a writer."

"Well, that's nice for you, but what business do you have with me?"

He rubbed his eyes and decided the cigarette smoke was worse than the incense. "Well, I write books about murder and mayhem and as such I'm looking into the murder of a man named Mike Rossi." He grinned. "Doing some research, you might say. I understand you knew Mr. Rossi."

Her expression remained unchanged. He dropped the grin.

"I see. And who or what gives you license to go around investigating murders, questioning people as if you had a right to do so?"

He nodded like it was a question he expected. "Well, ma'am, I guess the answer to that is no one. But I happened to be with Mr. Rossi the afternoon of the day he was killed, and I have been summoned by the police to tell them what I know tomorrow," he lied. "I have talked with some other people in the meantime, and I happen to know that Rossi was blackmailing you."

He watched Helfrich's eyes for a reaction. Nothing. If Jimbo was telling the truth, Alexis was pretty cool about it.

She took a long drag from the cigarette holder and blew the smoke toward him. He didn't know they even sold the things anymore. Except for FDR and the old forties movies, he'd never seen one.

"You don't beat around the bush, do you Mr. Wallace?" She turned to the woman on the sofa. "Did you hear that, Carole? This gentleman says Mr. Rossi was blackmailing me. Now where do think he could have heard such nonsense?"

She nodded her head, just a tad, but Sam picked up on it. The woman slid off the sofa and headed toward him. He watched her approach and blinked twice. Was this amazon Alexis' Cecil?

She had to be at least six-two, maybe six-three. Her arms bulged under the T-shirt she wore. The thighs of a linebacker threatened to rip open her tennis shorts. With her shoulder length blond hair, she looked like Samson, except there was no questioning her gender. This was a gorgeous hunk of woman.

She stood next to his chair, looking at Alexis. Was she waiting for a signal to mangle him? She hovered over him. He smiled. "Hi."

She walked behind him and planted herself. He could no longer see her, but the perfume he smelled somehow comforted him. She's only a woman, he reminded himself.

Alexis watched with a half smile, apparently enjoying the scene. He wondered if he'd been too direct with Alexis.

"Carole, Mr. Wallace looks tense. Perhaps you could give him a nice massage."

Before he could move, her fingers dug into his shoulder blades. He tried to get up but she clamped him back down and began massaging his shoulders. The powerful hands moved across his shoulders and down his back, kneading deep into his flesh. They moved up and down his back and across his shoulders again toward his neck. If not for wondering when they would clamp around his throat, he found the sensation rather sensuous.

As abruptly as she began, she stopped. Sam turned and looked up at her. "Thank you, Carole. That was very nice," he said before another sneeze erupted.

"That's one of the things we do here, Mr. Wallace," Alexis said. "Let's just assume that's what you came for. This one is on the house. Come back again and we'll give you the full treatment. Now Carole, would you escort Mr. Wallace to the door?"

Carole helped him to his feet and turned him around. His eyes were even with her chin. She smiled, showing perfect white teeth. "It's been nice working you over," she said in the deep voice he would have expected from a woman this big.

On the way home he decided that he'd accomplished about what he set out to. He'd met and sized up the two ladies he'd been hearing so much about from people who were somewhat less than objective.

Having done so and formed his own opinions, he could better evaluate what he had heard. Alexis Helfrich had a very hard edge to her. Could she and her sidekick be guilty of murder? Who knows? But there was something about her that made the hairs on the back of his neck stand up. Instinct?

He also had the distinct feeling he'd been warned. Or was it threatened?

20

Francis J. Wilson banged his cane on the marble floor of his foyer and squealed. When Francis was angry he squealed. It was his way of venting.

He pressed a button on his remote again and again, throttling the tiny instrument. "Where is that fool Cecil when I need him?" he muttered.

The sun streaming through the windows hit him in the eyes. He squinted, flicked the remote, and dispatched the sun behind his blinds.

He went into the living room and aimed a kick at a pillow lying on the floor. His little foot swung wide of the mark and he toppled over.

Cecil appeared in the foyer and hurried to lift Francis to his feet. "You all right, Mr. Wilson?" he asked, his hands extended on either side of Francis, ready to catch him should he topple again.

Francis wiggled his shoulders and flailed his arms. Cecil backed off.

"I'm all right, but I want to know how that pillow got on the floor." He moved toward Cecil and planted his cane. "Have you been sitting on the sofa, Cecil?"

Cecil took another step backward, started to speak, then lowered his head, and stood in silence.

Francis pounded his cane. "Cecil, I asked you a question."

Cecil's head popped up. "Yes sir. I was cleaning up in here and felt a little dizzy, so I sat for a minute. Must have knocked the pillow off when I got up. I'm very sorry, Mr. Wilson." He retrieved the pillow, fluffed it twice, and returned it to the sofa.

Francis walked to the foyer, turned and glowered at Cecil, cringing next to the sofa "Cecil, I am very upset. Melody is here in Sarasota. It would appear that she never left. Did you or did you not, put her on the plane to Zanesville?"

"Yes, sir, I did, Mr. Wilson. Took her to the boarding area and watched her hand her ticket over and enter the plane."

"Did you wait until it took off?"

Cecil shifted from one foot to the other. "No sir, didn't think it was necessary."

Francis beat the cane and squealed again before laying into Cecil. "Cecil, you idiot. As soon as you left, she must have deplaned. She apparently created quite a scene at the Hilton Hotel on Longboat Key."

Cecil moved behind the sofa and nodded.

"One of my dear friends, Jeffrey Poindexter, who also happens to be chairman of the Save the Speckled Possum fundraising committee, was present at the outside bar having a cocktail with friends and witnessed the entire spectacle.

"Melody apparently threw a drink at the bartender and engaged in a hair pulling melee with a female customer." Francis paused, trying to compose himself. He walked over to Cecil and hissed out the words. "She was ejected from the premises."

Cecil edged further behind the sofa, keeping it between him and Francis.

Francis continued. "How could she choose Longboat Key to humiliate me? She knows that all the important people live there? Mr. Poindexter, who was one of the honored guests at my lavish affair for the Cultural Center, was kind enough to call me. Can you possibly know how mortifying this is to me, Cecil?"

"Yes sir, I do, Mr. Wilson."

Francis lowered his voice. "Cecil, we must find her. She is out there somewhere, a danger to my reputation. Francis J. Wilson is a pillar of this community, an integral part of the most elite segment of Sarasota society, a man admired by his friends and colleagues. I cannot and will not be embarrassed further by this . . . this trollop. You must find her, Cecil. I cannot have her out there, jeopardizing everything I have worked to accomplish." He waved his cane. "Now, go find her. Check every bar and den of iniquity in Sarasota and find her."

Cecil gave Francis a puzzled look, mumbled to himself, and left.

Francis slumped onto the sofa and sighed. Alone with his thoughts

134

and no one to bluster at, he felt the old self-loathing, self-pity returning. He had endured so much with that dreadful Redding woman, hoping that one day she would make him a rich man and he would be somebody. He would wear his tuxedo and socialize with the in crowd. He would have his name in Cynthia Mayfair's column. He would be invited to the finest parties and be a significant part of the real Sarasota.

His fundraiser, the social event of the year, was attended by everyone who was anyone. His announcement of his own five million dollar donation was to be the defining moment launching him into the inner circle. And that slut Melody nearly ruined everything. He was working hard to restore his dignity, keeping in touch with his friends, supporting all the important causes.

He interrupted his reverie with a loud squeal and kicked his dangling legs back and forth against the sofa. Today's newspaper contained the ultimate humiliation.

Cynthia's entire column was devoted to a smashing party, the social event of the year (how could she use that phrase?) given at the home of Joshua Fishman. The names of all the important people who attended were mentioned in bold type. He had not even been invited.

He could be in danger of not being invited to the coveted Patrons' Circle at the Grand Ball this year.

He had thought of calling Joshua but decided against it. It would have been gauche of him, and he was a man of style.

He did call Cynthia just to chat and bring her up to date on his own activities. Complimented her on her fine column and adroitly maneuvered the conversation around to today's column.

She sounded uncomfortable, evasive. Tried to change the subject. She then asked about Melody and he had the distinct impression she was intimating that the Fishmans might have been concerned that Francis would bring Melody if he attended.

She didn't come right out and say that, but he knew. He knew.

* * *

Alexis Helfrich sipped her Perrier Jouet champagne. The champagne warmed and relaxed her. Perrier Jouet—only for people with taste and the money to indulge.

She had always had the taste and now, after some difficult years she had built her business to the point where expensive luxuries were easily affordable. She held the crystal flute to her lips and smiled. The fools in this town had no idea how lucrative her business had become. And it was all cash.

She'd had an excellent spring and early summer when most establishments were struggling. When the tourist season begins in late December, her business would quadruple. Yes, life was good now that the one threat to her livelihood was gone—by a stroke of good fortune.

This writer, Wallace, could be a trouble maker. Where was he getting his information? Ever since his visit, she'd been upset, worried that some bastard is shooting off his mouth to nosy strangers like this amateur wannabe detective.

She looked across the room at Carole, filing her nails, relaxing with her champagne. Devoted, loyal Carole. Enjoying the good life, too. And not about to have it threatened. "Carole, come over here and sit."

Carole put her file down, walked over, and sat next to Alexis.

Alexis smiled. "Hmm, you're wearing a different perfume. I like it. Tell me, Carole, what do you make of this Mr. Wallace?"

"I think he's a nosy troublemaker," she said and held her glass out for more champagne.

Alexis filled both their glasses. "Yes, I believe he is. Now, where do you suppose he's been getting his information?"

Carole took a walnut from a bowl on Alexis' desk, crushed it in her hand, and began picking the walnut meat from the crumpled shell. "I don't know, but I think we need to find out, don't you?"

Alexis nodded. "Yes, we need to find out."

21

Sam was wide awake, his plans for sleeping in, crushed by Henry, who hovered over him, licking his face. "Go away," he grumbled and slid his head under the covers.

Henry crept under, found Sam's nose, and got in a few more licks. Sam sat up and dropped him off the bed. Henry whimpered and trotted off toward the kitchen.

Sam closed his eyes and pulled a pillow over his head. A minute later Henry was back, barking at the foot of the bed.

Sam knew the routine. He sat up and sure enough, the little rascal stood there with his dog dish in front of him, yapping at Sam. He'd done it again, pushed the dish along with his nose, making sure Sam got the message. "You know Henry, sometimes you can be a little pain in the ass." He got up, picked up the dish, and padded into the kitchen with Henry trailing behind.

After feeding Henry, he stepped out to the balcony with his coffee: 6:30. The workmen hadn't arrived yet, and he sat enjoying the silence and the soft pinks and pale blues of the early morning sky. The air was like crystal. The sun's rays were already filtering through the fleecy clouds, heralding the beginning of another beautiful day in Paradise.

There was a lot to like here, if you kept an open mind, and Sarasota was growing on him. It was certainly a cut above the fast food, cracker image he and his friends had of Florida, where the latest amusement park passes for high culture.

And God knows he'd met an intriguing cross section of characters. There was much more to the place than Francis' bevy of self-styled celebrities.

Part of the appeal has to be the challenge he's finding, poking into Rossi's murder. Never got the cop out of his system, which is probably why he started writing cops and robbers books. Playing amateur sleuth is just what the doctor ordered for keeping his mind off Whately and the other thing—as he'd come to refer to his broken marriage—and hopefully, writing better books.

Back inside he found Henry standing in front of the door, holding his leash. The dog communicated better than most people. "OK, buddy, let me get some clothes on and we're outta here."

After a brisk walk around the property with two stops at Henry's favorite bush, they returned to the apartment. Henry retired to his room and Sam sat at the computer. His second book was finished and off to the publisher. He'd outlined a couple of plot ideas for the third but couldn't get excited about either one. With so much going on, he was having trouble focusing. Writer's block after two books?

Why not write about Sarasota and Mike's murder? He's already using it as a laboratory for hands-on research. Create a plot around it and he's got his next book. It could help him to deal with yet another transition in his life, and hopefully provide some substance and meaning to his stay in Sarasota.

He thought about the people he met. One squeezed everybody else out, and he suddenly felt a need to see her. He picked up the phone and punched in her number.

You do things like this, he thought. You're going to call her up and ask her out to dinner. Tonight. No advance notice, no setting up a date ahead of time, the civilized way to approach a classy lady. Just call and expect her to say yes.

"Hello."

"Hi Jennifer. This is Sam."

"Hi, there."

Nice upbeat in her voice. He liked that. Never know when you call somebody at work. "I won't ask if you're busy, because I'm sure you are, but I called because I need a Jennifer fix. The one I got at our lunch is wearing off and needs renewing."

"Didn't last very long. It's only been two days since we had lunch."

"Oh. I'd have sworn it was a month. Anyway, I'd love to see you, and I have a wonderful idea."

"And what's that?"

"You have dinner with me at the Summerhouse, the restaurant I've been hearing good things about."

"The Summerhouse is a lovely place. When did you have in mind?"

"Tonight."

Long pause. "Tonight?"

"Er, yeah, I thought—"

"You call me up and ask me to have dinner with you tonight? No advance notice, no setting up a date ahead of time, just call and expect me to say yes."

You blew it, jerk.

"Is that what you expect?" A sternness there.

"Well, I guess I—"

"Anyway, the answer is yes."

He grinned. "Had to work me over a little there first, huh?"

"Well, you deserved it. I'll do it this time because I'm hungry and I don't have anything to eat in the house."

"That's what I like, a woman with romance in her soul. Pick you up at seven?"

"Make it 6:30. I told you I'm hungry."

"You want the top up or down?"

"Down."

He hung up the phone and smiled. He had one more call to make, if he wanted to stay on the good side of the cops.

"This is Detective Lewis."

"Sam Wallace here, Detective Lewis," he said with a bravado he didn't feel.

"Oh yes, Mr. Wallace, the ersatz private eye. What can I do for you?"

Ooh. The woman can be direct. "Ersatz, huh? Good word."

She made a sound that was either a snicker or a half-hearted laugh. He wasn't sure. "I promised I would keep you up to date on my activities, and that's why I'm calling."

"Well, I can't talk with you now. Can you come down to the station at eleven?"

"Sure."

At eleven sharp, Detective Lewis came out to collect him from the reception area. She shook his hand with the same crunch as last time. He was again struck by the mixture of toughness and femininity. She wore a soft charcoal colored blouse with gray cotton pants and black slides. Her hair, pulled back the last time they met, hung loosely over her shoulders. She wore no makeup.

He followed her, thinking that even though he's a writer, conditioned to observing people, would he have been so observant if she were a man or a nondescript woman. Probably not.

"This is my office, Mr. Wallace. It's not much, but at least it's private. Sit down and tell me what's on your mind."

He told her about his conversation with Jimbo first. She smiled when he got to the part about Alexis and Carole but said nothing. He picked up on the smile and stopped. "You know Alexis and her business, I assume?"

"Of course I do. But she's very clever and has friends in high places. Anyway, there are many such operations in and around Sarasota. We've targeted a few but it's very difficult to justify closing them down. Occasionally we get lucky, but for every one we nail, two more spring up."

"And did you know that Rossi had been blackmailing her?"

She seemed to hesitate for a moment. "Hmm, not exactly. What else do you have, Mr. Wallace?"

Pondering what she had just said, he scratched his arms and tugged aimlessly at his hair. No matter which way he maneuvered his hair, the excitable curls popped willfully back to where they began.

Not exactly. What the hell does that mean, he wondered. Detective Lewis is playing it close to the vest, taking whatever he can provide but giving back nothing. That's her prerogative, but it would be nice to make this a two way street. "You know, I've enjoyed getting to know you a little. I think you're a very good cop—for whatever that's worth to you." He watched her face. Did it soften just a tad or was he reaching? "How about calling me Sam. Mr. Wallace is what my students called me, and I'm trying to forget them for a while." He grinned. "OK?"

She surprised him by returning his grin. He decided to push his luck. "May I call you Diane?"

The grin disappeared, but she nodded. "OK, tell me what else you have."

"I went to see Alexis and her friend, Carole. Told them what Jimbo said about the blackmail. She wasn't happy and warned me in so many words to lay off. She's a tough customer, Diane, and I think the lady is capable of anything." He spread his hands out and shrugged. "Well, that's about it. Probably not much, but I told you I would share with you everything I do and hear."

She listened but said nothing.

"Whatever I hear will be for your ears only. As a former police officer, I fully understand the need for confidentiality, and you can trust me. I can also help." He gave it his best shot and waited to see if it got him anywhere. Hard to tell with Detective Lewis. Diane.

She studied him for a moment before replying. "All of that sounds good, but I'm only buying it because I checked you out with the Boston P.D. I must say they gave you high marks. Said you left a promising career behind when you resigned."

"Thank you, Diane. High praise, I must say."

"Don't get carried away. It's not coming from me."

He laughed. "Damn! Every time I think I'm getting somewhere with you, you shoot me down."

"Maybe you should keep trying," she said.

Something in that brief exchange told him he had rounded a corner with her, maybe enough to push further. "Do you have anything for me?"

She twisted her topaz ring and slid it back and forth along her finger. "I listened to your little speech, Sam. Now you listen to mine. I should tell you nothing. You of all people know how risky it is to give out information on an open investigation. If we ever hope to pin down who did this and get an indictment, we can't afford the investigation being compromised, and have a defense attorney blow our case apart. You do know that, don't you?"

Sam nodded. He was getting to like this lady. "Yes, I do."

"OK, now having said that, I'm going to take a chance with you."

He started to speak, but she waved him off and interrupted. "Why am I doing this? Selfish reasons, pure and simple. I think you might be able to help us. I gather from things you've said, that you and Jimbo Conlin have become friendly."

"Yes, I'd say so."

"Well, we have already talked with your friend, Jimbo. As you seem to know, there was bad blood between him and Rossi. He has also had some run-ins with Alexis Helfrich. Even though they have a business relationship with him leasing his building to her, there's no love lost between them. It's not surprising that he would bad-mouth Helfrich."

"Why is there no love lost between them?"

"There's no point in going into detail. Let's just say that Conlin has been infatuated with Carole for some time. No problem with Helfrich as long as he was only Carole's client, but when she learned there was more to it—at least on Conlin's part—she clamped down and told Carole no more seeing Jimbo."

"Why would she do that?" Sam asked, knowing it was a rhetorical question.

His naiveté didn't fool Lewis. "Oh, come on, Sam. Don't play games. Conlin has not been happy, being shut off from Carole, who I understand has no use for him anyway."

"Interesting. Jimbo and I are going fishing in a couple days. Anything else I should know?"

"Just be careful what you say to Mr. Conlin." She got up, walked to the other side of the room and stood with her back to Sam.

Was this a sign of dismissal? He waited.

She turned, walked toward him, and sat on the edge of her desk. "There is one other thing I will tell you, Sam. Jimbo Conlin is a suspect in Mike Rossi's murder. Please keep this in mind as you spend time and talk with him."

"How is he a suspect?"

She got up off the desk. "I think I've shared enough information with you. Now, I have a meeting in a few minutes. Thanks for coming." She nodded toward the door.

"OK," he said. "I'll keep in touch. He started to leave, feeling good about their meeting.

"Sam!"

He had the door half open and closed it. "Yes?"

"If any of this leaks to the media or anyplace else, I'll have you in a jail cell so fast you won't know what hit you."

22

Jennifer greeted Sam at the door and closed it behind her. When she did so, it occurred to him that she still had not invited him inside her house.

That was his second thought, coming after the usual impact she had on him. Her red hair and everything about her looked freshly scrubbed, highlighted by the pastel colored dress she wore. "You look like a strawberry ice cream cone," he said.

She cocked her head and frowned. "Come on Sam, you're a writer. You can do better than that."

"I thought it was pretty good." He looked around the yard. "Place looks great, all freshly manicured, weeded, and mulched. You must have a good gardener."

"I do. I'm it."

"I thought you worked all the time."

"I do a little each day. Fiddled with it for a half hour today after work. It's my therapy."

"Didn't know you needed therapy." He held the door open for her and she slid in.

"Everybody needs therapy, Sam. Even you, I bet."

He nodded but said nothing. Best not to go any further down that path.

The drive from Lido to Siesta Key went along Lido Beach and the Gulf, over the bridge across Sarasota Bay, along Bayfront Drive with the park and the bay to their right, then over the North Bridge onto Siesta Key.

He loved driving over the bridges, admiring the city's skyline, perched over the aquamarine waters, catching the sun's rays. With the combination of the sun and the reflection of the water, the buildings actually seemed to glisten. As they crossed the North Bridge, a breeze from the west brought with it the smells of the Key, filling the car with a potpourri of fresh sea air, jasmine and frangipani.

Jennifer said little. She sat back, her head resting against the seat back, eyes closed, a half smile letting him know she was enjoying the ride. He knew he was, driving across the water on a perfect summer night, with the beautiful Jennifer sitting beside him.

They shared the comfortable silence until Jennifer opened her eyes and sat forward. "Sam, I love your car," she announced.

Her simple declaration of love for the old 280 SE clinched it for him. This was going to be a great evening. "Thank you, Jennifer, I can see that you and my car are soul mates. We must be coming up on the Summerhouse pretty soon, aren't we? I take it you've been here before."

"Yes, we are coming up on it and yes, I have. There, watch for the sign on your left."

He pulled into a narrow shell road nestled between thick foliage and there was the restaurant on his left, looming majestically out of the woods. Three young parking attendants in shorts eyed his car with predatory looks.

"Uh, Sam, if I were you I would not allow any of those cowboys anywhere near this car. They park cars like they're in the Indy 500."

Sam nodded and drove further down the road into a parking space under a gathering of moss covered oak trees. Past the trees, exquisite gardens rolled out to a tranquil body of water.

"That's Little Sarasota Bay out there," Jennifer said.

Just beyond a panoply of more oak trees, they reached the restaurant, which looked like an elegant tree house. Towering walls of glass blended into the trees overlooking colorful plants and queen palms, a true tropical setting.

Jennifer turned toward him and smiled broadly. "You like it?"

"It's like a fairy tale," he said.

They walked under a green awning festooned with twinkling lights. Colored lamps enhanced the natural beauty of the foliage, creating hues of orange and blue and yellow.

When they reached the front door, Sam stopped. "Food's gotta be lousy," he said. "Must be a catch somewhere."

"Uh, uh, the food is fabulous. Face it, Sam. You picked a winner."

They settled into a table and ordered a bottle of wine. Jennifer was still smiling at him.

"OK," he said. "I know you're getting a big chuckle out of me oohing and ahing over this place. Guess I'm just a hick city boy at heart, used to lots of concrete and cars honking around my restaurants."

"It's OK, Sam. Everybody reacts the same way to this place the first time they see it. Cheers."

They clinked glasses and Sam wondered if he would ever see Boston again.

Jennifer interrupted his thoughts. "You look nice, Sam. I like your outfit."

He lowered his head to check out what he had on. He'd forgotten. Wasn't much. A white polo shirt, tan slacks, and a blue blazer. Funny how women always refer to the clothes a person has on as an outfit—no matter if it's nothing more than shorts and a T-shirt. Men rarely use that word.

"Oh, thanks," he said. His hand went to the back of his head and he idly arranged a few strands of hair. "So, how's your red tide research coming?" he asked.

She made a face and sipped her wine. "It's nasty stuff, Sam. Dangerous to both humans and marine life."

"How dangerous?"

"Well, a few years ago 162 Dolphins washed up on Mexican beaches. Police suspected drug gangs of dumping chemicals at sea. A few months later they found the real killers; billions of toxic one celled organisms that formed a poison net across Mexico's Sea of Cortez."

"Red tide?"

"An isolated form of it, yes."

"How serious is the threat to this area?"

"Very. In 1996 a red tide onslaught killed 300 Manatees in Southwest Florida. They died when their diaphragms stopped working because of nerve damage from the toxin producing dinoflagellates. The manatees weren't the only marine life affected. Dead fish floating on the water were so thick you could almost walk on them."

"And that's the kind of thing we're looking at this year?"

"Worse." She watched his expression and a thin smile crossed her face. "Oh, Sam, I know I sound like the grim reaper, but this thing could be disastrous in so many ways. And please don't repeat anything I've been telling you."

Sam put his hands over hers. The act drew a quick glance from her, but her hands stayed put. "Jennifer, you don't sound like the grim reaper. You sound like the dedicated scientist you are. And I won't say anything to anyone."

He squeezed her hand and felt a gentle squeeze back. "But hey, I didn't ask you out to dinner to get you off on something you've been up to your ears in all day. You're having a busman's holiday and that's not what I had in mind."

She grinned and winked at him. "Oh? What'd you have in mind?"

She caught him off guard and he fumbled for a reply. "I don't know, charming you into falling in love with me. Something like that."

She laughed, a great, long lazy laugh, and he wanted to hug her just for the sound of it. Her face lit up like there wasn't a dinoflagellate in the world. "Hmm, you've got your work cut out for you, I'd say."

Walked into it again. But at least her hands were still there.

Neither said anything for a moment. He could feel her mind clicking. "What are you thinking?"

She turned serious again and slid her hands from under his. "Sam, at the risk of boring you, I really would like to tell you more about this red tide business. I need to talk about it with somebody other than the colleagues involved with me on it." She returned her hands, only this time over his. "You're smart and you're a good listener."

148

"Flattery will get you everywhere. Continue."

"These dinoflagellates occur naturally in the Gulf and normally consist of only one cell per organism, which produce neurotoxin chemicals. When the number of cells increases from only a few cells per quart of sea water to thousands and even millions, a red tide occurs, causing massive fish kills, contamination of shellfish, and severe respiratory problems to people on shore. At concentrations greater than one million cells per quart of sea water, it colors the water and makes it appear red or rusty brown."

He nodded and poured them both more wine.

"The worst outbreaks of red tide recorded measured about 180 million cells per quart of sea water. Our latest tests show that we're now up to 150 million and increasing every day. When it reaches here, it could be a half billion or more."

"Has there ever been a red tide that virulent?"

"No, not to our knowledge. There was a severe outbreak here in 1971, and an extensive survey of economic damage placed it at over twenty million dollars. Scientists at that time predicted that a future outbreak of equal severity could cause up to fifty percent more economic damage. One of greater severity could easily triple the damage. Remember now, that's in 1971 dollars."

"Ah, we're talking dollars and cents, the magic word down here —tourism."

"Right. That outbreak in '71 left a swath of environmental destruction. Dead fish floating in the water, beaches heaped with their rotting carcasses. The bacterial count escalated, flies multiplied by the billions, the stinking air was laden with toxic particles, which irritated the eyes and respiratory tracts of humans, many of whom, especially those with asthma and similar problems, got very ill. Not a pretty picture, is it?"

"No, and I can see the punch line coming."

Her head bobbed up and down. "Exactly. We're projecting this one to measure four times the number of toxic cells per quart of sea water."

23

Sam finished his salmon along with a final swallow of chardonnay and smiled. The dinner was right up there with the ambiance. He watched Jennifer still lost in thought. He silently cursed himself for bringing up her work, but let up when he realized it wouldn't have made any difference. She'd have gotten into it anyway.

She's a pro, totally dedicated to her work. Got to be why this gorgeous, brainy woman is so unattached. Was it always so? he wondered.

"Jennifer, tell me something," he said.

She still had nearly all of her wine and took a sip that wouldn't have made a dent in the stomach of a wren. She looked up with her crooked little smile. "You mean I haven't bored you enough?"

"First of all, you haven't bored me. Quite the contrary. Until I met you, I had no idea how threatening red tide could be to the economy of an area, not to mention people's health. Anyway, that's not what I wanted to ask you about."

"Good, I'm ready to change the subject." She ran both hands through her hair and sat back. "Shoot."

"Tell me more about the other side of you. Ever been married?"

"No."

"Ever been close to it?"

"Yes."

He raised the wine glass to his lips, forgetting it was empty, and stole a glance at the empty bottle. This isn't going to be easy, he thought. Maybe better to go back to red tide. "Hey, I don't mean to be prying. If I am, tell me to bug off."

She covered his hand again. Even though she could be distant, she was a toucher. He liked that.

"I'm sorry, Sam. You're not prying." She took another of her bird like sips and peered over the glass at him. "And I don't want you to bug off."

He grinned and tried to think of something to say. Nothing came.

She rescued him. "I was engaged four years ago to a marine biologist. Not a Galt colleague. He worked for NOAA in the Tampa area."

She stopped and he wondered if that was the end of story. She seemed to struggle even with that little bit. "What happened?"

"We had a June wedding planned. I bought my wedding dress, had the church reserved, picked my maid of honor, bridesmaids, the whole bit." She lifted her glass and took a slug that would have drowned the wren. "And one day in March, he told me he was having buyer's remorse."

"Buyer's remorse?"

"Yeah. Romantic expression, huh?"

"And that was it?"

"Yup. But there was a sequel."

"And what was that?"

"Well, I was devastated, inconsolable—and pissed off—for months. And then, just as I was getting over it, he called. Said he realized he'd made a big mistake, could I ever forgive him—blah, blah, blah."

"And?"

"I surprised myself. He had hurt me so badly, I guess I lost all feeling or respect—or whatever—for him. I'm not sure, even now. I just know I said, 'No way.' He came back on strongly, but that was the end for me. It was over."

"Did you ever see him after that?"

"Yes. He kept calling, and I finally agreed to have lunch with him. It's funny, Sam, but there was just nothing there for me. I had been wronged and it simply drained all my feeling for him. I couldn't wait for the lunch to end. He called a couple of times after that, but it went nowhere. I think he went back to New England."

Why was he not surprised? Given what he'd observed about Jennifer, it was not difficult to picture her having too much integrity to go back to a man who had dumped her. That was much of what he admired in her.

They lingered over coffee, enjoying the comfortable atmosphere of the restaurant, and each other. Jennifer looked around and smiled, "Sam?"

"Yes?"

"Have you noticed, we're the only ones in the restaurant?"

"Nope, didn't notice. I was having too much fun."

"My God, it's quarter of ten. We've been here for almost three hours."

"Where'd everybody go?" he asked.

"Sarasota's an early town, Sam. Nobody stays up late. And that includes me. I'm a working girl, remember?"

He got the hint, called for the check, and they left. The drive back was even more beautiful, with the salty sea breezes seasoning the gentle night air. Dinner had been a dance, and he still floated in time to the music. He drove slowly, in no rush to get her home. He wished she lived forty miles away. It was that kind of night.

"So what about you, Sam? We haven't talked much about you. You write books and you said you were a teacher. What else do you do? Tell me some more about yourself."

He glanced at her. Somehow, she had managed to curl those long legs under her and was turned facing him. At the moment, he didn't feel like talking about Whately. Better to stay with Sarasota. "Right now, I guess I've got myself hooked on this Mike Rossi murder, and I've been playing amateur detective." He told her about his conversations with Jimbo, Alexis, and Detective Lewis.

"My, you've been busy. Is it because you're a writer or just nosy?"

"A little bit of both, I suppose. Maybe I come by it naturally, having once been a cop."

She uncoiled her legs and sat up. "You were a cop?"

"Yes, for four years. I actually liked it a lot, but I got itchy to go back to school and finish my degree. Then I went on to grad school, where I did some teaching and got hooked on it."

She was still erect, looking at him. "So you were a cop. You're full of surprises, aren't you?"

They drove over the North Bridge and he gasped at the setting. A full moon illuminated the water and silhouetted a sailboat moored off to the left of the Intracoastal. Palm trees swayed in the background on shore.

"Jennifer, don't tell anyone up north about this place. Let's just keep it to ourselves."

She ignored his comment and went silent for several minutes. He watched her face from the corner of his eye. Something was troubling her, and he decided to wait it out to see if she would tell him.

"Sam, if you insist on getting involved in this, I suppose there's something I should share with you." She leaned over and touched his arm. "This thing seems to have all kinds of tentacles."

"What do you mean?"

"Three of us at the Galt share a secretary. She and I have become friendly and she told me something yesterday."

"What's that?" They were coming to the bridge onto Lido, just a few miles from her house. He slowed the car, stretching out their time together.

"Well, she had dated Rossi recently. I thought she had better taste, but anyway, she of course, knows about my research and yesterday she came to me and closed the door. Told me she mentioned it to Rossi, and then started to cry."

"Afraid you'd fire her?"

"Yes, and because she felt guilty. She apologized profusely, I lectured her on confidentiality, and thought that was the end of it."

"But it wasn't."

"No. On the day before the murder, he bragged to her that he was going to have lunch with Tim Lester, who, if you don't already know, is a very influential columnist in this town."

"Yes, I've been reading him."

"Anyway, she said Rossi was crowing that he was really going to put the screws to certain people. His words, by the way."

"And she said nothing to you until yesterday."

"No, and that's what's been eating away at her. Ergo, the confession to me."

"Do you have any idea who she meant by 'certain people'?"

"Not really, and I don't want to speculate."

"Come on, Jennifer. Speculate."

She shook her head, and he knew better than to press her.

"'Put the screws to certain people', meaning, I assume, that Lester would spread the word in his column and scare the bejesus out of everybody. Word spreads like wildfire—which it would—and bingo! Sarasota's season is finished before it starts." He pulled the car into her driveway and turned off the motor. To his relief, she showed no sign of getting out.

She nodded. "That's exactly why the confidentiality of my work is important. I told you what happened in 1971, and I don't want to be responsible for keeping people away until we're absolutely certain it's going to hit here. When I am, I'll go on national television if I have to, to warn people."

"OK, so it's not a certainty. When will you know that it is?"

"I'm not sure. And I do have to go." She placed her hand on the door handle but didn't open it.

He eyed her hand on the door, and wondered how much time he could buy. "Have you informed the police about what your secretary told you?"

"No, I was out on the Gulf all day on a field trip and just plopped into bed when I got home. I've been in meetings all day today." She turned and grinned at him. "And then, you."

He continued to watch the door handle. Her hand was still on it. No time for any wise remarks about her last comment. "Well, the police need to know about this."

"Yes, of course. I'll call them tomorrow."

He thought for a moment. "Jennifer, I've been working with the detective in charge of the Rossi case. I should say, trying to work with her. We're not exactly colleagues. Anyway, would you mind if I tell her?"

She turned to him. He didn't like the look she gave him, but at least she took her hand off the door handle.

"You?"

"Yes. I'm trying to develop some credibility with her, and the more information I can pass on to her, the more I think she'll trust me and open up a little more." He smiled, scratched at his arms, ran his hand through his hair and nodded his head hopefully, not sure she was buying this. "I won't tell her how I know this. I'll simply tell her that I know Rossi was scheduled to have lunch with Lester and why. I'm sure Lester will confirm all of it with Detective Lewis. That way there's no need for you, your secretary, or anyone from the Galt to get involved."

He watched while she digested all of what he'd just said and hoped it made some sense to her. If it didn't, he knew she would let him know in her inimitable way.

She shook her head and laughed. "OK, Dick Tracy. And thanks for a lovely evening."

"Thank you, Jennifer. And would you believe it if I told you it was the best night I've had in a long time?"

"I think so, and sometime you'll have to tell me why."

"Why it was such a great night? That's easy."

"No, why it's been so long." She kissed him on the cheek and left.

24

Jennifer had just sat down at her desk the next morning when Cliff called. "Jennifer, can you come in and see me?"

She grabbed her notes and coffee and headed down the hall, in no mood to deal with Cliff. What was he going to give her a hard time about now?

She still smarted from the ugly conversation they had less than a week ago. After first praising the good work she was doing, he gave her a lecture about keeping it top secret until the last minute and then implying that maybe she should say nothing. Unbelievable!

"Ah, Jennifer, come in." He came out from behind his desk and led her to the small sofa he used for his informal chats. "I see you already have your coffee, so please sit down, relax."

He sat next to her, and she instinctively moved to the end of the sofa and leaned forward. Informal chat or whatever, she knew what would come out of his mouth next.

"Give me an update on your work. What are the latest test results?"

She glanced at her notes and set them down. "We're now showing over three hundred billion cells per quart, Cliff and they're still on track to hit this area."

"Same time frame?"

"Pretty much. Somewhere between late December and mid February."

Cliff winced and she braced herself.

"Jennifer, I've thought a lot about our last conversation when you brought me up to date on your findings, and I said we needed to talk. Do you remember what I said?"

"Of course I remember what you said, Cliff. Subtlety has never been your strong suit. You expressed concern about the 'economic devastation' that will hit the area when I release my findings."

"Yes, and what I said about the impact is certainly true, and we are going to have some very powerful people around here very upset." He paused and their eyes met and held for a moment.

Her stomach knotted and she looked away. "Where are we going with this, Cliff?" she asked in a voice flat and without emotion.

"What I just said, notwithstanding, we can't allow that to influence the work we do here as marine biologists. You're a pro Jennifer, one of the best we have. You keep up your good work, and we'll do what's necessary."

She stared at him, watching his face, allowing his words to sink in. This was Cliff Johnson, the distinguished scientist who first attracted her to the Galt talking, not some sycophant sucking up to the wealthy business interests in town. "Thank you, Cliff," she said, simply. "That means a lot."

He began methodically filling his pipe with tobacco and smiled at the wary look on her face. "Don't worry, Jennifer. I won't light it until you leave." He got up and walked across the room, turned, and paced back.

Jennifer waited. He was in his lecture mode.

"I was wrong, Jennifer to let myself get caught up in the need for constant funding, allowing my concerns for the sensitivities of our contributors to take precedence over my scientific responsibilities. This has been a wake up call." He returned to his desk and sat down.

That was it. She left, feeling like a large monkey had been taken off her back. The best part was the reawakening of this fine scholar and scientist.

After Jennifer left, Cliff smoked his pipe and reflected on their conversation. It had been brief and to the point, the way he liked it. He was not a man of words. Science was his forte, and he was a very good scientist. It was why he could attract outstanding people like Jennifer Belding to the Galt.

If he was to become Director of the Galt, it would be because of his stature in his profession, enabling and inspiring the best in his people. He had been a fool to think otherwise. The directorship was not worth his compromising his professional integrity. The phone rang and his sixth sense told him who it was. "Yes, Johnson here."

"Hey, Buddy-Boy," Jimbo's voice boomed through the receiver. "This old Jimbo here. What's the good word?"

"Hello, Jimbo. Nice to hear from you. How are you?" He set the pipe down and watched the smoke drift out in little curly-cues.

"What's this 'nice to hear from you, how are you' shit? Think I called just to bat the breeze? Come on, Buddy-Boy. You know why I'm callin'. You put the clamps on that Belding broad yet?"

Cliff closed his eyes and shook his head. 'Put the clamps on that Belding broad'. How nice. "No, Jimbo, I haven't," he said softly.

"What do you mean, you haven't," Jimbo roared. "She still fuckin' around with that red tide shit? Getting ready to scare everybody away from Sarasota? Break old Jimbo? She still doin that? Huh?"

"Jennifer's work continues, Jimbo. She is still tracking the red tide, and I must say she has made some significant breakthroughs in some areas we have not previously been able to identify. This is very important work she is doing and it will benefit all of us in the long run."

"Hey, Buddy-Boy, don't give me that mumbo-jumbo. She wants to track red tide, then good for her. But she starts shootin' her mouth off, then you'n me got a problem. You get my drift, Cliffie?"

"Jimbo, listen—"

"No, you listen." The forced bonhomie was long gone from his voice. "You tell me now that you're gonna keep her quiet at least until late February when I got my place fully booked, and it's too late for refunds, then I tell you my check's in the mail to you boys. It's that simple, Cliffie. That's how much I trust you and depend on you. Just gimmee your word."

Cliff picked up his pipe and puffed the dying embers back to life. He knew that the end of this conversation would be one he would long remember.

"You hear me, Cliffie?"

"Yes, Jimbo, I hear you. I can't and I won't lie to you. Jennifer Belding's work is far too important for me to suppress it. Her work will continue and if she is absolutely certain that the red tide will hit this area, she has the professional and moral responsibility to make her discovery public. I will support her one hundred percent. And please don't call me Cliffie anymore. My name is Cliff."

* * *

It was after 8:30 when Jennifer sat down at her computer and stuffed some notes into her briefcase. Another twelve hour day, and she felt the exhaustion gradually creep across her mind and body.

She drank from her water bottle, leaned back, put her feet up on the desk, closed her eyes, and purged all the day's work and stress from her mind. She let Sam Wallace into her thoughts and moved the other stuff out. Last night had been a lovely evening, a nice diversion from her work which took up most of her life. Some gardening. A little jogging, a rare day at the beach, that was about it.

She knew that focusing on her job to the exclusion of most other things was a conscious decision. She knew she was afraid to get involved romantically again, and had become a workaholic. The work itself had taken on a life of its own, and she went along with the flow.

Sam was an interesting man, smart and fun to be with. She smiled, thinking of how he would instinctively shoot up to his little bald spot and try to push the hair over it. Some vanity there, which she found kind of cute.

She'd rattled on about the damn red tide for half the night. Probably bored him to death, but he's too much of a gentleman to say so. Yet, there was something about Sam that made it easy to talk about it with him. He was a good listener and seemed to genuinely care about her work.

They had talked about going canoeing on the Myakka, and she waited for him to bring it up at dinner. But he didn't. Maybe she should have. It would be nice to get away for a day, into the wilderness area of Myakka. A day alone with Sam. Get to know him, and maybe find out what's there.

She stretched her arms and yawned, still thinking about Sam. Neither one of them had really opened up yet. She'd told him a little about herself, even got into the business of Richard jilting her. Probably tried to be a little too cavalier about it, afraid to drop her guard and let him know how much she had been hurt.

She'd noticed how quickly Sam changed the subject when she asked him about himself—how smoothly he'd shifted into the Rossi murder. Is he hiding something? He seems so open about everything else. Are there skeletons he wants to keep in his closet? She slammed the briefcase shut and zipped it, angry with herself for letting the old paranoia and distrust of men slip in. She was long over Richard. But he'd left his mark.

Darkness had set in when she finally left the building, and there was only one other car in the lot. It was at the far end, where hardly anyone ever parked, too far away to recognize whose it was. She shrugged and started her car.

When she pulled out of the lot and headed down the road toward John Ringling Parkway, she noticed a car behind her with no lights. It had to be the one from the lot, but why would the lights be out?

She turned left onto John Ringling and slowed down. The car with no lights had to wait for another to drive past before it, too, could turn left. She saw that the lights were now on.

Who in the world was it? Was she showing another kind of paranoia? The car actually could have come from any one of a number of places back there. The restaurant, the condos. Who says it had to be the car from the Galt lot?

She relaxed and cruised toward home. There were only a few cars on St. Armand's Circle. She drove halfway around and turned right toward Lido. She'd gone about a hundred yards when a car turned and continued behind her.

She drove along the beach, the other car staying a respectable distance behind her. When she reached her street she turned left and slowed down, waiting to see if the car was still behind her.

There it was, cruising along, maintaining the same distance. She debated for a moment, wondering if she should keep going, and go back to the Circle.

Bullshit! This was stupid. So there's another car driving the same way she is. Big deal. Happens all the time. She was going home to bed.

She pulled into her driveway and watched as the car drove slowly past.

25 Jennifer had two messages on her machine, one from Sam and one from Sarah Hanson, a friend from college. God! She had totally forgotten that Sarah was coming on Friday. She double checked her calendar and there it was. "Sarah, Delta flight 27, arr. 3pm."

She was losing control of her life, forgetting a long scheduled visit from an old friend. Crazy. She simply had to take a day or two off and relax.

Sam's message was so like Sam. "Hi, Jennifer, this is Dick Tracy, tracer of lost souls. No, that was somebody else. Never mind. Call me back. Miss you."

She surprised herself at how quickly she picked up the phone and dialed his number.

"Hello."

Sam's voice, upbeat and cheerful, lifted her spirits. "You're dating yourself, Sam. The guy who was the tracer of lost persons was an old radio program my dad used to listen to. I forget the guy's name but you would know."

"Come on, Jennifer. Be nice to the elderly. How are you?"

"Tired. I just got home."

"You're working too hard. That's what I called about—to take you away from it all. Canoeing on Sunday, remember?"

"Oh, Sam, I'm sorry but I completely forgot I have an old college friend coming in from Massachusetts on Friday. I can't just run off with you two days later."

"What's her name?"

"How do you know it's a her?"

"Power of positive thinking."

She laughed, the first time all day. "Her name is Sarah, and she's staying with me for a week."

"OK, Sunday's out. How about taking a day off during the week? Maybe by Tuesday you and Sarah will have run out of conversation."

He was probably right. She hadn't seen Sarah in several years and they might welcome a break from each other by Tuesday. And she was just thinking how much she needs a day or two off. It would be a lot less crowded at Myakka during the week. "OK, you talked me into it, you silver-tongued devil. Call them for reservations and let me know what time you'll pick me up. Top down."

* * *

On Friday morning Francis J. Wilson arrived at the Sarasota Yacht Club at ten on the dot. Francis was excited about being invited for a cruise on Joshua Fishman's yacht.

Word must have got around that Francis was disappointed at not being invited to the elegant event at Joshua's home. And now that Francis had let it be known that he was no longer the squire of the trouble making Melody, he was back where he belonged, with the cream of Sarasota society.

Francis frowned, thinking of Melody, out there somewhere, ticking like a time bomb waiting to embarrass him again. He knew it would just be a matter of time before Cynthia would be referring to him in her column as a celeb—if Melody didn't do something to ruin everything.

Cecil pulled up to the entrance of the yacht club and escorted Francis in. They were immediately met by a man wearing a red blazer bearing the Sarasota Yacht Club insignia. The man's head drew back, and his nose twitched several times. "Is there something I can help you with?" the man asked.

Francis raised himself to his full height, squared his shoulders, and announced in his most imperious voice, "I am Francis J. Wilson, a guest of Mr. Joshua Fishman, and this gentleman is my chauffeur."

The man's expression changed. He managed a half smile and beckoned to a door at the other side of the room. "How do you do.

Mr. Fishman is expecting you. He and the others are on the boat. Allow me to take you there."

Francis grunted and excused Cecil. He glanced around at the people inside and was pleased to see that the attire he had selected appeared to be appropriate. His double breasted blazer with the brass buttons, white trousers, and new white sneakers fit in well with the ambiance of the club. The maroon ascot tucked into the collar of his white linen shirt was a nice touch. Casual, but elegant.

Joshua greeted him at the boat. "Nice to see you, Francis. Hop aboard." Francis observed Joshua's khaki Bermuda shorts and navy polo shirt. Others milled about the boat in similar attire and he wondered if he had overdressed.

Joshua set his mind at ease. "Francis, you look very spiffy. The consummate yachtsman. Come on and say hello to everyone. I believe you know most of the folks here."

"This is a handsome boat, Joshua," Francis said. He had never seen such a yacht up close. "What's the length of your boat, Joshua, and how many knots will she do?" Francis asked, hoping to sound knowledgeable about such things.

"This baby's a sixty footer, Francis. I've had 'em bigger, but I like the way this one handles. I never really opened her up, but she can fly, believe me. Come on inside."

They entered one of the salons and encountered Dexter and Susan Kingman. Francis noticed they appeared to be looking beyond him. Both looked apprehensive. Were they expecting Melody? He wouldn't blame them for being wary, considering Melody's disgraceful behavior at Mickey's on West.

He walked over and extended his hand. "A pleasure to see you both," he said.

Dexter Kingman surprised him by grabbing his hand warmly and flashing enviably white teeth at him. Francis wondered if they were capped. "Nice to see you again, Francis. I must have you out to the

college soon and show you around. We're pretty proud of our Sarasota University.

"Indeed, from what I hear, you should be, Dexter. It would be a
pleasure to visit." Francis said, pleased that Joshua had heard Dexter's
gracious invitation.

Mrs. Kingman smiled and mouthed, "Hello."

Francis wiggled his fingers goodbye as Joshua ushered him along
to the sprawling main salon. Everyone was there. Leona Cavendish,
Finley Spaulding, President of the Sarasota Opera, the Braunfelds,
Winifred Gwynn, Grande Dame of Sarasota Society, Bradford Feld-
man, Chairman of the Radford Museum Board, the President of the
Sarasota Ballet, whose name Francis had forgotten. Across the room,
Francis spotted Cynthia Mayfair. He tried to get her eye, but he was
afraid she couldn't see him.

A steward handed Francis a glass of orange juice and held a
bottle of champagne at the ready. Francis nodded and the man spiked
his juice.

All of the city's cultural and society leaders were on board to
share the lovely day with Francis. His heart filled with pride.

A man wearing a Sarasota Yacht Club polo shirt with the word
"Commodore" just above the logo approached Francis. "Welcome
aboard, Francis. Pleasure to meet you. I've heard a lot about you. We
must get together some time. We'll have lunch at the club and I'll fill
you in on our rich history. Yes, yes, we'll do that. Excuse me, Francis.
Got to give a hand with the lines. We're about to cast off."

Lunch with the Commodore of the Sarasota Yacht Club, one of
the most prominent people in all of Sarasota. Francis could barely
contain himself as he sipped his mimosa and continued greeting his
friends.

He was soon surrounded by the cultural doyens of Sarasota,
the powers behind the ballet, the opera, the Henzle, all the major
theatres. Even Mayor Cudworth came over to join them. Francis
could feel the boat moving but he was so busy chatting with his

166

friends, nibbling on hors d'oeuvres and enjoying his mimosa, he had no idea where they were headed—nor did he care.

Minerva Griffith, chairperson of the Sarasota Arts Council, had also joined the group and began extolling Francis' virtues. "Francis J. Wilson is one of our city's most generous benefactors as well as being a man of culture and refinement."

Everyone nodded and murmured agreement.

Francis smiled and chatted easily with his friends. How foolish he had been to think they had deserted him. His initial nervousness had disappeared along with his first mimosa. He nursed his second, mindful of the moderation he usually practiced. But today he was in a celebratory mood, back where he belonged.

After several hours and a glorious lunch, Joshua invited Francis to join him atop the flying bridge. "We're cruising in the Gulf along the shoreline of Longboat Key. This is where I like to take over the wheel from my captain. The view from up on the bridge is fantastic. Come on up with me, Francis. You're going to love it."

Francis was touched, but hesitant. Joshua noticed, leaned over, and put his arm around him. "Don't worry, Francis, I had a lift installed to help people up top. Come on."

Francis had never been on the flying bridge of such a vessel. Joshua was correct. The view was impressive. He found it interesting, viewing the beautiful mansions and resorts from the water.

"That's your place over there, isn't it, Francis?"

Off to the right, he spotted his house, looking like a Moorish castle. It was indeed an impressive sight, far more so from the water than he could have imagined. "Yes, that's my house, Joshua. How did you know?"

Joshua laughed. "Oh, we all know a good deal about you, Francis."

Francis responded with a cordial laugh of his own.

"Looking forward to having you third row center for opening night of *The Matchmaker*. Of course we'll be paying special tribute to you for your generosity in being a co-producer," Joshua said.

After a last look at his house, he turned and faced his host. "That's kind of you, Joshua. Of course, as you know, I have a warm spot in my heart for the Grande."

"Yes, we know that, and I thought you would be interested in knowing that we're, uh thinking of adding a couple of more people to our Board. Joshua lowered his voice and looked around the small pilot house where he and Francis stood. "Your name has come up and I want you to know you're under very serious consideration."

Francis wanted to respond, but he was unable to quell the excitement building within him. He finally regained his composure enough to squeak out a hushed thank you.

"We have some major challenges ahead of us over these next several years and we need people of vision, intelligence, theatrical insight, and—generosity.

"Next year in particular will present a major financial challenge. We are planning two extravaganzas whose budgets will be daunting. As you know, we're committed to a new sound system and other renovations. We're going to need all the help we can get from our supporters."

Francis looked up at Joshua at the wheel of his elegant boat, his seaman's cap at a jaunty angle piloting his way through the waters of the Gulf of Mexico alongside the beautiful shoreline of exclusive Longboat Key. Never in his life had he felt such pride of belonging. "You can count on me, Joshua," he said solemnly.

Joshua smiled and reached down to shake Francis' hand. "I knew I could, Francis."

Several people milled about below on the bow deck. Cynthia Mayfair looked up and waved at Francis and Joshua, alone on the flying bridge, talking business. Francis waved back. He wondered if he should subtly leak to Cynthia the news of his being considered for the Board.

"Francis, there is something else I think you should know,"

Joshua said, his voice again lowered to the hushed, conspiratorial tone he'd used in discussing Francis' board consideration.

"What's that, Joshua?"

"Several days ago I pulled into Marina Jack's with the boat. Brad Feldman and his wife were with Esther and me. We had stopped for a bite to eat. Your friend Melody was there, having lunch with a large, muscular blonde woman."

"Oh, oh," Francis thought.

Joshua leaned over and lowered his voice more. "Melody was clearly drunk, and it was obvious that she and her companion were having an argument. Suddenly Melody began screaming obscenities at the other woman, creating quite a scene."

"Oh, dear," Francis said. "I sent Melody back to Ohio, but she has obviously returned."

"Indeed she has, Francis. The scene was ugly, so the four of us got up to leave. The thing you should know is that Melody began using your name. In fact the last thing we heard as we were leaving was, 'I'll have my boyfriend, Francis J. Wilson take care of you'."

Francis winced and attempted to speak, but Joshua continued over him. "This is not good, Francis. I know the Feldmans were upset, and I must say, concerned. They were concerned for you, Francis, and frankly so were Esther and I." Joshua made a face, like it was hurting him to continue. "Doesn't look good, if you know what I mean."

By the time the party returned to the yacht club, Francis was no longer in high spirits. He said goodbye to his friends and climbed into the car with the waiting Cecil. Sitting in the back, alone and depressed, he knew it was now more critical than ever that Melody be found.

26

Donald Frazier kicked the wastebasket in his office, sending the contents sprawling over the floor. Three unsatisfying, frustrating conversations in one day were enough for any man. First Cliff calls him in and tells him he'd better be prepared for a call from Jimbo Conlin, then to his horror, Cliff tells him he'd just told Jimbo to go to hell in so many words.

The biggest individual contributor they have, and Cliff blithely informs him that it's his tough luck if the release of Jennifer Belding's findings scares people away from Sarasota and Jimbo's resort goes down the tubes. Jimbo stiffs the Galt and Donald takes the fall for badly missing his fundraising goal. It was so unfair.

He got nowhere with Belding. She practically blew him out of her office, and without Cliff's backing, he no longer has any leverage with her.

And then comes the end of a perfect day with Jimbo screaming at him like he's some kind of lackey. All he'd worked for, crumbling in front of him. Not fair. Shit, it's just not fair.

* * *

Sam put the finishing touches on chapter four of his new book and shut off the computer. He leaned back in his chair, took off his glasses, and rubbed his neck and eyes. Four productive hours and it was only noon.

The call from his editor was just what he needed. She had a way of gently needling him into guilt feelings—like he was letting himself, the company, and of course, her down. But she did it with style and good humor, and Sam always felt recharged after talking with her.

Henry galloped in from his bedroom and skidded to a halt next to Sam. Something about the computer, Henry didn't like. Sam figured it was probably the clicking of the keys. Whenever he stopped typing and turned off the machine, Henry appeared from wherever he'd retreated.

Sam took stock of himself, unshaven, sitting in his underwear, sipping on cold, stale coffee. Back in Boston, he would have just finished class and be joining his colleagues over lunch at the faculty club. He let his thoughts linger for a while over the repartee and the spirited discussions they enjoyed.

He missed it all, but he was making a life for himself here in Sarasota, temporary though it may be. "Tell you what, Henry, let's you and I go to Dog Beach." Henry, who knew the two magic words, leaped into Sam's lap and began licking his nose. Sam set him down, and he ran off to the bedroom and reappeared with his leash.

Sam parked the car in one of the two places in front of Jimbo's unoccupied cottage. "Park there anytime you want, Sam," Jimbo had told him.

The short, two block walk to the beach took fifteen minutes. Henry stopped and sniffed at every bush, mailbox, and person they passed. Sam liked the attention Henry got as much as Henry did, everyone telling him how adorable his dog was and stopping to pet and fondle him.

Some of the people, by now, knew Henry's name, even if they didn't know Sam's. Henry was more wary of the other animals they passed. He was strictly a people dog.

Under the shade of a palm tree, they settled into the beach, which to Sam's surprise was uncrowded. After a few flings with the Frisbee, they spread out on a blanket. Sam ate a sandwich he'd brought and Henry munched on his dog biscuits. Sam lay back and closed his eyes. He wasn't due to meet Diane Lewis until 3:30. Plenty of time to veg out and think.

Rossi getting killed the night before he was to meet with the reporter couldn't have been a coincidence. Someone knew about that meeting. He was dying to talk to Jennifer's secretary, but that was a no-no. It wasn't worth jeopardizing his relationship with Jennifer.

He rubbed on more sun block and tipped the straw hat further over his eyes. Henry lay across his lap, all four legs splayed out flat.

Any one of at least three people he's already met and talked with could have killed Rossi. Jimbo certainly had good reason to even the score with him or shut him up. He hated to think that Jimbo could be a murderer.

He would much rather have it turn out to be Alexis who was a lot harder to like than Jimbo. Francis J.? He didn't want to think of Francis as a killer, either, but the little guy had motive enough. Probably more than anyone.

Diane Lewis was leaning toward Jimbo. She was too smart to even mention it to him if she didn't have something pretty solid to go on. She also knew a lot more than she was letting on to him,

He knew she was giving him just enough cooperation and encouragement to see what he could come up with, another little arm out there for her. Was he merely some meddling ex-cop, tilting at windmills, making a jerk out of himself? Dick Tracy.

He smiled and thought of Jennifer. Only a few days until Tuesday, when they would have a full day together, canoeing on the Myakka. And speaking of making a fool out of himself, he wasn't exactly Captain Nemo. Supposing he tipped over the canoe in a nest of alligators?

The sun was high in a cloudless sky and, it seared into him. A sirocco wind came off the Gulf, bringing with it a sultry oppressiveness. Sweat rolled off his body, and he was covered with wind blown sand. He felt drawn of energy, feeling his age, and more. Henry squirmed and nibbled at the sand coating his fur. Fun at the beach had run its course.

* * *

Diane Lewis herself came out and greeted Sam in the reception area of the police station. "Come on, Sam, I need a break. Let's go to Carrie's and have a Coke."

Sam put down the copy of *SRQ Magazine* and was on his feet, appraising Lewis. She wore a nondescript looking pair of chinos, flat sandals, and a sleeveless cotton sweater that was seductively tight for an all business cop.

Why does he always have to check out what she's wearing? He wished he didn't do it. But he did. "Sounds good to me, Diane," he said, relieved to be sprung from the dreary station house.

Carrie's was a long narrow café on Ringling Boulevard across from the police station. Tables lined one side while a cafeteria style counter ran along the other.

A hardy looking fiftyish woman standing behind the counter greeted Lewis. "Hi, Diane. Go on back and sit. What can I bring you?"

"Diet Coke for me, Carrie, and a tuna salad sandwich on whole wheat. And," she looked at Sam.

"I'll just have a Coke."

They settled into one of three empty tables in a small back room. "We can talk here," Lewis said. "Carrie won't bring anyone else back."

She took a hefty swig of her Coke and watched him. "You have a little sunburn," she said. "You look like a tourist," she said, giving him a gentle needle.

Sam nodded. She was actually making small talk. Maybe it was Carrie's ambiance. "Yeah, I took my dog to the beach and we fell asleep for a while."

"You have a dog?" she asked with a lilt that was definitely not her cop's voice. "What kind?"

"Aw, he's just a little mutt, but he's a smart little guy. You like dogs?"

"Love 'em. I love all animals. I have a yellow lab and a cat. I'm a big fan of the Humane Society here. So, what have you got for me?" The cop's voice was back.

He smiled. What was it he called himself in this partnership? Another little arm out there for her. "Well, since we're, uh, sharing, let me tell you my latest." He paused for effect. "Tim Lester, the columnist, had an appointment with Mike Rossi the day after Rossi was killed." He searched her face to see how she would react to that one.

"And for what reason?" she asked flatly.

He sipped his Coke and noticed that Diane had finished off both her drink and sandwich. He wasn't surprised that she had a lusty appetite. "I'm not sure, but I do know that he told a friend he was going to put the screws to certain people."

This time she raised her eyebrows like maybe he had connected with her. "And did he tell this friend what certain people he was talking about?"

"No, but I'm sure you would have your thoughts on that."

She picked up a remnant of tuna salad with her fork and downed it. "The trouble is, Sam, that there are a lot of people that Mr. Rossi would have liked to 'put the screws to'. And I might say, vice versa."

He watched her fruitless search for more tuna on the empty plate. She's a cool customer. Gives him nothing, not even a reaction to the information he'd just given her. He turned away, then back to her with a sideward glance. "Did you know about the appointment Rossi had with Lester?"

She smiled. "Yes. I also know where you got your information."

He frowned and studied her for several beats. The woman was scary.

"You said I was a good cop, Sam. I know you've been seeing the biologist at the Galt, Miss Belding. I also know her secretary was dating Rossi."

"How do you know I'm seeing Miss Belding?" He was working at containing the anger building. Her smile was beginning to piss him off.

"Look, I know you were once a cop, Sam. And I know, as I told you, that your former colleagues had great respect for you. But I also know I can't have you running around like a loose cannon, now can I?"

Maybe it was the patronizing tone that tipped him over the edge. He slammed his glass down. "Goddamn it, Diane, I thought we were working together, and now you tell me you've had me followed. I think you're enjoying making a fool out of me. Well, screw you!" He slid his chair back and started to leave.

"Come back here," she snapped.

He turned and hesitated.

"Sit down," the cop in her commanded.

He counted to ten like his father had taught him to do when he was angry. After a count of twelve, he trusted himself to return. He sat, pouting.

"First of all, I'm not making a fool out of you. Second, I respect and value whatever help you can provide. Third, I have not had you followed. One of my colleagues happened to be at the Summerhouse the night you were there with Miss Belding. He knows her. They belong to the same running club. I haven't had you followed, Sam."

She hesitated. "I like you, and as I told you before, I think you can be of help to me. I'm afraid I couldn't resist pulling your chain a little." She hesitated again and gave him a genuine smile this time. "Sorry."

He relaxed but stayed with the pout for a few more seconds before letting her off the hook. "OK, sorry I blew up. How do you know where I got my information?

"Fair question. Tim Lester told me about the appointment he had with Rossi. He didn't know why, but he knew that Rossi had a grudge against Conlin, and he also knew about his troubles with the midget, Wilson, as well as some others. He assumed the meeting might have something to do with all that."

"Did 'some others' include Alexis Helfrich?"

She nodded. "There's very little that goes on in this town that Tim Lester doesn't know about. He knew that Rossi was dating a secretary at the Galt. And since I knew you were seeing Belding, I simply put two and two together. Am I right?"

Sam shrugged. He was still miffed, but he had to give the devil her due.

"When are you going fishing with Conlin?" she asked.

"Oh, um, not for a few days now."

"OK, I'm going to tell you something now, because I trust you and maybe because I feel a little guilty for putting you on a few minutes ago. Remember I told you Jimbo Conlin was a suspect, and you asked me why?"

"Yes?"

"Well, what I will tell you is that we have some evidence that indicates Conlin may have been in Rossi's yard and in his house on or about the day he was killed. That's all I can tell you now." She was up and starting to leave. "I have to get back to work."

Sam got off his chair and stood facing her. Standing next to her, he smelled a different fragrance, stronger and sensuous, unlike the jasmine. "Should I be flattered or offended that you don't consider me work?"

They stood eyeball to eyeball for a moment. "I'm not sure," she said. "Let's go."

45

Melody headed for home after another unsatisfying evening. Home. What a joke referring to the flea trap of a motel as home.

She'd been staying in that dump for over a week now, sharing it with the roaches and the mold, and she was getting goddamned sick of it. She missed Francis and their beautiful home on Lido. That's what Francis called it, their home. And it was, until she went and fucked up everything.

And that big asshole tries to hit on her in the bar tonight. Big loudmouth. Even though she was horny, she wasn't having any of him. The clown wouldn't take no for an answer, but did she have to throw the drink in his face before leaving?

She was getting out of control, drinking too much, fighting with everybody, insulting people. The scene with that pig, Carole was disgusting, even for her. That should have been her wake up call, threatening her, throwing Francis' name around. Making a complete fool out of herself and embarrassing Francis.

She recognized that guy Fishman from the party. He probably told Francis and got him even more pissed at her. He must have known she was back in Sarasota anyway.

It wasn't too late to try and make up with Francis. He could be an obnoxious little shit, but he was so good to her. And even though there wasn't much to him, he knew little ways to satisfy her in bed, enough to keep her going until she got the real thing elsewhere— which was often enough.

Damn! She had a good thing going with Francis and here she was living in a smelly dump with cockroaches and running out of money. It was time to go back and apologize, promise never to fuck up again. Sit down with Francis, rub him a little, put his hand where he liked it, get him worked up, and he'd be hers again.

Jesus, it was dark out. She was having trouble seeing. Too many stingers? No, she'd only had two. Or was it three. Where the hell was that motel? Nothing looked familiar at all. Christ, the road was dark. Nothing around. Nothing. She must have taken a wrong turn. No motels here. Nothing but blackness and woods. How did she get here?

She was struggling now to focus, keep her eyes open. She remembered taking a right turn to head back toward 41. But then was she supposed to take another right or left? Can't remember.

Shit. She was drunk again. Driving in the dark after midnight, drunk, lost, all fucked up.

Another car coming in back of her. At least somebody else on this road to nowhere. Got his brights on. Dim your lights, you dumb shit. Can't see. Where the hell am I? Road's bearing right. Dim your lights, you prick.

She was off the road, crashing through bushes, trees coming up on her. Turn the wheel. She turned the wheel sharply, hit something hard, and felt the car rolling over. It stopped and everything was quiet.

She felt around inside. Her seat belt was still on, and she didn't feel any broken bones. But she was up in the air in a funny position. Car's on its side.

She unhooked the seat belt and fell off to the right onto the floor. The door was open and she rolled herself out.

The car was hissing and smoking. Roll away from it. Where was she? Lots of thick bushes and small trees everywhere.

She lay still, wondering if she would be able to get up. And how was she ever going to get out of here?

Some light shining through the woods. Car headlights? She tried to move but her body throbbed with pain. She could raise herself only a foot or two—enough to see someone walking through the woods. Thank God! The asshole with the bright lights.

Coming closer. "Yes, yes, here I am," she half whispered. "Here, here. Thank God." The figure moved in close and she fell back, waiting to be rescued.

* * *

At eleven a.m. Jimbo Conlin pulled his car into the parking lot of Alexis Helfrich's building. He snickered, thinking of how she always referred to her place as an "establishment."

"It's a whorehouse, Alexis, baby." he liked to remind her, just to piss her off. "Ain't no establishment, it's a whorehouse." Actually, he knew it wasn't really. Alexis ran an escort service. He liked to needle her anyway.

The door was locked, but he used his key to enter. Shit, it was his building. He had a right.

He walked through to Alexis' office and opened the door. She arrived every morning to do her paperwork and man the phones. Jimbo knew her routine as well as everything else about her.

Alexis looked up sharply from her desk when Jimbo walked in. "Don't you ever knock?" she asked.

Jimbo strolled over to an easy chair, flopped into it, and put his feet up on the coffee table. "Alexis, honey, that ain't no way to talk to your ol' buddy, Jimbo."

Alexis eyed the muddy, heavy soled boots defiling her table. "That's a hand-carved, one of a kind coffee table you're wiping your boots on," she said.

"Ooh, must be expensive. Lady has that kinda money, outta be able to pay her rent. You're a month behind, sweetie. Thought I'd drop by, pay my respects and save you some postage."

She continued to glare at the boots on her table. "Jimbo, it's been slow this month. How about if I include this month with next month's rent. We have some heavy hitting clients coming into town."

Jimbo gave her a Texas size laugh. "Sheeit, now that your friend Rossi's no longer around blackmailin' you, you must have plenty of money to take care your obligations. Convenient for you, I'd say, getting that scumbag off your back."

Alexis flew off the chair and was in his face. "Listen, you sonofabitch. You've been spreading that ugly kind of talk all over this town. You even told that self-styled gumshoe, what's his name—Wallace—that I had something to do with Rossi's death. Now, I'm warning you to stop it and stop it now."

Jimbo took his boots off the table and stood. "You threatenin' me. Lady?"

"Take it anyway you want. I'm just telling you to stop filling people with your filthy lies. I'll have your rent for you this afternoon. You can come by and get it then. Now get the hell out of here. You're smelling up my establishment."

* * *

Charles Williams drove his Home Depot truck with a load of lumber down Laurel Road toward the Myakka River. Charles loved this area of Sarasota where it was still rural and peaceful.

He neared the end of the paved road, about to run onto the dirt section when he noticed a number of bushes and small trees mashed over like a car or something had shot through and mowed them down. He'd delivered another load yesterday to the guys building the two houses along the river and everything was normal then. He sure would have noticed a swath like that.

Charles pulled his truck over and got out.

* * *

Jimbo paid his check and nursed his beer. He liked sitting on the deck of the Old Salty Dog, looking out across the Gulf of Mexico. Music filled the air with upbeat island sounds. Why not? He was on City Island.

He glanced back across the marina and boat shop toward the Galt. His meeting with Donald was a little tense, and the couple of beers and fresh sea air provided the relaxation he needed.

The important thing is he was satisfied that Donald got the message. He wasn't sure after their phone conversation, but he felt a little better after today. Always best to handle things in person. He checked his watch. Time to pick up his rent money.

Carole was sitting at Alexis' desk when Jimbo walked in. He hadn't seen her in quite a while, not since Alexis put the kybosh on her seeing him. Jesus, she still looks sensational. That big broad always did turn him on somethin' terrible. For the moment he forgot what he came in for.

Carole looked up from whatever she was doing and greeted him. "Hello, Jimbo," she said in the husky voice that did weird things to him.

"Hey Carole. Long time, no see." He stood, feeling like a helpless puppy.

"Alexis had to go on some errands. She left me holding the fort. I've got your rent check."

He watched her move toward him, wearing those short shorts. The man's shirt tied around her midriff was open at least four buttons down, exposing everything but her nipples. He let out a moan and wondered if she heard it.

She reached him and held out the check. "Here's your money, Jimbo." She moved in a step closer and ran her tongue across her upper lip.

Hot damn! She was havin' fun with him. Teasing. She knew what she did to him. He looked at her hand holding the check, looked at those luscious, milk white boobs, struggling to break out of the shirt. "Keep it and come see me tonight." He barely managed to get the words out.

She looked down at the check and back to Jimbo and smiled. "Jimbo, you know Alexis has forbidden me to see you." She still held the check.

"How's she gonna know. Ain't no way she's gotta know. You'n me have always had some fun, Carole. How 'bout it? For old times sake." He placed his hand over hers and rolled her hand into a fist over the check. "What do you say, honey?"

She handed the check toward him. "Jimbo, the check is made out to you and signed by Alexis. How do I benefit?"

Jimbo laughed and shook his head. "Ole Jimbo must be losin' it. You're right." He reached into his pocket, pulled out a wad of hundred dollar bills, counted out the amount of the check, and placed them in Carole's hand. "Here, sweetie. Now you can give me m' check."

She moved her fist up and down, assaying its contents, and pursed her lips in thought. Jimbo held his breath. She opened her hand and tucked the bills inside her cleavage.

Jimbo slowly exhaled and smiled. "That's my girl."

28

Sam and Henry had developed a morning routine that seemed to suit them. They were becoming a recognizable duo around Siesta Key village. Sam liked that. He liked the neighborliness of the village and enjoyed being part of it.

Each morning, after feeding Henry, they drove to Jimbo's cottage, parked the car, and walked to Dog Beach. Along the way Henry went through his sniffing routine and found one of his favorite bushes where he did his business. Sam scraped it into one of his ever present plastic bags, and they joined the gang at Dog Beach.

Henry had taken a shine to a cocker spaniel, and once they worked through their wariness, they bonded. Sam enjoyed chatting with the cocker's owner, a retired doctor from England, who moved to Florida to get away from the nasty weather in London and all those bloody Englishmen.

Henry and Reggie, the cocker, frolicked about the beach, while Sam and Doctor Tabner exchanged pleasantries. The doctor's wife didn't like the beach, thought Florida was too hot, and missed England. "But we're coping," he said pleasantly. "She likes the dog track and Disney World."

After walking the few blocks to the village center, Sam picked up a copy of the *Sarasota Herald*, and he and Henry settled into a table on the outside patio of the Broken Egg restaurant.

"The usual, Sam?" the waitress asked.

"The usual, Polly."

She returned with a coffee and raisin bagel for Sam and three milk bones for Henry, who lay spread out under the table, behaving himself. Sam thumbed through the paper and frowned. He hadn't yet acclimated himself to the local journal.

The twelve page main news section consisted mostly of ads.

A section called Florida West, which offered articles about food, some recipes, a TV section, comics, and a few other tidbits mixed in with the ads, did little for him. The sports section was a potpourri of local sports, extensive coverage of Florida's college football mills, the Gators and Noles, a reverential homage to car racing, and a smattering of references to national sports. The section called "Sarasota" contained the usual local news, obituaries, a half page of weather, and of course, the ads.

The thing he liked best about the paper was its extensive stock listings, which included many stocks rarely found in papers serving much larger cities. Not surprising, given the wealth of Sarasotans.

He'd heard that the paper, owned by the *New York Times*, was reputed to be the most profitable of any of the *Times'* papers. Figures, he thought, given the ratio of ads to news.

He scanned the paper, which like most newspapers, had a heavy dose of bad news. Good news must be boring, he mused.

A couple of auto accidents caught his eye. A hit and run driver hit a child on a bicycle and took off. Nice. A woman, as yet unidentified, was killed in a car crash off Laurel Road. Neck broken. He winced, put the paper down, and thought of more pleasant subjects, like his upcoming canoe trip with Jennifer.

* * *

Jennifer scanned her computer, tracking red tide's path. No change. It continued inexorably toward the West Coast of Florida. Her calculations indicated a coverage stretching from Tampa to Naples, placing Sarasota directly in the middle of it. She knew it was still possible for it to change course, but at this point, not likely.

"Excuse me, Jennifer, may I come in?"

She looked up and saw Donald standing in the doorway. "Damn," she thought. "Why didn't I close the door?" Cliff liked to foster an open door policy among his staff and himself. If a person's door was closed, it was a message he or she was not to be disturbed.

She nodded, turned back to the computer screen, and began scribbling notes. Maybe Donald would get the message.

He entered and sat in the chair next to her desk. She continued writing.

"I know how busy you are these days, Jennifer, so I won't take a lot of your time." He paused, waiting for her to look up.

She put her pen down and turned to him. "Yes, I really am terribly busy, Donald, so can we keep it brief?" Not a very gracious welcome, she thought, but Donald brought out the worst in her. She did manage a smile. "What's up?"

"Well, first of all, I want to compliment you on the landmark work you've been doing in tracking red tide, and particularly the research you've done on predicting. It's something that no one has ever been able to accomplish from what I understand."

She said nothing, having no desire to engage in a discussion of her work with Donald.

"Uh, isn't that right?" he persisted.

"Yes."

"Uh—"

She waited, knowing now where he was heading.

"Well, what I mean is how can you be certain that this breakthrough of yours is valid? I mean, to my knowledge, we haven't really had any concrete experience in predicting the direction and timing of red tide, and having it validated, have we?"

She looked at her watch and swiveled her chair back to the computer. "Donald, I really am busy. If you want to question the scientific validity of my work, I suggest you do it with Cliff. He'll explain it nice and clearly, so that even you will understand." She began punching keys on the computer, expecting him to leave, given her last remark. He stayed put.

"I don't appreciate your attitude, Jennifer," the oily friendliness now gone from his voice. "I may not be a scientist, but the work I do is very important. If I may be blunt, it pays your salary and goes a long way toward funding your research."

She knew he was exaggerating, but she was not about to argue with him. Best to ignore him now.

"All I was trying to say is that if you prematurely release your findings and frighten people away, the Galt stands to lose a very substantial portion of the funds on which we all rely. I believe there is an ethical, moral responsibility involved here."

She rolled her chair back and was on her feet. "Who the hell are you to preach to me about moral, ethical responsibilities? I don't answer to you. I answer to Doctor Cliff Bracken. Now please leave. I have work to do."

After Donald left she stared at the computer, unable to concentrate, thinking about her flare-up at him. She pulled her water bottle out of the desk drawer and downed half of it. Donald was an over-reaching fundraiser on the make. She knew what his problem was. Jimbo Conlin and some of the other developers were getting nervous. These were the heavy hitters around town and the source of Donald's clout at the Galt. His ambition meant more to him than people's safety and health. Thank God Cliff took a different view. She would not be intimidated by the likes of Donald Frazier.

But his point about her having an ethical, moral responsibility was certainly valid. She needed to be careful not to allow her enthusiasm for her research turn her into an over-reaching scientist on the make.

Oh, God! Sarah's flight was due in forty-five minutes. She almost forgot with all of Frazier's nonsense. She turned off the computer and headed for the airport.

Twenty-five minutes later, she was at the airport, waiting for Sarah. She said she'd be wearing a University of Massachusetts T-shirt, so she shouldn't be hard to spot. Anyway, she would recognize her. How long had it been? Nine years. Nobody changes that much in nine years. She hoped she hadn't.

Sarah's flight was on time, and Jennifer spotted her immediately. Tall and slender, still wearing the blonde hair long, and sporting her UMass shirt, she had actually changed very little.

They greeted each other with the hugs and enthusiasm of old friends. After Jennifer's obligatory, "How was your flight?" and other small talk, they collected her bags and drove home.

Jennifer remembered Sarah as being easy to talk with, and was not surprised she hadn't changed in that respect either. She thought it best to wait a day or so before telling her she would be gone all day and evening on Tuesday.

At the house, Sarah unpacked several bottles of a California Merlot. "Sarah, how thoughtful. You remembered my favorite wine."

"It's after five," Sarah said. "Perfectly respectable time to enjoy it. Shall we open a bottle?"

They sat on Jennifer's small terrace, drinking wine, getting reacquainted. Sarah cupped a hand to her ear. "You can hear the Gulf from here. Hmm, you can smell it too. What a wonderful spot this is, Jennifer."

Over the wine Jennifer learned more from Sarah about her job as an associate professor of biology at University of Massachusetts and that she'd been married for four years, and recently divorced.

"What about you, Jennifer? Anybody special in your life?"

"No, not really. I guess I've just been too wrapped up in my work. I don't know, I—" She stopped abruptly and grinned. "Actually, there is a guy who has possibilities."

"Oh?"

"He's a writer. Wrote a mystery novel that's actually quite good. I happened to be reading it when I met him at the beach."

"No!"

"Yes, it was quite a coincidence."

"A writer? How many books has he written?"

Jennifer laughed. "Hey, slow down. I really don't know a heck of a lot about him, to tell the truth. But he's interesting and fun. You relax, Sarah. I'm going to put the water on for some pasta. Be out in a few minutes."

Sarah started to get up.

"Uh, uh. You stay put. Relax. I'll be right back."

Inside the kitchen she thought about Sarah's question. There wasn't much she could answer, because there wasn't much she could tell her. A little embarrassing when you've just said he's a guy who's kind of in your life, but you don't know much about him. She would make it a point to rectify that on Tuesday.

29

Saturday's paper identified the woman killed in the car accident as Melody Griggs. Sam had to read the article twice to be certain she was Francis' Melody. He never did know her last name, but there was no question about it. The address given for her was Francis'. Probably taken from her driver's license. And the article said she was from Zanesville, Ohio. It was Melody. He looked up Francis' number and called him.

"Hello," a gruff voice answered. Cecil.

"Hello, may I speak with Francis?"

"Who's callin'?"

"This is Sam Wallace."

"Mr. Wilson don't wish to talk with nobody today."

"I just read the terrible news in the paper about Melody. I knew Melody, and of course, Francis. Please tell him I'm very sorry."

"I know who you are. He don't wanna talk today." He hung up.

Sam pondered the two articles he'd read about the accident. Apparently the car went off the road into the woods. High alcohol content. Neck broken. Had Melody's drinking finally caught up with her? He dialed Diane Lewis.

"Detective Lewis here."

"Hi, Diane. This is Sam."

"Well, Sarasota's answer to Sam Spade. How are you, Sam?"

He could have done without the first crack, but the "How are you?" sounded friendly enough. "I'm fine, but what do you think about Francis Wilson's friend, Melody, being killed in a car accident?"

"What do you mean, what do I think?"

She was being a hard ass again. "I mean—do you think there's a possibility it wasn't an accident?"

Long pause. Not a good sign. He fidgeted.

"Sam, you're getting carried away with this private eye thing. No, it doesn't appear to be anything but a tragic automobile accident. The woman was drunk. She had enough alcohol in her blood for two drunks."

"But you're investigating it aren't you, like any fatal accident?"

The sigh from the other end told him he'd pushed her too far. "Am I personally investigating it? No. Is the department conducting a routine investigation? Of course. Call me when you have something to tell me, Sam, not ask me."

He got himself another cup of coffee and went out to the balcony. Diane Lewis was still tough to figure out. You never knew which Detective Lewis you're going to get, he thought. Today he got the ball buster. Maybe working on Sunday put her in a bad mood.

He wondered how Francis was taking this. Not well, judging from Cecil's comments. He could have other reasons for not wanting to talk to anyone. Melody was a loose cannon out there. He knew that from his own encounter with her. Maybe Francis saw her as a threat to his social aspirations. Naw. Melody was a drunk. The only two times he saw her, she was loaded. And from what Diane said, she was drunk again, driving late at night. Probably fell asleep.

Henry came over and hopped on his lap. Sam scratched behind his ears and under his chin. Henry closed his eyes, gave a little moan, and snuggled his head against Sam's chest. He'd had his breakfast, went for a walk, pooped and peed. "Happy Henry," Sam said.

Henry turned his head and opened one eye. "It's OK, buddy, go back to sleep." Sam closed his own eyes and let some of Henry's contentment rub off on him.

He had just dozed off when the jangling phone brought his head up. Henry reacted at the same time and leaped off Sam's lap.

"Sam, have you seen today's paper?" Jennifer asked.

"Uh, today's paper?"

"You sound like I just woke you up."

"You sort of did. Henry and I were taking a little snooze on the balcony. Yes, I have read the paper. You read about Melody?"

"Oh God, yes. The poor woman. What a shame."

They talked about Melody for a while. He told of seeing her at the Hilton on Longboat Key, and they agreed that she'd probably been drinking and fell asleep or lost control of the car.

"What a shame. I'm so sorry." Jennifer said.

Neither said anything for a moment, until Jennifer changed the subject. "My friend Sarah is here, Sam. We're having brunch at the Colony and then going to the museum today. Tomorrow, Sarah has to go down to Fort Myers on some business. She'll be gone most of the day. Tuesday is the last day of the Monet exhibit at the St. Petersburg Museum of Modern Art and we both want to see that. And I have to go back to work on Wednesday."

"Wait. Slow down. You're losing me. I'm still in Fort Myers."

She laughed, "Sorry. What I'm getting at is can we go canoeing tomorrow instead of Tuesday?"

"Whew! Took a while to work our way through that one, but it's a no brainer. Of course we can. Sounds like you're enjoying Sarah."

"Yes, Sarah's great. She's even nicer than I remembered her. And I'm looking forward to canoeing tomorrow. Promise you won't fall out?"

Oh, oh, she's on to me, he thought. "If I do I'll hold on to my oar, so I can fight off the gators."

"We're in trouble already. They're called paddles."

"Oh. Well, I knew that. Just wanted to see if you were listening."

30

At eleven a.m. Sam pulled into Jennifer's driveway wearing his straw hat, sunglasses, shorts, and a Siesta Key T-shirt. Jennifer popped out of the front door and gave him a big smile and a wave.

He watched her pause to pinch some weeds from her perfect little flower garden, and lope toward the car, carrying her water bottle and a small back pack. He smiled. More water and her cell phone. She looked as fresh as the flowers in her garden. It was going to be a great day.

They drove along the beach, inhaling the clean morning air. He turned to her, caught her eye, and squinted. "Can I ask you a strictly hypothetical question, Jennifer?"

"Sure."

"How can a woman look freshly scrubbed, wholesome, and sensuous at the same time?"

"Strictly hypothetical?"

"Strictly."

"Probably has to do with her genes. Let me ask you a question. You like wholesome or sensuous?"

"Both."

She giggled. "Sounds like we're back where we started."

They left Lido, drove over the Ringling Bridge, cruised along Bayfront Drive, with the bay off to the right, dappled in sunlight. Jennifer undid her ponytail, and her hair floated behind her like a crimson kite. Sam sneaked peaks at her from time to time.

"Did you bring your oars?" Jennifer asked.

"Come on, Jennifer. I was just being cute. I know they're paddles. You think I'm some kind of rookie?"

She giggled again. "Yes."

The giggling was something new. He liked it, a nice contrast to

195

the buttoned down Jennifer. He was tempted to ask her if she was having fun, but decided it wouldn't be cool.

"OK, we're going canoeing on the Myakka. Tell me what you know about the Myakka River."

Her head snapped up like he'd said the magic words. "You want a little history?"

"Sure."

"Antonio De Herrera. Know who he was?"

"He was a Spanish writer."

"Yes, and he was the historiographer for King Phillip of Spain. He wrote of the Myakka as the river that provided rejuvenation. It was said to have the same replenishing effect as the Nile in Egypt."

"Interesting. Continue."

She slid her legs under her, a movement he was beginning to realize signaled her getting into the conversation. "How would you like to have written this, Sam? 'Many a haggard face has grown calm and less wretched from a soothing sojourn on the Myakka, and many frivolous, unthinking souls have grown more noble.' "

"That's very nice, but are you trying to tell me something? By the way, that doesn't sound like Herrera's writing."

She nodded. "You're right. It was written by a man named Ned Wyatt Chapline from a book published in 1914. I love that passage."

"So you memorized it?"

"Yes."

"Do you always do that when you read something you like?"

"Not always, but often. By the way, Warm Mineral Springs, two miles east of the Myakka River Basin is widely assumed to be the Fountain of Youth renowned among the Indians—the one Ponce de Leon was looking for."

"That's for me. Let's go."

"Be serious. I'm trying to educate you. The river and the whole region are very old. Rock samples taken from the Myakka tell us the river existed over a million years ago. Man's presence in the area over ten thousand years ago has been confirmed from human skeletal material."

"He's the guy who found the Fountain of Youth. Probably just died last year."

"You're impossible," she said. "Trainable, but definitely not educable."

He glanced at her. "Sorry for being flip. Actually, the more I see and hear of Florida, the more I appreciate the sense of history surrounding it. What you're telling me about this river is a good example."

She nodded. "Maybe there is hope for you. Oops, there's the sign ahead. Turn left."

The park was about what Sam hoped it would be—and more. Giant oaks with tentacles of moss dripping off them bent over the road, forming a tropical tunnel. They drove under the oaks, sable palmettos, and slash pines for about three miles before reaching Upper Myakka Lake. A small concession stand offered canoes for rent.

They got their canoe and were soon on their way. Sam gasped at the array of tropical birds. They were everywhere. Jennifer identified each of them, pointing out herons, egrets, sand billed cranes, red shouldered hawks, ibis, spoonbills, and even two flamingos.

"The flamingos don't live here, Sam. They're transient, but aren't they beautiful?"

Sam nodded, his mouth open, eyes staring at the wonderland surrounding them. They glided within a boat length of a great blue heron. The heron looked up and resumed poking his bill into the water, fishing.

Several alligators sunned themselves along the banks. Occasionally one would slide into the water, heading slowly toward them before submerging. Sam eyed the water, expecting the gator to surface under the canoe and plunge them into his jaws.

"It's OK, Sam. They're more leery of us than we are of them."

Sam shrugged. "Oh, sure, I know. They don't bother me."

The sun was now high in the sky, but a cool breeze kept them comfortable, as they meandered along the shallow ribbon of water patched with clusters of bulrush, golden blooms of marsh marigold, and pink spikes of smartweed. Jennifer knew them all.

They paddled around a sharp bend with slash pines growing from the water's edge. Large oaks bent at ninety degree angles over the water.

"This is called Alligator Point," Jennifer said.

"Oh? And, uh, why is that?"

"There, that's why." She pointed to the bank ten yards in front of them.

"Jeeesus," Sam cried. "That has to be the largest alligator in the world." He watched the creature watching them and decided it was much bigger than their canoe. He thought of *Jaws* when the Great White got into the boat and swallowed Quint.

Jennifer nodded. "Yes, I'd say he's fifteen, sixteen feet. We'd better give him a wide berth."

They paddled around the bend, keeping as far away from the alligator as possible. As they rounded the curve, a half dozen more of them came into view, swimming only a few yards ahead of them. The river narrowed, and to continue forward, they would pass close to the alligators, all of which were at least as large as the first one.

Sam thought of Quint again. To his relief, Jennifer back paddled and suggested they turn around.

"We've been out here for almost four hours. We'll have the wind with us on the way back, but it'll still take us well over three hours. Let's turn around."

"OK," Sam said, trying to sound casual. "If that's what you want to do."

They turned and Sam put a little extra juice into his paddling. He glanced back at the alligators receding into the distance, and relaxed. "Hey, I could get into this canoeing. I think I'm getting pretty good."

"Yes, I'm proud of you, Sam. You haven't tipped it over yet."

They pulled in their paddles, turned and faced each other, and let the river slowly move them along. After eating the sandwiches and fruit Sam brought and drifting in silence for several minutes, Jennifer finally broke it.

"Sam. You haven't told me a whole lot about yourself. You've managed to squeeze more out of me than most people do, so—"

"How about evening things up?"

She hesitated. "Yes, as a matter of fact."

"Seems fair enough. What do you want me to tell you?"

"I don't know. This isn't an inquisition. Tell me anything you want to." Again, she hesitated. "I'm interested."

"Well," he said, dragging out the word. "I'm divorced. Happened about five months ago."

"Oh?"

"Yeah, I came home unexpectedly one afternoon and found my wife in bed with another gentleman, a colleague of mine, in fact."

"Oh, Sam. I'm so sorry."

"Yeah, well as you might expect, that put a dent in our marital bliss. Turned out they'd been having an affair, so since three is considered a crowd, I shuffled off the scene."

She took his hand and squeezed it. "Oh, Sam."

"It was a bit of a surprise, but not as bad as it sounds. Lisa and I had been drifting apart, and I guess in retrospect I should have seen something like this coming. I'm getting over it." He shrugged and wondered if she bought the last part.

To his relief, Jennifer changed the subject. "Boston is such a great city—so different from Florida. But you seem to be adjusting. Are you?"

He thought for a moment and nodded. "Yes, I'm surprising myself. I was never big on change, but since I've been here I'm finding new things about myself."

"Like what?"

"Well, for one, I'm not as resistant to change as I thought, and for several reasons I think what's happened could turn out for the best."

"How do you mean?"

"I was getting complacent, probably smug. It happens to people. I've only been here over a week, but as I look back now, I think I can see things more clearly. I probably would have stayed in a deteriorating marriage for one thing. Path of least resistance.

"I was a good teacher, but I don't think I was growing all that much. It came easily, and I didn't have to work hard at it.

"Boston was the hub of my universe, but now I'm beginning to think getting away from it, even if only temporarily, is going to be a good thing." He hesitated. "There's another reason, but I think I'll save it for later."

Jennifer grinned. "Oh?"

He returned her grin, satisfied that she knew what he meant. "Anyway, I think we've heard enough about me." He checked the river, making sure they were still drifting on course. "You said I squeezed more out of you than most people do, but it wasn't really a whole lot. Can I squeeze some more?"

She hesitated before answering. "Depends. What do you want to know?"

He wasn't sure how to proceed, and decided to start with something safe. "Family?"

A little smile glistened on her lips like dew on a petal. "There was always just my mom and I.

"What about your dad?"

"My father walked out on her when I was two."

That was a curve ball—not the safe subject he thought. Just threw it out there in her typical, no b.s. way. It was his turn to touch her hand. "Did you ever see him after that?"

She shook her head hard. "No, neither did my mother. He just— disappeared."

Sam caught her expression, which didn't match the matter of fact tone in her voice. "No brothers and sisters."

"No, but my mom and I had a good life together. We were best pals. She was a great lady."

Past tense. A longing for her surged through him like a grease fire. "Your mother has passed away?"

The canoe began to drift off course, and they resumed paddling, still facing each other. Sam paddled the wrong way for a moment before adjusting to the change. Jennifer didn't skip a beat.

"Yes, she died two years ago of breast cancer. She was only fifty-five. She had moved down here when I did. Had a small condo on Lido, so we saw each other nearly every day."

Sam smiled. "And I bet she had red hair."

Jennifer returned his smile. "She did."

Things went quiet again.

Jennifer turned back to normal paddling position. "It's getting late. Let's get serious about moving the canoe."

Neither of them said much during the drive back from Myakka. For Sam it was a combination of healthy fatigue and feeling mellow from the wonderful day on the water, alone with Jennifer. He was also digesting what she had told him.

For Jennifer, a better insight into Sam, Sam with the wise guy answer for everything, keeping those defenses up. His casual shrug did little to hide the hurt he must be still feeling.

Sam glanced toward her. She looked deep in thought. He wondered what was going on inside that fertile mind of hers. Dinoflagellates? The Galt? New horizons to conquer? Him?

31

Sarah Hanson pulled the Jeep into Jennifer's driveway, turned off the ignition, and stretched. She'd had a long day, and with road construction and accident traffic on I-75, the drive from Fort Myers had taken her three and a half hours. Jen had been so generous to loan her the Jeep, but it wasn't the most restful car to drive.

All she wanted now was a long hot shower and a good night's sleep. The St. Pete Museum with Jen tomorrow would be a fun day, and she wanted to be rested and ready.

She locked the Jeep and stood in the driveway for a moment, stretching and getting the kinks out. From the corner of her eye she saw something move along the house and turned to see a queen palm swaying gently back and forth, sending shadows flickering through the yard.

She smiled, feeling a trace of envy over Jennifer's little piece of heaven, unlocked the door, and went inside. The house was dark except for the small table lamp Jennifer had left on, and Sarah went straight to her room. She sat on the bed, peeled off her clothes, lay back and closed her eyes.

* * *

The man walked casually along the quiet street. At 9:30, he had the neighborhood to himself. A resident out for an evening stroll before retiring.

Three blocks away his car sat in the crowded parking lot of the Beachview Hotel, where he had parked. He was a careful man, smarter than people gave him credit for, and tonight he would do what needed to be done, efficiently, thoroughly.

The wind picked up and whistled down the narrow road. Dead leaves blew across his sneakers as he walked silently along the street. He tightened his cap as a sudden gust picked up a plastic bag from a nearby lawn. The man watched it blow and disappear into the darkness like a hitchhiking ghost.

He reached his destination and stopped, listening, all senses alert. His eyes darted up and down the street and across the yard. There was no sound, except his own breathing—and the wind.

* * *

Sarah opened her eyes. She had dozed off for a few minutes. God! She was lucky she hadn't fallen into a deep sleep without the shower she badly needed. She removed her contacts and sat up, rubbing the dryness from her eyes. She shivered and ran her hands over her body. Her skin felt clammy, sweaty. She eased herself off the bed and padded into the bathroom.

The hot shower she'd looked forward to all evening performed its magic. She closed her eyes and turned her face up to the soothing waters.

* * *

The man walked along the side of the house, past her car. He avoided the shell driveway, preferring to tread quietly across the grass. Adrenaline raged through his body, forcing him to stop and calm himself. The whole clockwork of his existence was in danger. He could make no mistake. He leaned against a tree, blending into the darkness until the adrenaline slowed, replaced by a strange sense of power from what he was about to do.

* * *

Sarah dried her hair and wrapped the bath towel in a turban around her head. She grabbed her terry cloth robe from the hook, reveling in its soft, clean feel against her body. Her hair smelled of herbal essence, aloe vera, and passion flower. She smiled, wondering if there really was such an ingredient as passion flower.

Inside the bedroom, she felt revitalized, restored, and suddenly wide awake. She glanced through the newspaper and noticed that one of her favorite Cary Grant movies, *An Affair to Remember*, had started a few minutes ago.

She loved the old romantic comedies and the sly intelligence they brought to the pursuit of love. They made her own heart beat faster—even more so now since Frank had walked out on her and she was alone. They made it easy for her to fantasize, to recreate a world she no longer had, but could still wish for. She wandered into Jen's small den and turned on the TV.

* * *

He tipped his head back like a dog, testing for scent. Everything clicked into place in his mind. It was time.

Around the back of the house he found what he'd hoped for. A set of French doors led from the patio into the house. He slid along the side of the building until he reached the doors, and peered inside.

* * *

Sarah slouched deep into the big comfortable leather chair, munching a carrot. She loved the dark coziness of the small room, the only light coming from the TV. She leaned forward as Cary pulled Deborah Kerr against his body and kissed her passionately. Deborah responded and Sarah moaned along with her.

* * *

The man reached inside the small bag he held and extracted a brass circle glass cutter. Inside the bag he also carried a length of rope and a serrated knife. He hoped he would not have to use the knife.

He placed the rope in his pocket, slid the knife under his belt, folded the bag, and pocketed it. The glass cutter was a precision machine, designed to quietly cut through the strongest glass. The flimsy glass on the French doors would cut like butter.

He put on a pair of thin leather gloves and secured the suction pad firmly to the glass pane and set the bar scale of the turret to a circle large enough for him to insert his hand. He then grasped the ball grip handle and slowly turned it, watching the six finely honed steel wheels cut a perfect circular hole. After removing the glass circle, he reached in and unlocked the door.

His heart pounded, and sweat rolled down his face as he stood in the kitchen. He was in the house and she couldn't be more than a few yards away from him. It was going to happen. So much thinking, so much hesitation and questioning himself, but now there was no turn-ing back.

His head snapped around. A light flickered from just outside the kitchen. Voices. He froze. More flickering. The television. She was watching TV.

Except for the light from the TV and a dim light in the living room, the rest of the house appeared to be dark. He moved slowly along the kitchen to the doorway and saw where the TV flickering came from—a room across the hall from the kitchen.

On his hands and knees he crawled across the hall to where he could see inside the television room. She sat in a chair facing the screen, her back to him. Perfect.

As he rose to his feet, his knees cracked, sounding like a rifle shot to him. He hugged the wall and held his breath She squirmed in her chair. Had she heard him? He gripped the knife in his belt.

* * *

Did she hear something out there? She muted the television, turned, and listened. The house was still. Silly. She would get a coke and check around at the next commercial. Like she was going to find some phantom lurking in the closet. Anyway, this was her favorite scene coming up. She returned the sound and snuggled back into her chair.

* * *

Struggling to contain the harsh asthmatic breathing that threat-ened to expose him, he could wait no longer. He stepped into the room, slipped the cord around her neck, and pulled with all his strength.

32

Sam and Jennifer stopped at a trendy little down-town restaurant called Epicure and ate dinner outside on the sidewalk. Driving along Main Street, Sam had noticed several interesting looking out-door cafés. Sarasota was a continuing surprise. Every day he found something new and different to like.

After dinner they crossed the bridge to Lido, and the lights of Sarasota's skyline glowed off to the right and danced along the water. It was one of those nights when he felt like he could drive forever. As if reading his mind, Jennifer said, "I think you're getting to like Sara-sota, aren't you?"

"You took the thought right out of my head. I was liking it before today. Love it now."

She smiled and he watched the wheels turning. "When do you have to go back?" she asked.

They drove along Lido Beach, and he was tempted to ask her to sit with him on the beach for a while. It was getting late, and he decided against it. "I don't have any special timetable," he said and turned onto her street.

She gave him a puzzled look. "Don't you have to get back to school?"

"No."

"Why not? What about your job?"

He pulled into her driveway. "I don't have a job."

"I thought you were a professor."

"I was. Let's go inside and I'll tell you about being fired."

They sat in the car, staring at each other, the silence broken only by the idling engine. He saw the questioning in Jennifer's eyes before she spoke.

"Are you sure you want to?"

He nodded and smiled. "Are you going to invite me in for coffee?"

She studied him for a moment more before replying. "OK. I see the car's back, but Sarah's probably asleep. Anyway, we can talk on the patio."

She unlocked the front door and led the way inside. The night light was still on, and she could see flickering of the television from the den. "The TV is still on," she said. "I bet Sarah fell asleep watching it."

Sam closed the door and locked it as Jennifer's voice came from the den. "Hey, sleepy head, wake up. Time for beddy-bye."

Sam snapped on a light in the living room and flopped on the couch. He rubbed his shoulders and decided he'd had enough of canoeing for a while.

Jennifer's voice rang out again. "Come on, Sarah. You'll hate yourself and me in the morning if I let you sleep all night in this chair. Come on. You—"

Sam had just closed his eyes when Jennifer's scream tore through the house. He leaped off the couch and ran into the den. Jennifer, still screaming, sat in the leather chair, cradling Sarah. She dropped her friend back onto the chair and fell to the floor, pounding her fists on the rug. "Oh God, Sarah. No. No. No."

Sam's eyes flicked back and forth between the two women, not sure which one to minister to first. A man on TV brayed about the low prices of his automobiles.

Sam switched on a light, turned off the television, helped Jennifer from the floor onto a chair, and examined Sarah. The first thing he noticed was the deep ugly groove in her neck—and her eyes, filled with small red dots, minute blood clots, indicating the presence of petechial hemorrhages, all of which told him Sarah Hanson had been strangled.

He turned to Jennifer, who stared at the wall, sobbing, and muttering, "No, please no" over and over. He led her into the living room, where they sat on the sofa and he whispered into her ear and held her, until the sobbing subsided and she stopped shaking.

They sat on the couch, rocking back and forth, until Jennifer spoke. "Who could have done this, Sam? Why?" And she let go again.

He handed her his handkerchief. "Here. Blow."

She blew her nose, which somehow calmed her. "She is dead, isn't she, Sam?"

"Yes, I'm afraid she is. She's been strangled."

She lowered her eyes and nodded, like she knew.

"The first thing we have to do is call the police," he said. "Don't touch anything. Just sit." He led her into the living room and gently settled her onto the sofa. "Where's your phone?"

Sam reached Diane Lewis and told her of the murder. Lewis said she would notify the Sarasota City Police, as Lido was in their jurisdiction, and she would come with them.

Fifteen minutes later the house was illuminated with the headlights of cars pulling into the driveway. Sam went to the door and faced a tall fortyish man with a marine style crew cut and a bushy mustache. Diane Lewis stood next to him.

"You do get around, Sam, " Lewis said flatly. She and the tall man entered the house and six other men and women followed. Lewis pointed to the man with her. "This is Detective Roberts with the Sarasota City Police. He will be in charge of the investigation."

Sam looked at Roberts, who nodded and gestured toward the others. "These are forensic people. Where is the body?"

Sam led them to the den and returned to Jennifer, sitting on the sofa staring into space. He took her by the arm. "Come on, Jen. I want you to go lie down."

She offered no resistance as he helped her into the bedroom. He removed her shoes, settled her into the bed, and joined Lewis and the others in the kitchen.

He watched the forensic people doing their thing, photographing and videotaping the body and everything else in the room. A fingerprint specialist dusted for prints, while another worked with a laser to pick up fibers, hair samples, and anything else that could help in identifying who might have been in the house besides Jennifer and Sarah.

Murder in Boston was an everyday event, and law enforcement people had a lot of practice at being very effective. In spite of Sarah being the third possible murder since he'd arrived in Sarasota, he was certain it was not a common occurrence. All the more reason to be impressed with the professionalism with which this team worked.

Lewis looked up at him. "Please go into the living room and wait for me there, Sam," she ordered. He sat on the living room sofa, puzzling over the tragic death of Jennifer's friend.

The groove in her neck was very deep. She must have been caught from behind by someone who was very strong.

Such a pretty young woman. She actually resembled Jennifer a little. Why would anyone want to kill her? A burglar? He tried to avoid thinking the obvious, but it wouldn't go away.

He buried his face in his hands for a moment, and when he looked up, Detectives Lewis and Roberts stood over him. "Fill us in, Sam," Lewis said and sat down.

He told her of the canoe trip, dinner, and returning to find Sarah.

Roberts scribbled in his note pad. "Did you know the victim?"

"No, I never met her. She arrived on Friday, I believe, to spend a week or so with Jennifer. They were friends from college. That's all I can tell you about her. Does it appear to you she was murdered?"

Roberts put his pad down and eyed Sam for a couple of beats. "I'll ask the questions, sir. She's been strangled. I'm sure you noticed the groove bruises on her neck, both front and back. What do you think?"

He nodded, knowing Roberts wasn't expecting an answer. It wasn't a real question, more of a sarcastic put down. Anyway, there was no question in his mind. Of course she was murdered. He knew that the minute he saw her neck.

"Where is Miss Belding?"

"She's in her bedroom, lying down."

"Would you get her. I'm sorry, but I'm going to have to ask her some questions. By the way, does she have somewhere she can stay tonight, maybe for a couple of days? She can't stay here until we have completed our investigation of the premises."

"Yes, I'm sure we can find some place. I'll get her."

Sam was impressed with Jennifer's composure as she responded to Roberts and Lewis' questions. No, Sarah had never been to Sarasota before. No, she knew of no one other than herself that Sarah knew in town. No, she knew of no one anywhere who would have a reason to murder Sarah. No, Sarah had not met anyone in Sarasota since she arrived here. No, she didn't know why Sarah went to Fort Myers. "She simply said she had some business there. I didn't ask her what business."

And then came the question Sam knew would eventually be asked. "Can you think of anyone at all who would want to hurt—to kill you?"

Sam winced as Jennifer finally lost her composure. Her face flushed and she stammered the words out. "Kill me? Why would anyone want—? Oh, my God, you think whoever did this thought they were killing me?"

"We don't know that, Miss Belding." Roberts said. "We're not even one hundred percent sure that your friend was murdered. However, we do have to consider all possibilities, and I'm sorry but it's not unreasonable to consider the possibility that you were the intended victim."

Jennifer shook her head and her face flushed. "I—"

Sam broke in. "Look, Miss Belding has had a horrific shock, finding her friend, her house guest murdered—I'm sorry, dead. You've now introduced the possibility that the killer was after her. I think that's a bit much for anyone to swallow in one sitting. Can we continue this tomorrow after Miss Belding has had some sleep?" He addressed the questions to both Roberts and Lewis.

Lewis glared at him. Shooting off his mouth, he'd probably screwed himself with her for good, ruined whatever rapport he'd established. Fuck it. Jennifer's well being was more important.

"It's all right, Sam," Jennifer said softly.

He turned to her, surprised at the calmness in her voice. She seemed to have pulled herself together.

"I'll try to answer your questions as best I can. What is it you want to ask?"

Lewis glanced at Roberts who nodded. Lewis asked, "Can you think of anyone, anyone at all, who could have reason to want you dead?"

Jennifer thought for a moment. Sam slumped down in the chair and folded his arms in front of him.

"Don't pout, Sam," Lewis needled him.

"Detective, I've been conducting research on the red tide," Jennifer began. She described the results of her work to date and her warnings. "I'm afraid the dire forecast I've made regarding the potential negative impact on this area during the upcoming vacation season has some people upset."

Lewis moved from her chair and sat next to Jennifer on the sofa. "Who specifically are you referring to when you say 'some people,' Miss Belding?"

"Well, we've tried to keep my findings quiet so as not to alarm everyone until we're certain that the red tide will hit here." She told of her conversations with Cliff and Donald and Donald's concern about certain heavy contributors to the Galt.

"Who in particular was he referring to?"

Jennifer pondered the question and glanced at Sam. Sam raised his eyebrows and shrugged.

"I know from conversations that both Dr. Johnson and Mr. Frazier have had with the developer, Jimbo Conlin that Conlin is very upset about my work and the impact it could have on his new resort. Mr. Conlin is a rather heavy contributor to the Galt."

Lewis sat back and crossed her legs. "I see. Anyone else?"

"Well, to be honest with you, Mr. Conlin's is the only name specifically mentioned, but both Dr. Johnson and Mr. Frazier have said there would be a lot of people hurt, when and if it becomes an absolute certainty the tide will hit here and we go public."

"I can understand why people like Conlin would be concerned. Certainly others who depend heavily on the invasion of tourists this winter would be equally upset, right?"

"Yes."

"The area would lose millions of dollars worth of business, wouldn't it?"

"Yes, and I'm very sensitive to that. But as a scientist, I can't let it influence me."

"I'm not questioning your motives, Miss Belding. Can you be specific as to any others whose business would be hurt, who are aware of your findings, who have expressed concern?"

She thought for a moment before replying. "No, I can't."

"Has Mr. Conlin spoken to you about his problem with your work?"

Jennifer sighed and glanced at Sam. "No, but as I said he has spoken to both my boss, Dr. Cliff Johnson and to our financial development director, Donald Frazier."

Sam watched Jennifer's body language. She was wearing thin and looked like she'd had it for the night. "Diane—"

Roberts interrupted him. "What did Mr. Conlin say?"

Jennifer took a deep breath and looked again toward Sam. "Well as I said, Mr. Conlin is a major financial supporter of the Galt, has been for years. As a result, I think he feels he has some kind of clout, and . . ." She shook her head, "I don't know, I don't know what he said."

Sam got up. "OK, I think that's enough for tonight. Jennifer will cooperate in every way she can, but she needs to get some sleep now." He walked over and stood next to Jennifer, who looked up and smiled at him.

Lewis watched the by-play between the two of them and stood up. She looked towards Roberts.

"All right, you can go," Roberts said.

"What do you mean, go?" Jennifer asked.

Sam explained to her why she couldn't stay.

"I can't stay in my own house? Where am I going to go? What about Sarah?"

"Do you know where we can contact her family?" Roberts asked.

Jennifer looked back toward the kitchen. "No, I don't even know if she has a family. Except for an ex-husband, whose name I don't know."

"I see from her ID that she's a professor at the University of Massachusetts," Roberts said. "We will contact them in the morning. Meanwhile, Mr. Wallace is right. You need to try and get some sleep." He looked at Sam and nodded.

Jennifer grabbed a few things from her bedroom and they left. Inside the car, Jennifer sat stiffly, her eyes straight ahead. Sam put his arm around her until she collapsed into his shoulder.

"I'm going to take you to my place. You can sleep in Henry's bedroom. He won't mind. He likes the ladies."

She sniffled and blew her nose. "You mean I finally get to meet the famous Henry?"

"Yep, and you're gonna love him. Everybody does."

Jennifer sat back and closed her eyes. Sam pondered over the evening's events. There was no sign of any burglary. No indication of a sexual attack. Sarah was still fully clothed, and he doubted the medical examiner would find any evidence that she'd been sexually assaulted.

No, someone got into that house and killed her. And it wasn't Sarah they were after.

33 Henry was waiting at the front door when Sam and Jennifer entered the apartment. He bolted into the bedroom, returned with his leash, and dropped it at Sam's feet. "I have to take him downstairs so he can pee. Let me show you the bedroom first."

Henry seemed to forget nature's call for the moment, as he sniffed around Jennifer, and looked up at Sam like, "Who's this?"

"It's OK, Henry," Sam said. "This is Jennifer."

Henry nudged his nose against her and sat on her feet.

"Oh, Sam, he's adorable."

"Told you he likes the ladies. You go and lie down, while I take him out."

When he returned, Jennifer was sitting on the bed. She had changed into a pair of pajamas, and sat staring at the wall. Sam sat next to her and held her hand.

Henry hopped onto the bed and perched next to Jennifer, who was fighting tears. "Sam, this is just awful. I still can't believe it. Sarah was so full of life, with everything to live for." And then she let go.

He put his arm around her and rocked her back and forth. "It's all right, Jen. Just let it come."

When she had spent herself, she looked up at him. "I don't know what I would have done, Sam, if you hadn't been with me.'"

Suddenly she slid her arm around his neck and pulled him to her. She kissed him on the lips, at first gently, then passionately.

Taken by surprise, he returned her kiss, and gently disengaged himself from her. "Jennifer, that was sweet and wonderful, and I'd like nothing better than to lie here and kiss you, and hold you all night. I hope that will come. But tonight you need to get some sleep." He kissed her again and tucked her into the bed.

She lay back and watched him with eyes that understood. "Thanks, Sam," she said and closed her eyes.

* * *

Francis J. Wilson sat on the patio drinking his morning coffee. He had just finished a most satisfying phone conversation.

Leonard Rich himself had personally called him, and they had a lively chat. What a fine gentleman Leonard was.

Francis hadn't yet met Leonard, but he certainly knew who he was. Everyone knew who Leonard Rich was. His name was always in Cynthia Mayfair's column, and pictures of him and his wife, Myrtle, were constantly in the newspapers.

Leonard was one of the wealthiest people in Sarasota. Yes, Francis knew all about Leonard Rich. He inherited the family business, based in Racine, Wisconsin. The Rich's were the largest manufacturers of condoms in the world, Francis proudly announced to Cecil after his phone conversation.

Leonard sold the business for a very substantial amount of money and moved to Sarasota, where he quickly became a patron of the arts. And now, Francis J. Wilson would take his place next to Leonard Rich at the Gala Grand Opening of the Sarasota Ritz Hotel.

"Yes, Francis, I'm putting together a table of—shall we say—heavy hitters, and quite naturally I thought of you. There'll be the Fishmans, Josh and Edna, the Spauldings, Alistair Worthington and his lovely wife, Buffy, and of course, Sid Golden and Selma. Tickets are fifteen hundred a pop, but, ha-ha, I guess we can afford it, eh Francis? Talk to you soon."

Francis could scarcely believe his ears. He hoped he had responded articulately through his excitement. The gala was to be a benefit for something, but Leonard couldn't remember what. Francis was sure it was a worthy cause. The grand opening of the Ritz! People were already referring to it as the social event of the century. And Francis J. Wilson would be a part of this historic event.

He was becoming quite a patron of the arts himself. The Cultural

216

Center was coming along just fine and certainly Francis' million dollar endowment to the Grande Theatre caught people's attention. Leonard had commented on it over the phone and jokingly scolded Francis for overlooking the opera. Well, Francis would fix that.

He was sure Cynthia Mayfair would be at the Ritz affair, and certainly there would be photographs taken of Leonard's table. Francis reflected for a moment on his good fortune, and thought of Melody.

Melody could have been a part of all this if only she had behaved like a decent human being. He would miss her, but his life would be easier now, free of the constant threat of humiliation that could have alienated him from his dear friends.

* * *

In the morning Sam called the police and learned they had completed their investigation of the alleged murder scene and it was OK for Jennifer to return home. They piled Henry into the car and the three of them drove to Lido.

Henry insisted on sitting in Jennifer's lap during the trip. "I figured you two would bond," Sam said.

Sam watched her as they drove. She was much better already, in control of herself, probably focusing now on who might have killed Sarah and why.

"It makes sense, Sam. It was me the killer was after."

"Jennifer, remember, the police haven't said yet for sure that she was murdered."

"Oh, come on, Sam." She said, rearranging the squirming Henry.

"Well, if she was murdered, you shouldn't be going back there."

"Because the killer was after me?"

Sam slowed the car, turned, and looked her in the eye. "Yes."

She went silent, as if digesting what he had just said. Neither of them spoke for nearly a mile. "Thanks for your concern, Sam, but I am not going to be driven out of my own home."

"Okay. Then Henry and I will stay there with you. You have a guest bedroom. We'll be your guests."

"Hey, you're getting kind of pushy, aren't you? Oh, I'm sorry, Sam. That was uncalled for. You were so sweet last night. You might have been able to take advantage of me, you know." She smiled, the first one he'd seen since they found Sarah.

"It occurred to me."

"I remember what you said. Do you?"

"You mean about kissing you and holding you all night?"

"Yes, and do you remember what you said after that?"

"Yes," he said. "Do you?"

"Very much so."

"Good, let's keep it in mind."

She didn't reply.

"Anyway, I don't want you to be alone, Jennifer. Let me stay with you. I promise to be good."

"No, Sam. I'm not ready for that, even for the reason you suggest. I can take care of myself."

"I hate to ask you this, but do you have a gun?"

"No, I don't believe in them. But I do have a softball bat, and if it will make you feel any better, I'll sleep with it."

He shook his head. "You are a very stubborn lady. Do you know that?"

"Yes."

"One other thing."

"What?"

"You're a good kisser."

A yellow crime scene ribbon ringed the house and a police officer stood in front. They identified themselves and went inside.

Inside the entry way, they stood quietly for a moment. Could this lovely little house ever be the same again for Jennifer? Sam wondered.

They walked past the den and into the kitchen. Neither of them spoke. Sam watched the color drain from Jennifer's face, as she leaned against the sink.

"Jennifer, you can't stay here. You—"

"Sam! I am going to stay here. This is my house."

"OK." He said, and walked out the door. "How long will you be here?" he asked the police officer.

"I'm supposed to stay for the day or until you all return," he said.

"Will there be anyone stationed here overnight?"

"No sir."

Jennifer met him at the door when he went back inside. "Sam, I'm going to the office. I need to get my mind off this and work is the best medicine."

"OK. I'll call you later."

They stood facing each other. Jennifer cupped his face in her hands and kissed him. Before he could respond she took her lips away.

"Thanks for everything, Sam. I'll talk to you this afternoon."

"You be careful," he said and left.

"Hey."

"What?"

"I think we need to finish the conversation we started before we found Sarah."

"We will," he said and resumed walking.

"Hey."

He turned.

"You're a pretty good kisser yourself."

Driving over the causeway, Sam failed to notice the perfect formation of pelicans gliding over the bay. He ignored the sailboat with spinnaker flying, gracefully skimming across the water.

Unsettling thoughts ricocheted around his head. Jennifer stubbornly insisting on staying in her house. Who killed Sarah? Jennifer poking into his past. Who killed Sarah? Jennifer's kisses. How did the song go? "Kisses Sweeter Than Wine."

Was there a connection between Sarah and Melody's deaths? One had a broken neck, the other strangled. Three possible murders in two weeks. Were they connected? Who killed Sarah? Why? If they were after Jennifer and brazen enough to go to her house, they would likely try again.

He stopped at the red light at Bayfront Drive and 41 and a car pulled up beside him. The driver's window slid down. Sam knew what was coming.

"Hey buddy, what year is that car?"

"It's a '69."

"She's a beauty."

"Thanks."

He decided to drive up Main Street instead of heading straight home. Epicure, where he and Jennifer ate last night, came into view, and thoughts of their mellow, carefree dinner flooded over him.

Across the street, he spotted Sarasota News and Books. He'd been planning to call them about a book signing. With so much going on now, he would never get around to it. Might as well drop in now. He pulled up directly in front of the store and parked. Try doing that in Boston.

Several tables and chairs were spread invitingly on the sidewalk. Henry hopped onto his lap, settled his paws over the car window, and plopped his face on it, checking things out.

"Henry, you be a good fella and sit here. I'm going to have a coffee." He recognized Henry's frown and winked. "I'll slip you a piece of my doughnut."

He loved the rich, Cuban coffee, the first he'd had in Sarasota. Henry polished off his piece of doughnut and nearly fell out of the car, sniffing out Sam's.

"Ernie said you wanted to see me?"

He looked up to see an attractive blonde woman smiling at him. The first thing he noticed was her beautiful complexion. "Oh, yes. Are you the owner?"

"Yes, I'm Carla Logan." She extended her hand.

He introduced himself and asked about a book signing.

"Absolutely. Your book has been selling surprisingly well. In fact I'm about to reorder."

He wanted to ask her why it was surprising. Instead he asked if she had heard about the murder on Lido.

"Oh, my God, no. When?"

"Some time yesterday or last night." He felt like a ghoul, but he'd seen Logan's name and picture in the paper a couple of times in the brief period he'd been in Sarasota. She obviously got around, and he was curious what, if any, observations she might have on all that had happened.

"Who was it who was killed?"

He told her about Sarah. "She was a house guest of her friend, Jennifer Belding."

"Jennifer Belding. The name sounds familiar."

"She works at the Galt. She's — "

"Of course. She's the marine biologist, the one predicting the invasion of red tide this season."

"How do you know that?"

"I run a business, my dear. My place does a very large chunk of its yearly sales during the four months of the season here. You can bet I'm going to know about a potential outbreak of red tide in season." She grinned. "And there's not a whole lot that goes on in this town that I don't know about."

He returned her smile. "Are you saying that her work has become fairly common knowledge?"

"I'm saying I know about it." She smiled again. "Hey, what are you doing, research for another book?"

He smiled. "I guess I just have a writer's curiosity."

Logan snapped her fingers, startling him. "Was Belding home at the time?"

"No, she was gone for the day. Why do you ask?"

"You think someone wanted to kill her and made a mistake?"

"I don't know. What do you think?"

Logan nodded her head slowly. "Could very well be. I have to get back inside.

"Uh, how about the book signing?"

"Oh, yes. Let me run in and check my calendar."

He was still pondering her last comment when she popped her head out. "Let's do it on the 26th."

Driving back to Siesta Key, his mind was everywhere but on the road. Twice cars behind him honked for driving too slow.

He thought of his conversation with Logan. She was a savvy lady, and already concluded that Jennifer was the target of the killer. Damn! She was in danger and too stubborn to admit it.

Who could benefit from killing Jennifer? If somebody was worried about her research and what would happen to business down here, what good would it do killing her? That wouldn't stop the red tide. Her boss and probably others at the Galt know about her work.

Maybe Sarah really was the intended victim. She didn't tell Jennifer what her business was in Fort Myers. Could it have something to do with her being killed? Jennifer said she hadn't seen her in, what, nine years? So she really knew nothing about her.

And how could Sarah's death be connected with Melody's? With Mike Rossi's? That's a real stretch.

Henry hopped onto his lap and began licking his face. Sam shoved him back onto the passenger seat. "Don't do that, Henry. You'll get us wrapped around a tree."

Inside the condo he sat down at his computer and tried to write. Nothing came. Too many distractions.

He checked the refrigerator. One egg, two cans of beer, a shriveled up apple, and a half bag of potato chips. How did they get in the refrigerator? He was living like he did in college. Out of nowhere, Lisa came back. The empty refrigerator. Lisa was a fanatic about keeping a well stocked pantry and was a great cook. Way back when things were good with them, she even taught him to cook. He slammed the door. There was more to marriage than a full refrigerator.

Sam looked around the apartment. Dreary cookie cutter, two bedroom, two bath condo. A million like them here in Sarasota and all over the country.

The drilling, pounding, and scraping outside sounded louder than ever. Voices of the workmen echoed between his building and the one going up. The sky clouded over and his mood darkened with it.

Henry came over and checked him out. "Hi ya buddy," Sam said. He bent down and Henry got in a few quick licks. Sam picked him up and sat at the kitchen table. Henry curled into his favorite position and snuggled in.

Funny, Sam thought, how people's worlds can get turned upside down and suddenly nothing is the way it used to be. He had become a creature of habit. He knew that, and he also knew he didn't like change. He had read somewhere that the three leaders on a person's trauma scale were death of a loved one, divorce, and loss of your job. Two out of three.

Henry squeaked and moaned as Sam scratched under his chin and behind his ears. He rolled over and pumped one leg up and down like a little piston.

Sam closed his eyes and let his mind drift. Before he knew it he was back in Boston, back in the classroom, surrounded by his adoring students. He opened his eyes and got up. "Uh, uh. Cut that shit right now."

The self pity wasn't like him, but he had it figured out. He was starting to be happy again, and now he was worried about Jennifer. What if something happened to her? He grabbed his car keys and flew out the door.

34

Standing in the station house reception area, Sam worried that he should have called first. When Diane Lewis appeared, her cocked head and exaggerated sigh told him he was right to worry.

"Sam, you, of all people should know better than to come bursting in here unannounced. I'm very busy. What do you want?"

His old colleague wasn't acting very collegial. Best get right to the point. "Can we talk somewhere? Five minutes, that's all."

Again the sigh. She pointed to a door off the corridor. "Come in here."

"Diane, I'm sorry to break in like this without calling first, but I'm worried about Jennifer Belding. I don't think there's any doubt her friend was murdered, and I also think it's very likely Jennifer was the target." He watched her eyes to make sure he still had her attention. He had a feeling she would hold him to the five minute pledge.

"She insists on staying in her house alone, and I think she's in danger."

Before he could continue, Lewis interrupted him. "I would have thought you'd have happily volunteered to protect her."

Something about the way she said it put him off, but he pressed on. "I've offered, but she refused. Could you have one of your people cruise by a few times during the night—just to be kind of a presence? I'll be happy to pay the department for the time." He checked his watch. Still two minutes to go.

"Sorry, I can't do that, Sam. I just don't have the manpower." She paused and studied him for a moment. "I will tell you this, however. We think we know who did this and we're putting enough pressure on that person so you can rest easy. The individual will make no effort to visit Jennifer's house. Trust me."

"Who is it?"

She smiled and shook her head. "Sorry, Sam. You know I can't tell you that." She pointed to the wall clock. "Time's up. Gotta go."

On the way home, he felt emotionally and physically exhausted. Canoeing all day, discovering Sarah's body, and getting little sleep had all caught up to him.

Diane had all the friendliness of a cobra, and that crack about his being happy to protect Jennifer. Sounded more like a woman than a cop. Was he flattering himself, thinking something stupid like that?

They think they know who did it. Who could it be? Had to be something they found at the house. If they're right, he could relax about Jennifer. If they're not?

By the time he entered the condo he could barely keep his eyes open. He went into the bedroom, slipped out of his chinos, and noticed two coffee stains and fraying at the pockets. He frowned, peeled off the rest of his clothes, and fell onto the bed.

The ringing phone woke him. He forced his eyes open and looked around the room, trying to get his bearings. The room was in semi-darkness. What the hell time was it? The phone refused to quit.

He groped for the receiver. "Hello."

"Sam, this Jimbo. You sound like I woke you up."

"That's because you did."

"Sam, I gotta see you."

"What time is it?"

"It's 6:30. What're you doin', sleepin' off a drunk?"

He was coming to and thought of Jennifer. He told her he would call. "I'm not sleeping off a drunk, Jimbo. What's up?"

"Sam, I gotta see ya. Can I come over? I know where your place is."

Henry leaped onto the bed and sat eyeballing Sam. "Uh, yeah, sure. I have to feed my dog and make a call. Give me half an hour or so. I'm in 8-A."

He got up and threw the frayed pants in a bag. He was getting a bit too casual. Give them to the Good Will.

Jennifer answered on the first ring. "Hey, I thought you were going to call me at work."

"Sorry, I fell asleep. Just woke up." He pulled a pair of shorts from the drawer and hopped around, trying to get them on with one hand. "Ow!"

"What's the matter?"

"Aw, nothing. Just stubbed my toe. How are you doing?"

"I feel like a truck hit me. I just finished having some soup and I'm going straight to bed."

He tried to convince her to let him come over, but got nowhere.

"I'll be fine, Sam. I've got all the doors and windows locked, and I'll be snuggled in bed next to my softball bat."

"There's a line there somewhere, but I'll leave it alone."

"Good idea. Call me in the morning."

He went into the kitchen, opened a can of Henry's dog food, and went through his routine of mixing the dry and wet food while Henry stood at attention. What does Jimbo want? He wondered while feeding Henry. He didn't sound like himself.

After Henry ate, he took him for a walk, then tended to himself. He brushed his teeth and checked his bald spot. Was it getting bigger? He used to be able to ask Lisa stuff like that. He wondered if Piro asks her if his belly is expanding.

The buzzer sounded and he buzzed back, letting Jimbo in the building. He opened the door, grabbed one of the two beers in the fridge, and waited.

"Hey, Buddy-Boy, you got one of them for ol' Jimbo?"

Sam grinned when he looked up and saw him in the doorway, looking Jimboish in his black high tops, cut-off shorts, and a Tampa Bay Bucs' T-shirt.

"Come in, Jimbo and tell me what's going on. You didn't sound like yourself on the phone." Sam led him to the balcony, where it was quiet again, and watched warily as Jimbo plopped his bulk on the fragile lawn chair.

"I ain't myself, Sam," Jimbo said, taking a swig of his beer.

Sam sat and nodded, waiting for him to elaborate.

"The cops are givin' me a bad time. They're tryin' to pin them murders on me."

"What?"

Jimbo finished his beer and crushed the can in half. "Sonsa-bitches."

Sam stared at the mangled can and thought of Sarah's neck. He remembered Jimbo's expression at Marina Jack's when he talked about Rossi. "Which murders, Jimbo?"

"That lady at your friend Jennifer's house." His shoulders sagged and he slumped into the chair.

Sam watched his body language, all the swagger and confidence gone from it, not the Jimbo he had come to know. Be careful how you handle this, he reminded himself. "How do you know Jennifer is my friend?"

"This is a small town, Sam."

"Yes, I've heard that. You mentioned murders. What others?"

"Them fuckers are tryin' to pin Rossi's murder on me, too."

Sam asked the obvious question. "Why?"

"Don't know. They had me down the police station, askin' me all kinds of questions."

"Like what?"

Jimbo looked back toward the kitchen. "You got another one of them beers, Sam?"

"Sorry, I only had two left."

"It's OK. Anyway, they wanted to know where I was last night, what was I doin'."

Sam's eyes narrowed. "What did you tell them?"

"Told them the truth. I was on the job all day, supervising fin-ishing touches on my new resort. Went to bed early, 'bout nine. Slept like a baby."

"What did they say?"

"Asked me if I'd ever been to Jennifer Belding's house. Asked me if I knew her. Asked me if anyone could corroborate that I was home all night last night. Kept askin' me all kinds of questions like that, like they were tryin' to trip me up, you know? Like in them TV shows?"

Sam said nothing. He watched Jimbo for a moment before speaking. "Have you ever been to Jennifer Belding's house?"

Jimbo dropped his eyes and shuffled his feet. He lifted the mutilated beer can to his mouth, frowned, and threw it in the trash can. "Yeah, I went there yesterday."

Sam stood up. "Yesterday? She was murdered yesterday."

"Relax, Sam. I went there to see if I could talk to her, find out about this red tide shit—see just how realistic it is that it's gonna hit here. I been hearing from everybody else, and I just wanted to get it —you know—straight from the horse's mouth."

"So you went to her home."

"I called her office and they said she was off for a couple days. I figured if I phoned her at home, she'd tell me to get lost. So I said, fuck it, and drove on over."

"How'd you know where she lives?"

"Looked her up in the phone book."

Sam nodded. Why should he believe anything this guy tells him? "Did you tell the police?"

Jimbo hesitated and looked down at his feet again. Sam waited.

"I did a dumb thing, Sam. They were pressing me, trying to pin stuff on me, tryin' to crucify me. I guess I kind of panicked and said no, I never been there. As soon as I said it, I knew it was a mistake, but I had to stick to my story. Figured I was already in deep shit."

"That wasn't too smart, Jimbo," Sam said and sat again.

"I know it wasn't Sam. But . . . I mean, it was last night they were talking about, and I wasn't there last night. I was home."

Sam studied the big man. His last statement came out in a long whine. This big, cocky tough guy was acting like a child accused of taking cookies. Acting very . . . unstable. "OK, what else did they ask you?"

"They kept askin' me what kinds of details I was supervisin' at my place."

Sam watched the sky changing colors off to the west as the sun disappeared. He pictured the beautiful sunset it was creating off Siesta Beach and wished he were there, instead of sitting, discussing murders. "You think they were doubting you were at work?"

"Naw. That part's easy. The guys saw me there all day. Mostly, I was keepin' tabs on them finishin' up the tennis courts and the fencing and landscaping around them. Then I was just kind of fine tuning a whole bunch of shit."

"What about Rossi?"

Jimbo frowned and turned back toward the kitchen again. Sam was glad he had no more beer left.

"They asked me a lot questions about the night he was killed. Then they said something that really bothered me."

"What was that?"

"They said they had reason to believe I had been at Rossi's around the time he was killed."

Sam changed positions in his chair and studied the big man for several beats. He liked Jimbo, liked his country boy directness. He was different from anyone he had known. Could he be a murderer? "They tell you why?"

"No, they're pretty cagey. Said they will when the time comes."

"Have you been there?" He waited to see how Jimbo would handle that one, watched his face for a clue. What he got was a look of disappointment that seemed genuine.

"Aw, come on, Sam." Jimbo drawled. "I never been to that scumbag's house. I don't know what the hell they're talkin' about."

"Uh, you might help your case a little, Jimbo, if you stop referring to Rossi as a scumbag." He got up and walked across the balcony and peeked at the patch of Gulf that had been spared by the encroaching building. "Why are you telling me all this, Jimbo?"

"Figured you'd get around to that. It's pretty simple. I like you, Sam, and I like to think we're friends. I didn't want you hearing from someone else that Jimbo Conlin is suspected of killing your friend's guest." He hesitated for a moment before continuing. "Or that he really meant to kill Jennifer."

Sam started to speak, but Jimbo held up his hand and interrupted. "That's what the cops were really getting around to."

Sam shook his head in disbelief. He had just listened to a different man. The good old country boy had transformed into an articulate gentle persuader. Interesting.

Jimbo got off his chair, walked over, and placed his hand on Sam's shoulder. "It's important to me, Sam, that you believe I had absolutely nothing to do with any of this."

Sam looked him in the eye and wanted to say he believed him. Instead he returned to his chair and sat. He motioned for Jimbo to join him. "Did they ask you about pressuring the Galt people to stifle Jennifer's work?"

Jimbo remained standing. "Sure, they did. I got everything I own ridin' on this. Sam. I was gettin' mighty scared. Still am. But I realize I acted like an asshole and I'm sorry about that. Killing Jennifer ain't gonna save my ass if the tide hits here."

He was drifting back into the old Jimbo. Sam was curious but let it ride. "Did they talk to you about Melody?" he asked.

"Yeah, but I didn't even know that broad."

"How did you know who I meant?"

Jimbo gave him the look he'd seen when Rossi's name came up at Marina Jack's. "The fuck is this, Sam? You playin' cop now, too?"

Sam said nothing.

"I read the papers, Sam. I know who Melody Griggs was."

Jimbo's expression had changed again. He looked wounded, like his friend had betrayed him, and Sam felt strangely guilty for trying to trip him up. But he checked himself. Jimbo was clever, and Sam had the feeling he was very good at manipulating people. He didn't become rich by being a dumb country boy. He was not easy to read. "Any thoughts on who could have killed Jennifer's friend or Rossi?"

Jimbo shrugged. "Pick a name on Rossi. I dunno. I think I told you about him and Alexis Helfrich. She hated his guts, and she can be one nasty bitch."

"Do you know Francis J. Wilson?" Sam asked.

"The midget? Yeah, I know him. He came to me once about building him a house on some land I own on Longboat Key. We talked a few times before he found the place he lives in now. I've seen him a couple times at fundraisers. He's a weird little dude."

"What do you mean?"

Jimbo returned to his chair and sat. Sam winced as part of the chair's webbing snapped. "Well," Jimbo continued. "I went over to see him one day to talk about the house deal, and I made some off hand, wise-ass remark—don't even remember now what it was. Well, Jesus, the little shit went berserk. Screamed and hollered somethin' terrible. Over nothin'. That little fella's got some temper, and a mean streak in him. Ol' Jimbo can spot it."

"Could he be capable of murder?"

Jimbo shrugged. "Cops seem to think I am, and I ain't got near the temper little Francis has. He's an angry man. You never know about a guy like that."

Sam nodded and thought about the scene at Rossi's car place. He thought back to Melody and how she humiliated Francis.

What about Sarah? Jennifer? Hard to see any connection with anyone there. He could only think of one. Jimbo.

"So, how did they leave things when they finished questioning you?"

"Told me not to leave town. Told me they were going to want to talk with me some more. Only reason they let me go when they did was I finally said I wasn't gonna talk anymore 'til I talked with my lawyer."

"From the sound of all this, I think you'd better do that soon. And I think you'd better tell him you went to Jennifer's house yesterday. He's going to tell you to tell the cops, too. You know that, don't you?"

Jimbo nodded and got up. Sam eyed the remains of the chair.

"Going to. He's out of town 'til tomorrow. Anyway, thanks for listening, Sam." He put his hand out and looked Sam in the eye. "Sam, I had nothing to do with any of this stuff. I don't know why the cops think I did."

Sam had a feeling he was going to find out soon.

35

Jennifer laid the book across her chest and closed her eyes. She'd been in bed reading for forty minutes and couldn't remember a word she had read.

So many things rattling around her head. Sarah. Her parents. Her killer out there somewhere. Sam's concern about her staying alone in the house.

Sam is so nice, a lovely man. But what was that business about him being fired?

She opened her eyes, put the book on the nightstand and lay there, listening to the silence. The house was so quiet. It was what she loved about her little garden spot. But tonight the quiet was creepy.

She got up, slipped on her sandals, and double checked all the doors and windows. She'd already had the pane of glass replaced and installed a hasp and padlock on the French doors. Still . . . resentment and anger swept over her. Her house was her haven, her security blanket where she felt snug and safe. Now someone had destroyed that.

Through the living room window, she watched the graceful arc of a coconut palm bending in the moonlight. The small orange tree she planted vibrated as if being shaken by a giant hand. The wind had picked up, and she listened to it whistling through the trees.

She walked toward the French doors, rattling with the wind. The clacking of her sandals on the hardwood floor echoed across the room. "Damn," she thought. "Where did this wind come from?" She wedged a chair across the doors, and the rattling stopped.

Satisfied that the house was secure, she went back to bed and put out the light. She lay there, listening. The only sound now was the click of the ceiling fan. Her eyes closed and she drifted, waiting for peaceful sleep to envelop her.

Something awakened her. She had barely dozed off when she heard a noise. Not sure what, but— there it was again. A tapping at the window. Again. Oh God!

There. There it was again, more like a scratching this time. Someone was trying to get in her window.

She clutched her baseball bat and eased herself off the bed. With the curtains drawn, the room was in total darkness. She tiptoed to the window and stood quietly, listening. The scratching continued.

She took a deep breath and flung open the curtains. Nothing. Had the person ducked when she opened the drapes? Should she call the police?

An areca palm scratched against the window. The sound she'd been hearing. She smiled and made a note to trim it in the morning.

Back in bed she was wide awake. Her mind raced and she thought of the car that had followed her home. She had chalked it up as a non-event, hadn't even mentioned it to the police. Now, she wondered.

She closed her eyes, determined to get some sleep. She shivered and realized that her bed was soaked where she lay. The sheet was drenched and her nightgown clung to her, wet and soggy.

She would call Sam in the morning.

* * *

Sam awoke at six a.m. Unable to go back to sleep, he got up, made coffee, and turned on his computer. He sat in his underwear, sipping coffee, hoping to be productive. Nothing came.

His editor would be calling any day now looking for the manuscript. He would simply tell her he's interrupted his writing to do some more research. It was true, so why was he dreading the call? Have to get over letting her intimidate him.

Henry waddled in and joined him. He leaned against Sam's legs and closed his eyes. Sam shifted his leg and Henry toppled over.

"Still a little early for you, isn't it, buddy?" He picked up Henry, who settled onto Sam's lap and was out.

Sam closed his own eyes and drifted off. The jangling phone

brought him to his feet. Henry rolled off, scurried to his room, and returned with his leash.

Sam checked his watch. Seven a.m. Who could this be?

"Sam, I hope I didn't wake you up. This is Jennifer."

"Jennifer! My favorite wake up call. How are you?"

"Terrible. That's why I'm calling. I had a dreadful night."

"What do you mean? What happened? What—?"

"Slow down. Nothing happened, but I was a nervous wreck. Got hardly any sleep at all. I hate to admit it, but you were right."

"Of course. Sam knows all."

"Don't be a smart ass." She hesitated. "Uh, if the offer is still open, I accept your manly protection—at least for a while."

"The offer is still open. Do you want to come here, or you want me to come over to your place?"

"Would you mind coming here and camping out in the guest room? Bring your computer, and most importantly, bring Henry. You can come in mid-afternoon if you want. If I go to work, I'm not going to stay long."

When they hung up, Sam did a little two step and clicked his heels. He tripped over Henry and landed on his rump. Henry leaped on him and licked his face.

Jennifer's call energized Sam and he decided to take a drive. After feeding Henry and taking him for his morning stroll, he headed for his car when someone called his name.

Mrs. Bunting stood at the office window and beckoned him to her. He thought of Henry and cursed himself for letting him pig out on the doughnut yesterday.

"Yes, Mrs. Bunting. How are you? Haven't seen you for a while." She was back behind her counter, giving Sam the look he'd seen when they first met. He braced himself.

"I'm fine, thank you, but there is a matter I need to discuss with you."

What now? He'd been a model citizen. Had to be Henry. He straightened up, ready to face the music. "Yes, Ma'am."

"Mr. Wallace, one of our floor monitors observed you leaving the laundry room the other day."

"Yes. I, uh, used the facilities. I washed some clothes."

She slowly nodded, like his confession had cooked his goose. "You were observed not only leaving the door open when you left, but leaving the light on as well. That is a violation of article number twenty-two."

He was unable to contain the smile that crept across his face. "I'm sorry, Mrs. Bunting. It won't happen again."

"You may find it amusing, Mr. Wallace, but we have rules and regulations here that must be observed by all. We have a code by which we live here at Paradise Towers." She motioned to a sign on the wall behind her: "To counteract selfish behavior and the dissolving power of high intelligence and idiosyncrasies, society must codify itself—Henri Bergson."

He stared at the sign, wondering how he had missed it before. He turned his stare to Mrs. Bunting and closed his mouth, which had fallen open during the sign reading. "I'm terribly sorry, Mrs. Bunting. I promise to be more careful." He wanted to tell her that his smile was not one of disrespect, but of relief that Henry was not the cause of his summons. He thought better of it and left.

He drove past Marina Jack's, when a breeze swept across the bay and threatened to steal his straw hat. He pulled it down securely and decided that condo living was not for him. He understood the need for rules and regulations, but he had been around long enough to know that there are people in this world who feel it their high calling in life to regulate the lives of others.

He suspected that Paradise Towers was no worse than any other condo in Florida where cranky retirees with too much time on their hands have found a mission monitoring the conduct of their neighbors within the tightly constrained societies of condominiums and gated communities. That's OK and it works for those who find comfort in such societies. He was not one of them.

Questions continued to gnaw at him, but he was operating in such a limited sphere, he had no answers and nowhere to turn. His sources were limited. He decided to take another shot at one of them.

The parking lot at Hedonism was empty except for a Lexus sedan which he figured belonged to Alexis. In fact the license plate read "ALEXUS." Cute. The door was locked so he rang the doorbell.

A moment later Alexis appeared wearing a man's white shirt, jeans, and a scowl. He was taken back by how much older and coarser she looked without her make-up. Her face looked like a freshly laundered sheet that needs to be ironed.

"What do you want?" she asked in a voice that betrayed too many cigarettes. She was, in fact, holding one.

"Well, since you're one of the few friends I have in town, I thought I'd drop by for coffee."

"I'm busy, asshole. What do you want?" She held her hand firmly on the door.

He wasn't sure what he wanted, but he flashed his killer grin and decided to be direct. "Well, someone told me that you might be interested to know that a young woman was murdered at Jennifer Belding's home a couple of days ago. But I'm sure you read about it in the paper."

Her expression turned nasty. He preferred the scowl.

"Look, I don't know what kind of silly little game you're playing coming here, but this is harassment, pure and simple, and I can have you arrested. Do you understand that or are you too dim-witted?"

He stood his ground and gave her his cop stare. "From what I hear, the young woman who was killed wasn't the real target."

Alexis half closed the door. "I don't know who this phantom 'someone' is, except a figment of your overactive imagination. If you come here again, I will call the police." She started to close the door.

"I've already talked with them. And by the way, they're keeping a close watch on Ms. Belding's house." He got it all in before she slammed the door in his face.

He drove back down 41, not sure what he had accomplished by his brief visit with Alexis. It was what Dirk would do; what his own police experience had taught him. Rattle 'em, keep them off balance. He thought he'd accomplished that, but for what purpose?

She was right. She could charge him with harassment. But why would she wait for one more time. If she had nothing to hide, why not haul his ass in now?

Maybe she will. He had an ugly vision of Diane Lewis leading a swat team to his door.

A wave of depression swept over him. What the hell was he doing down here? Allowing himself to be insulted by people like Alexis Helfrich; being treated like an errant school boy by a cranky old woman; trying to ally himself with a cop who scolds him for bad behavior.

Driving along Bayfront Drive, he managed to resuscitate his spirits. Glistening in the sunlight, the waters of the bay took on shades of teal and aqua that rivaled the best of the Caribbean. The breeze coming off the salt water and across the park swept away the last of his negative thoughts. The 280 hummed contentedly along. He decided that life could be worse, and headed home.

It was three o'clock when he turned off his computer after the most productive session he'd had in a week. No writer's block there.

* * *

Jennifer unlocked the front door and collapsed on the living room couch. Her eyes and head ached and she had second thoughts about Sam coming over. Feeling as she did, being around anyone, even Sam, would be a trial.

Interesting developments today at the lab. A slight change in direction of the tide, moving now ever so slightly west. In spite of this potentially exciting shift, she couldn't take another minute of work, and left early. Her head throbbed. She rubbed her eyes, closed them, and was soon asleep.

* * *

Sam opened the refrigerator door, saw nothing he liked, walked through the living room, into his bedroom, across to Henry's, back through the living room, and into the kitchen. He opened the refrigerator again, peered in, shrugged, and closed it.

Henry stayed just behind him, sensing maybe something was up. Sam finally landed on a chair next to the phone. Henry spread out next to him.

With his suitcase packed and his computer ready to go, Sam checked his watch. Jennifer wouldn't be home for at least another couple of hours. He drummed his fingers on the table and watched the dust settling on the balcony railing, eyed the phone for a moment, picked it up, and dialed.

"Sheriff's department."

"Detective Lewis, please. This is Sam Wallace." He waited, wondering if Diane would come to the phone. Their partnership had yet to get off the ground.

"Hello Sam."

The usual all business tone was there, but he didn't think she sounded unfriendly. "Hi Diane. Just thought I'd check in and see what's up. Any new developments?" Not very good, but the best he could come up with.

He waited through another of her long pauses. What now?

"We arrested Jimbo Conlin two hours ago and charged him with the murder of Mike Rossi."

36

Sam went quiet for a moment, silently disbeliev-
ing what he had just heard. The disbelief turned
to sadness.

"Aw, shit," he muttered. "Why? What—?"

"I can't discuss it on the phone, Sam."

"Where is he?"

"Down here in our jail. He's being held without bail."

"Can I see him?"

"Not for a while. A couple of our people are still talking with
him. It'll be at least another hour."

He thought of Jimbo and him playing with the dogs on the
beach, sitting at the cottage drinking beer. "Diane, he and I had
become friends—I think. Can I come down and see you?"

Another pause. "Sam, you're getting to be a pest. You know that,
don't you."

"Come on, Diane. Just for a few minutes. I have to know more why
my pal has been charged with murder. Anyway, I like talking with
you. You're good at your job, and I think we're simpatico. And—"

"Sam, cut the bullshit. If you come down now, I'll see you for a
few minutes." She hung up.

Driving along 41, he thought of his conversation with Diane.
Maybe he laid it on a little thick, but it wasn't bullshit. He did enjoy
talking with her. She's a pro, a good cop.

He, too, was once a good cop. That's why he liked talking with
Lewis. He knew he could have had a fulfilling career in police work if
he hadn't decided to go to graduate school and fallen in love with
teaching. Funny, all the years he was teaching, he had no idea how
close to the surface the policeman in him lurked.

But he'd found his niche in teaching. The kids loved his classes
and liked him. Part of it was they found him a little eccentric, like not

hearing the class ending bell, when he was wound up and really into it. "Hey, where's everybody going?" He'd ask when the students got up to leave.

"Uh, Mr. Wallace, the bell rang."

Or doing fun stuff like making Cyrano de Bergerac come alive for them by wearing a plumed hat and fake nose, dueling an imaginary foe, while reciting lines from the play. They never forgot Cyrano.

He felt schizophrenic, starting a new life in Sarasota, so different from the sophistication of Boston. On the other hand, there was no denying the appeal of Sarasota. And as he told Jennifer, in retrospect he probably needed a change.

He thought again about change and its effect on people. Some thrive on change and actually need it. Others resist it, become disoriented and lost when the security blanket of familiar people and routines are taken away; find it hard to assimilate, make new friends, adapt to unfamiliar situations. He also believed that a person is defined by his work, and when that is taken away, he suffers a diminished sense of self, searching for a new identity.

Maybe that's what he was into now, circling back to his roots as a cop, seeking to find that other identity. It made sense, a perfect tie-in to his writing, and it helped him feel the involvement he's always needed. And thank God he had his writing. He was good, and he would get better.

Still, Sam Wallace, the bumbling private detective was a far cry from Professor Wallace, teacher of the year. What was it Diane Lewis called him? The ersatz private eye? Screw it. He pulled into a parking place directly in front of Diane's office.

Detective Lewis ushered him into her office, a step up from the dingy little room she'd stuffed him into the last time they talked. "I'm sorry about your friend, Sam, but we have some compelling evidence against him."

He nodded and speculated when Lewis had last slept. Her eyelids drooped, he noticed lines in her face that hadn't been there before, and there were perspiration stains under both arms. He wondered how Jimbo looked. "Can you talk about it?" he asked.

She walked to a coffee urn, poured a cup, and offered it to him. He shook his head, and she kept it for herself. "Since we have already confronted Mr. Conlin with it, I can tell you a little." She sipped the coffee, and kept her eyes trained on him. "First of all, we found several footprints in Rossi's yard and in the house.

"The footprints were from size twelve construction type boots. They had a unique rugged, circular design rubber soles and heels. Unusual. A reddish clay, the kind found on tennis courts had been imbedded in the soles and was found with the prints, both inside and out."

He frowned. Jimbo's tennis courts.

She walked past him, leaving behind a faint whiff of body odor, not at all unpleasant, he thought. He waited while she settled into her desk chair and scribbled something on a sheet of paper.

"The only red clay tennis courts on Siesta Key and in fact, all of Sarasota, are at Jimbo Conlin's new resort. Every tennis court in the area is either HarTru or concrete or a rubberized surface."

"That's still rather circumstantial, isn't it, Diane?"

She nodded. "Yes, except for one thing." She got up and walked over to him. "We searched Conlin's closet and found the boots in his closet."

Sam closed his eyes and shook his head. "The sonofabitch," he whispered.

She allowed herself a tight smile. "We have also compared the clay found at the murder scene with that on Conlin's boots and his tennis courts. They all match."

Sam slumped in his chair and thought of the lunch at Crab and Fin, when Jennifer admonished him for not being a good judge of people. "What else do you have?" he asked.

"We found size twelve footprints in Jennifer Belding's yard."

"The same boots with the clay?"

"No, these were sneakers." She leaned over her desk and looked down at Sam's feet. "What size shoe do you wear, Sam?"

"Ten. But wait a minute. Are you—?"

"Then someone besides you has been in Jennifer's yard very recently."

He closed his eyes and rubbed them. "Have you talked with her about this?"

"No, but we will."

He got up and poured himself some coffee. "Anything else?"

"Oh, there is more, Sam, but I think I've told you enough for now. Anyway, I have an appointment." She got up and beckoned him toward the door. "Do you still want to see Conlin?"

He finished his coffee and thought for a moment before answering. Could he keep his cool, talking with the bastard who meant to kill Jennifer and got Sarah instead? "Yeah, I want to talk to him."

* * *

Sam rang Jennifer's antique doorbell several times. No answer. When he called the office they told him she had left at mid-afternoon. He walked over to the living room window and peered in. Jennifer was sprawled on the couch, face down.

"Oh, God. No, no," he cried and ran to the front door, pushed and hurled his body against it, and bounced off. He rubbed his shoulder and ran to the window, grabbed a large rock, and smashed the widow. He unlocked it, and began climbing in.

Jennifer bolted to her feet. "Sam, what the hell are you doing?"

He hung suspended, half in, half out of the window, a blank look on his face. "You're all right."

"Of course I'm all right, you idiot. What were you *thinking* of, smashing my window?"

He slid a piece of glass from under his stomach. "Uh, can we talk inside?"

Inside the house they surveyed the carnage and Sam apologized. "I thought you were dead, and I'm afraid I lost it."

"I guess." She grinned. "You do make a dramatic entrance. Is this a sign of what I can expect from my new house guest?"

"No! You have any plywood?"

She smiled and shook her head. "Yes, there's some in my storeroom. You get it and I'll clean this glass up."

He covered the window with plywood and promised to have a new one installed in the morning. "Small price to pay for finding you alive."

"I'm sorry I barked at you, Sam." She crossed and kissed him on the cheek. "That was really very sweet of you. I'm not sure I can afford your protection, though."

"Let's have a drink. I have some interesting news for you," he said and plucked off another piece of glass.

Over drinks on the patio he told her of his meeting with Lewis and the news about Jimbo Conlin. "She claims they have more evidence than she told me about."

She put her hands over her face and shivered "Oh, God. I don't know what to say. I didn't really know him. I'd seen him around the Galt a few times, and I knew about him. I mean, everybody does. He's been a fixture in Sarasota forever. He's a little rough around the edges, but a murderer?"

He sipped his drink and watched her. He had expected her to rage at Jimbo for killing her friend, for probably intending to kill her. Instead she seemed sad that Jimbo Conlin could be a killer. He half expected her to say something like, "The poor man."

They sat quietly for several moments. Jennifer broke the silence.

"I could maybe understand him killing Rossi. That whole business with the gambling boat was common knowledge around town and so was the bad blood between them. And from what you had told me, he had as much reason as anyone to prevent the lunch Rossi had scheduled with Tim Lester. But Sarah? He didn't even know her."

Sam nodded and waited.

Her face hardened. "It wasn't Sarah he was after," she said softly. "I think he just flipped out over the red tide thing and projected everything onto me. I know about his rantings with Cliff and Donald. He was convinced he was going to lose everything and focused on me as the cause of it all. That's the only scenario I can come up with, Sam—whether it makes sense or not."

He took her hand and covered it with his. "I'm afraid it makes a lot of sense, Jen. The upside of it is, you can relax again. Oh, Jesus!" He jumped up and nearly knocked over a small table.

Jennifer followed him "What's the matter?"

"Henry's still in the car." He flew out of the house and returned with Henry in his arms. Henry looked confused and clung to Sam.

"Sam! What am I going to do with you? Give me that dog."

He gave her a sheepish look and handed over Henry. The little dog melted into her arms, threw his head over her shoulder, and glared at Sam.

"OK, OK, Henry. I'm sorry. I'll make it up to you." He went out to get Henry's things, while Jennifer gave him some water and a biscuit. Sam stashed Henry's stuff in the guest room and he and Jennifer fell onto the sofa.

Henry came out of the kitchen and hopped onto Jennifer's lap. She scratched his ears and hugged him.

Sam watched the display. "Looks like I may be suing you for alienation of affection," he said.

She shrugged and gave Henry another hug before setting him down. "I had an interesting day, too."

He wondered how long she'd been napping. The circles under her eyes and a wan pallor, so different from her usual robust appearance, worried him. "First tell me about last night."

She described the business with the scratching palm and her inability to get to sleep afterward. She also told him about the car that could have been following her.

"Could you tell what kind it was?"

"No, only that it was a large, dark sedan. It was probably nothing, which is why I didn't mention it. Anyway, it sounds like my worries are over." She glanced back toward the guest room.

Sam cupped his hands. "You're in good hands with Wallace."

"Let me tell you about today," she said. "Our tracking of the tide early this afternoon showed a slight change in course. It was headed northeast but now it appears to be veering a little west. It's still too early to tell, but it could wind up bypassing the West Coast of Florida and hitting somewhere off Texas."

37

Jennifer walked to the open door, and looked outside. She stood for several minutes without moving. The wind had picked up again and leaves scurried across the yard. She slammed the door and returned to Sam, still seated on the couch. "I've destroyed at least two lives, Sam. If Jimbo Conlin killed Sarah, thinking it was me, there can be only one reason.

"I've been so enthusiastic about my work. I put on a pair of blinders, and all I could see was the work I was doing. No thought to the human impact. No thought to people's emotions and concerns."

Sam got up and took her in his arms. "Come on, Jennifer. Get off it. You're a scientist, not a behavioral psychologist. You've acted like the professional you are. Don't beat up on yourself over this."

He watched her grab a tissue, blow her nose, and take a deep breath. No matter how smart and self-sufficient she is, he'd never seen her look so vulnerable. It was an appealing quality.

Whatever he said seemed to have worked. She brightened and said, "Come into the kitchen while I make a some supper for us."

They ate a quiet dinner of fresh pompano, baked potatoes, and a Caesar salad. Neither tried to capture the light hearted banter they enjoyed at other times. Sam's preoccupation with Jimbo Conlin kept getting in the way, and it wasn't hard to figure out Jennifer's silence.

He looked up from his wine and Jennifer seemed a million miles away, although she did have some color back into her face. Probably the wine, but it was good to see some of the old luster back. It had been especially trying when Sarah's parents came.

She was a beautiful woman, and the attraction he felt toward her was very real and stronger each time he saw her. She was smart, independent, athletic, and sexy. How sexy? It would be nice to find out, but he wouldn't push it. If it happens, it happens.

Jennifer, who had been diddling with her food, looked up at Sam watching her. Her face reddened. "My God, you've got me blushing," she said.

"Sorry, I was just thinking nice things about you."

She set her fork down and studied him for several beats.

"What's going on in that head of yours?" he asked.

She drained her glass and motioned for a refill. He poured her wine and waited. Was she loading up on alcohol to tell him what's on her mind? He had a feeling he knew.

"Sam, just before we came into the house and found Sarah, you told me you'd been fired from your teaching position. That must have been very hard for you."

It was his turn for more wine. He took a long sip, savoring it before replying. "It was."

"You liked teaching, didn't you?"

"Loved it." The pain in her face reminded him of Diane Sawyer and her agonizing empathy when asking probing personal questions of an interviewee. Jennifer's empathy was real, as was everything else about her.

She reached across the table and placed a hand over his. "Sam, I've only known you for a short time, but I'm a good judge of people. It's hard for me to imagine you being fired. Hard for me to imagine you being fired from a job you loved, and which I'm sure you were very good at." She waited for him to reply and when he didn't, she dropped it and resumed eating.

He started to say something when the phone rang. Jennifer answered it and turned to Sam with a puzzled look. "It's for you."

"Hello. Yes, yes, I do. Tomorrow? Isn't that rather quick? I see. OK, I'll be there in less than an hour. Thanks."

"What's up?"

"That was Detective Lewis. They're arraigning Conlin tomorrow. I had asked if I could see him. She says he definitely wants to talk to me, that it's important. She tells me I can see him tonight, but he won't be available tomorrow."

"How did she know to call you at my place?"

He turned to her and shrugged. "I don't know. She's a cop. Probably just played a hunch." He sighed and screwed up his face. "Jen, I really want to talk with him. I need to see what I can find out."

She got up and began clearing off the dishes. "Then I think you should."

He helped her carry things into the kitchen and stood facing her. "Look," he said, placing his hands on her shoulders, "I'm not going to leave you alone here. That was the whole point in my coming over. I want you to come with me. I'll drop you and Henry off at my place. You relax, take a nap, and I'll be back in about an hour. OK?"

She shook her head but before she could reply, he impulsively kissed her. She started to pull away, but then she slid her arms around his neck and returned the kiss. She was into it now, and pulled him in closer. He felt her tongue exploring him and he responded.

As abruptly as it began, she ended it. She backed off and held him at arms length. "Whew! You're full of surprises, Sam Wallace. Where'd that come from?"

"It's been hanging around since I saw you at the beach. Just waiting to pick its spot and strike, I guess. Surprised me, too."

She laughed, the musical, lyrical sound he'd heard before all the ugliness began. "That didn't strike me as a 'Let's go see Jimbo Conlin kiss.' But maybe we'd better do that." She picked up Henry.

Neither of them said much along the way. Sam savored the kiss with Jennifer and thought again of "Kisses Sweeter Than Wine." Yes!

He wondered how he would deal with Conlin now, knowing what he did about the evidence against him. Still, he grudgingly wanted to hear Jimbo's side of it all.

"You never mentioned if you liked my place," he said as they entered the condo.

"It's OK, but it's not you, Sam. Somehow, I picture you in some-thing a bit more rustic." She grinned. "More eccentric."

"Oh?" he said, not sure how to take that.

"Yes, this is a little too pat and sterile for you."

Henry, who had been streaking around the apartment, charged Jennifer, leaped against her thighs, ran toward his bedroom, turned, and waited.

"He's acting very seductive," Sam said. "Be careful."

"Must come by it naturally. Anyway, you go ahead. I'll feed Henry and take him for a walk." She walked him to the door, and he kissed her good-bye. No big deal. It just seemed like the thing to do.

* * *

Detective Lewis took Sam over to the jail and left him with one of the officers in charge. "You can let Mr. Wallace spend up to an hour with Conlin," she said and left.

In the cell area, Sam nearly gagged at the smell of urine and dried sweat. It had been a long time since he'd been in a city jail cell area, and he had forgotten how vile they were.

Jimbo sat on the bare mattress, staring at the wall. When he spotted Sam, he jumped up and held out his arms. "Sam," he said in a voice that was more a whisper than his usual bellow.

Sam nodded. "Hello, Jimbo."

Jimbo stood at the bars, both hands clutching them in the classic prisoner pose. "Thanks for coming, Sam," he said, shifting from one foot to the other, like he had to go to the bathroom.

The officer unlocked the door and Sam walked in. "You got an hour—max," the cop said and left.

Jimbo wasted no time. "I didn't kill anybody, Sam," he said, pacing around the small cell, and pounding his fist into the palm of his hand.

Sam sat on the bed and watched the big man venting, all nervous energy. He waited for Jimbo to calm down.

Finally, after punching the cell door, and snarling, "Fuckers!" he sat on the bed next to Sam and placed a hand on Sam's shoulder. He turned and looked directly into Sam's eyes. "Sam. I did not kill anybody. I ain't built that way."

Sam looked into Jimbo's eyes and held them for several beats. "Have you talked with your lawyer?"

"Sure, I talked with him. He tells me I'm in deep shit. Says he doesn't like what the cops are tellin' him, but right now he's workin' on trying to get bail set tomorrow. Says it don't look good."

Sam began to feel the oppressive heat in the cell, made worse by the claustrophobia brought on, squeezed next to Jimbo on the small bed. He got up and leaned against the wall, not sure if he could last an hour. "They seem to have a lot of evidence against you. How do you explain the footprints from your boots at Rossi's? They also have size twelve sneaker prints in Jennifer Belding's yard—your size, Jimbo. I guess you know that, too." He looked at Jimbo's feet—with the jail house slippers on them. "Where are your high tops?"

Jimbo got off the bed and started pacing again. Sam waited for an answer. Jimbo stopped and kicked off the slippers. "They took 'em and gave me these goddamn things. Probably figured I'd hang myself with the laces." He pointed to his waist. "Took my belt, too."

Sam nodded, trying to picture Jimbo's hulk dangling from a shoe lace. He studied the man he had once considered a friend, standing barefoot in a jail cell. His clothes were filthy and wrinkled, and with at least a two day beard, he looked more like an oversized Charles Manson than a wealthy developer. Sam shook his head. Amazing what a little time in the pokey can do to a person.

Jimbo walked over to Sam and stood facing him for a long moment. Sam returned his gaze, not sure if he should punch Jimbo or pity him.

Jimbo spoke softly. "Sam, I told you I could never kill anybody.

But I think I know why the cops think I did. Please listen to me carefully, while I tell you why I say that."

Thirty minutes later Sam called for the guard and left. He had just listened to a bizarre story, one that resonated all the way back to Siesta Key.

38

Jennifer declined Sam's offer to stay at his place. "Come on. You can share Henry's room," he said. "No Sam. I brought nothing with me. Everything I need that keeps a woman going is home. But you don't have to stay. I'll be fine now that the killer is in jail."

He thought about that. One way or the other, she was probably right. If Jimbo was the killer, she was indeed safe. If he was set up, the real killer would be foolish to harm her now with Jimbo stashed away taking the rap. But what Jimbo just told him refused to go away.

"OK, I'll take you home, but I think I should stay. We don't know for sure that Jimbo killed Sarah. He's only a suspect. If the real killer is out there, you may still need to be silenced in his mind."

She waited at the door. "Thanks a lot. You do know how to comfort a girl, Sam."

"I'm sorry. That didn't come out right. It must have sounded pretty insensitive."

She walked over to him and took his face in her hands. "I know what you're saying, Sam, and maybe you're right. It's sweet of you to offer to stay and protect me. Actually, I would feel better."

He started to say something, but she put her hand to his lips. "When we get there I'm going straight to bed. I'm exhausted and I have a big day tomorrow."

Again he tried to speak, but she overrode him. "And—more importantly, when we kissed back there, you triggered something that's been—to quote you—hanging around. I'm not sure I'm ready to let it out yet. I need to go slowly and ask you to be patient with me. OK?"

"Kisses Sweeter Than Wine. " The damn song kept rattling around his head. He stood eye to eye with her, inhaling the lush fragrance she must have put on while he was gone. He ran his fingers through that silky red hair and fought off the dizziness that threatened to buckle his knees. "Patience you want, patience you get." He said and kissed her gently. "Let's go."

True to her word, she headed straight for her bedroom when they reached the house. Henry trailed behind her. She stopped at the door and gave Sam a puzzled look. He shrugged and nodded. She threw him a kiss before she and Henry disappeared into the bedroom.

"Well, good for you, Henry," he muttered and trudged off to the other bedroom.

The next morning Jennifer went off to work, and while Sam waited for the window man, he formulated a plan that might be hairbrained, but he knew Dirk would approve.

By the time the guy arrived and replaced the window, it was nearly one o'clock. He made himself a sandwich, gathered up Henry, and left.

After dropping Henry at the condo, he went to a pay phone and placed a call. He concluded the conversation and smiled. "Tonight," he said aloud.

He went home and turned on the local TV news. Nothing about Jimbo yet. The cops were keeping it quiet for a while. He turned off the television, went into the bedroom, and sagged onto the bed. Henry hopped up next to him and they were soon asleep.

Instead of nightmares about murder, Sam's sleep was filled with sensuous dreams of Jennifer. She was in his arms, kissing him, first his lips, then his nose, cheeks, forehead. Wet, sloppy kisses. He awoke to find not Jennifer, but Henry, licking him from chin to forehead, not the affection he'd dreamed of. The little mutt was hungry.

He fed Henry, ate himself, and took a shower. Six o'clock. He was facing what could be a long, uncertain evening. Better call Jennifer. After getting no answer at home, he tried her office.

"Jennifer Belding."

"Jen, something has come up which is going to tie me up for much of the evening. I'll tell you about it when I see you, but I wanted to let you know that it's likely to be late by the time I get to your place." He felt like a jerk, being so vague.

"That's OK, Sam. I'm going to be working late myself, and then I'm going home and go right to bed. Just call me in the morning."

He tried to protest, but got nowhere. "All right, I'll call you to-morrow." He hung up, feeling guilty, but he couldn't let go now.

He punched in another number. "Detective Lewis is in a meeting right now, but she should be out in about fifteen minutes."

Close enough. He reached the station just as Lewis walked through the reception area. "Diane, can I see you? Five minutes, that's all."

When she put on her nasty face and started to turn away, he pulled a bouquet of flowers from behind him and presented them. "For you. Your office needs some color."

She stood, hands on hips, legs slightly apart, shaking her head. "Sam, you're crazy, you know that?"

He handed her the flowers and walked along with her to the office. She pulled a vase out of her desk drawer, filled it with water, and arranged the flowers. "OK, what can I do for you, Sam?"

He eyed the flowers and nodded. "Not bad. The place looks better already. They bring out the beige in the walls."

She rolled her eyes and started to say something, but he talked over her. "Diane, I have reason to believe that Jimbo Conlin could be innocent, and I hope to be able to prove that soon." He hoped he sounded convincing, but the look on her face told him different.

"Sam, before you waste my time with one of your cockamamie theories, let me tell you why I don't want to hear it." She picked up a folder from her desk and pointed it at him. "This is one time when I would love to be the prosecutor. We have enough evidence in here to put Mr. Conlin on death row." She held the folder high in the air and let it drop onto her desk. "This is a slam dunk, Sam."

"Maybe and maybe not. I think—"

"I don't care what you think. There is no room for discussion. I told you about the boots and the clay. What if I told you we have a glass found in Mike Rossi's house with Conlin's prints on it next to one with Rossi's prints? What if I told you we have a blood sample found at Rossi's house whose DNA matches Jimbo Conlin's? What if I told you we have hair follicles from the scene of Rossi's murder with Conlin's DNA? And what if I told you that Conlin was seen at Jennifer Belding's house the day Sarah Hanson was killed? Do you get the picture, Sam?"

He flopped into a chair and sat numbly, trying to process all of what she had just said. Was Diane right? Was he wasting her time as well as his own? Had he been taken in by Jimbo? He would do his best to find out.

Lewis opened the door and beckoned him toward it. "It's been a long day, Sam. When this is over, I'll take you out and buy you a drink. But right now, my long day continues, so go home and write a book."

39

It was a little after nine p.m. when Sam cruised past the house on Ninth Street near downtown Sarasota. He noted the empty carport and drove his car around the corner and parked.

He walked casually down Ninth Street. No need to rush. When he reached the house, he opened the wooden gate and walked through the courtyard to the front door.

He checked the door lock and was relieved to find it was a simple Kwickset lock. No problem. He inserted his tension wrench about a quarter inch into the base of the keyhole until the end of it grabbed the key cylinder. He applied tension and used his pick to rake each of the five pins into the shear line at which point he used the tension wrench to turn the cylinder to the open position.

The lock clicked, he opened the door and entered the house. He felt an odd sense of pride that he still remembered a skill he learned at the police academy so many years ago. But he was no longer a cop, and what he just did was blatant breaking and entering. Christ! He could go to jail. Inside, he leaned against the door, debating whether to open it, go back to his car and go home.

He thought of Diane Lewis' comment. "Sam, you're crazy, you know that?" Screw it. He had come this far, and he was not going to give up now.

The house was not totally dark. He could see a dim light coming from what was probably the kitchen. It was a weird feeling, standing uninvited in someone's home, violating their space. Bullshit! He was here to help solve a murder—or murders and hopefully, save an innocent man's life.

"Hello, anybody here? Hello." Silence.

He made his way past the kitchen, found the bedroom, and snapped on the light. The neatly made king-sized bed dominated the room. Everything about the room was neat and orderly. He checked the closet and found the same symmetry. Shoes carefully lined in a row, clothes on hangers, methodically arranged by classification, everything in its proper place. He examined the shoes and sneakers. All size twelve.

The closet turned up nothing so he went back to the bedroom, rummaged through the bureau drawers, and found a pair of handcuffs among the underwear. Hmm. Fun and games.

He closed the drawers and stood for a moment, pondering whether he should forget all this and get the hell out. He froze.

A noise, like shattering glass, came from another part of the house. He inched his way toward the front door, when a large cat bounded past him and into the bedroom.

He exhaled and listened. Nothing. He went to the kitchen found a broken glass in the sink.

Back in the bedroom, he checked his watch: 9:30. And so far, he'd come up empty, but he still had this nagging feeling that he was going to find something, somewhere that would tell him what he needed to know. He turned off the bedroom light and went into the bathroom.   * * *

Jennifer turned off her computer and relaxed in the semi-darkness of her office. Except for a small desk lamp, the computer itself was all the illumination she needed.

God! Almost 9:30. She threw her head back and closed her eyes. The time had flown by, and it was only now she realized she was exhausted. She had been sitting at that damn computer for hours, watching the ever so slight change in direction of the red tide.

Still too early to tell, but for the first time, she allowed herself to think there was actually a chance this thing would miss their area entirely. Too early to say anything—at least not for a few days.

Time to go home. The place was quiet as a tomb. She was the only one foolish enough to be still working this late.

* * *

The bathroom was immaculate—almost like no one used it. He searched the cabinets and drawers and found nothing out of the ordinary. He was tilting at windmills, and it was almost time to get out.

He shut off the bathroom light and went into the other bedroom, which appeared to be a combination bedroom and study. One wall of the room was lined with bookcases, housing an eclectic collection. He pulled several out and began looking through them, not sure what he expected to find. Nothing. It had all been a risky waste of time. He checked his watch. Time to leave. He began replacing the books he'd taken out, when something caught his eye.

* * *

Jennifer found a second wind, fascinated by what she saw on the computer. No longer tired and on a roll, she began scribbling notes on her yellow pad. She got up to pour some coffee, when the sound of a car driving along the shell road caught her attention. She wasn't sure, but it sounded like it stopped just outside her building.

* * *

Sam focused on the back wall of the bookcase. A small part of it, about a foot wide, appeared to be a different shade from the rest of the wall. He tapped it. Hollow. He poked the rest of the wall. Solid as a rock.

He pushed and probed the hollow section and, bingo! Nice and easy, the hollow section pivoted inward. He reached inside, felt a wooden object, and pulled out a small box.

Nice little spot to stash something, he thought, trying to control his excitement. He opened the box and stared at its contents. The two items gleaming inside brought a broad smile to his face, Mike Rossi's diamond ring set in platinum and a Cartier watch with the initials M.R. on the back.

"Holy shit." The sound of his voice startled him. Time to get out. He put the box in his pocket, closed the pivoting door, replaced the rest of the books, and turned to face Carole, standing in the doorway.

40

Sam froze where he stood as he and Carole faced each other. Neither said a word. He palmed the small box and slipped it into his pocket.

In spite of his predicament, his emotion at the moment was one of awe at the specimen standing before him. She wore a tank top, exposing the muscles in her shoulders and biceps, which seemed to ripple without her moving. The short shorts she wore gave him a view of legs that looked capable of snapping an oak tree. Her neck muscles strained and bulged, with what he feared was fury.

"What the hell are you doing in my home," she snarled in a voice that sounded like Pavarotti with laryngitis.

His timid smile had no mirth in it. "Hello, Carole. I came to talk to you, and the door was unlocked, so I walked in, thinking you were here. I apologize. Maybe we can talk another time." He started toward the door, but she moved into the room and hovered over him.

"You break into my house, I find you rummaging through my things, and I see you holding something that belongs to me." She nodded toward his pocket. "And you think you're going to just walk out of here?"

How long had she been standing in the doorway? He tried to walk past her, and she grabbed his arm and flung him across the room like a rag doll.

He hadn't worked out in over a year. The only exercise he'd had was walking Henry and hoisting drinks, and she outweighed him by at least twenty pounds. But he was ready to try his luck. Rush her and get the hell out of that house. He started to get up when she reached into her purse and withdrew a 38 revolver.

"My door wasn't unlocked. You broke in," she said, a smile on her face. She was enjoying this. "I think after I shoot you, I'm going to find lock picking tools in your pocket. You poor stupid bastard.

You think you can just go around breaking into decent people's homes and think you can get away with it? First you break into my home, and then you try to attack me."

He stood about four feet away, facing a pistol in the hands of a woman who may have killed at least two people and probably three. She would shoot him like she would swat a fly. Shit! He didn't come to Florida to be shot to death, breaking into a hooker's bedroom. He didn't want to die, and this was definitely not the way he'd planned to go.

Get her talking. He sensed some braggadocio there. Play on it. "Carole, are you curious to know why I came here?"

She shrugged the massive shoulders. "Why don't you just very carefully reach inside your pocket and take out the object you stole from me and throw it over here?"

"Oh, you mean Mike Rossi's watch and ring that you took after you killed him?"

"Just shut the fuck up and throw it over here."

The room was suddenly stifling, and he felt nauseous from the heavy perfume she wore. The entire situation would be ridiculous if he wasn't about to die. "Sure," he said. "I mean, if you're going to go around killing people for your boss, you might as well get something out of it, right?" He reached into his pocket.

She cocked the hammer on the revolver. "Careful," she said, holding the gun with both hands.

He extracted the box and tossed it to her.

She opened it, checked the contents, and smiled. "That's the good boy. Too bad you had to be so nosy." She ran her eyes up and down him. "We might have even had some fun together."

When he threw the box to her, he'd thrown it short, so she had to take a step forward to catch it. He calculated the distance between them now at no more than three feet. He also noticed she'd taken her left hand off the gun and now held it with only the right. Still, right hand or left, she couldn't miss at this range.

"I have to say, Carole, I'm amazed and impressed at how cleverly Alexis set up Jimbo. He told me he'd been set up and how Alexis masterminded it all. Smart lady, and she's lucky she has you to do the dirty work."

"Bullshit! Alexis masterminded it," she mocked. "Alexis masterminded nothing. She doesn't know enough to come in out of the rain. The whole thing was my idea. She can't go pee without my advice."

He was right about Carole. Got to keep playing that ego. "So, it was your idea to kill Rossi."

She inhaled, reminding him that her shoulders and arms weren't all that were massive on her upper body. "No, that was Alexis. She was tired of being blackmailed by that asshole. He was a bloodsucker, and we knew there would be no end to it."

He nodded and watched her gesticulating with the gun. She was getting careless. "And so she ordered you to get rid of him."

She snickered. "She didn't order me to do anything. I couldn't wait to take out that pig. I knew I could kill him and get rid of the other pig, Conlin at the same time. Alexis simply wanted Rossi dead. She hadn't a clue how to go about it."

"Very clever, Carole. Alexis should be working for you instead of the other way around."

She blinked a couple of times and flashed him a smile, as close to being coquettish as a six foot, two inch, 190 pound amazon can muster. "I know that, but we each have our respective roles in the relationship—if you know what I mean."

He let that one pass and shook his head in feigned admiration. "How'd you do it all, Carole? I mean, the footprints and clay at Rossi's, the fingerprints on the glass. You created an air tight case against Conlin. I have never seen anything like it."

"Yesss." She drew the word out, nodding as she did. "It was all very carefully thought out, if I do say so." The coquettish look returned, and her eyes moved up and down him again. "It was brilliant, wasn't it? But you have no idea how frustrating it's been to me to have no one to share it with, no one to admire my genius. I'm enjoying this. It's really too bad that I have to kill you."

He could have done without the last part, but he really had her pegged. He felt like the character in *Arabian Nights* or whatever. Keep the conversation going to stay alive. "What about Alexis? Can't you share it with her? You know, pillow talk?"

Her face hardened. "That bitch. She doesn't appreciate the genius in what I do. All she wants and sees are results. The fine touches I employ go right over her head."

The woman was obviously bright. But she was also nuts. She could shoot him in mid-sentence. "Tell me how you did it, Carole. I'm a writer, and you are living proof that truth is stranger than fiction. Start with the boots, the footprints and clay."

"Ah, that was beautiful. When I went to Conlin's house for a session a while ago, I spotted the boots in the laundry room and stuffed them into my tote bag. You see, I knew that we would eventually have to kill Rossi, and I saw the boots as a way to set up Conlin."

"You were already thinking that far ahead."

"Of course. I went to his resort one night and filled a bag with the clay they were using to surface his tennis courts. I made sure I had plenty of it on the soles of the boots, and I wore them to Rossi's house the night I killed him."

"And then you put the boots back in Conlin's closet."

She smiled and slowly nodded, like, "You got it."

"How about Jimbo's fingerprints on the glass in Rossi's house, the bloody handkerchief, the hair follicles? How'd you work all that?"

His mind raced as she laid everything out to him, obviously relishing the opportunity to share her brilliance with someone. He knew he would stay alive only as long as he could keep her bragging. "Why didn't you wear the boots again instead of sneakers, the night you went to Jennifer Belding's house and killed her friend? In fact, why did you kill Sarah Hanson?"

The smile disappeared. "I didn't kill that girl. I don't know any more about that than you do."

Sam shook his head, trying to clear the cobwebs forming. In spite of his predicament, his mind could only focus on what he had just heard. Why would she lie about Sarah Hanson's murder after just crowing about Rossi's. Did Jimbo kill her after all? What if he didn't?

Carole took a step toward him. "I think we've talked long enough." She held the gun with both hands.

Jesus! She was getting ready to shoot him. "One other question, Carole. Did you kill Melody?"

She waved her hand like that wasn't worth talking about. "She was a loudmouthed drunk who knew too much. But I don't want to go into that. I'm tired of this. You broke into my house, then tried to attack me. So I killed you in self-defense." She took a deep breath and her gun hand dipped down.

An audible click came from inside Sam's pocket. Carole's eyes widened and she screamed, "You sonofabitch, you've got a tape recorder. You bastard."

As she started to raise her gun hand, his foot flicked out and kicked the gun. It flew from her hand and skidded across the floor.

Her eyes followed the flight of the gun then returned to Sam. He froze, wondering what the hell to do now. She would have to retrieve the revolver. Maybe he could dash past her and out the door.

He watched her run her tongue along her lips as an animal might, eyeing a kill. The smile and dirty laugh told him she had no intention of scavenging for the gun.

She crouched, assuming a wrestler's pose and moved toward him. "Too bad for you, honey. A bullet would have been quicker. Now, this is going to be fun."

He backed away and went into his own crouch, hands out in front, feeling not only fear, but slightly ridiculous. As she moved slowly toward him, he kept reminding himself she was only a woman. It wasn't connecting.

She feinted to her right, and as he darted to avoid her, she clamped her arms around his stomach and lifted him off the floor. He pumped his legs, riding an imaginary bicycle going nowhere.

Pain seared through his body, and he gasped for breath that was no longer there. She pulled him to her and held him inches from her face. He watched the rivulets of sweat roll down her face, into her grinning mouth. She was having fun, squashing him like some kind of bug.

He gagged and coughed and felt the room spin. He knew he had to do something fast or it was all over for him, squashed to death by an AC-DC hooker.

He managed to get his hands under her chin and pushed at it with all his strength. The veins and muscles in her neck bulged, but to his horror, the chin and her head were unmoved. He felt like he was pushing a boulder uphill.

His hands slid up her face and found her eyes. He gouged a thumb into each eye, pushed in and pulled down. She screamed and flung him onto the bed. He landed on his stomach, and before he could roll over, she straddled him.

Again he felt the club like arms around him, this time his neck. He thought of the cops' description of Rossi's body. He thought of Melody's broken neck. He thought of Jennifer, Henry, his friends — all the good things in his life — and somehow found the strength to slide both his arms between hers and his neck, and force her to break her grip.

He rolled onto his back and swung his fists, catching her in the face with at least one wild punch. Again she screamed and cursed. The smile was gone and she hissed, "You'll pay for that, you bastard."

He managed to scramble to his knees and butted her face with his head. She reeled back, but as he rolled off the bed, she grabbed him in a hammer lock and wrestled him to the floor.

The two of them lay wedged between the bed and the wall. He was in deep trouble now with nowhere to go, no leverage and her powerful arms wrapped around his head. He felt the pressure increasing and was helpless to do anything about it. She slid her arms around his neck, zeroing in on his windpipe, using them as a garrote to squeeze the life from him.

She held him helpless now, one leg clamped over him. The other braced against the wall, her arms tightening around his throat.

He tried to raise his head and hit the underside of the bed. Christ! She had him stuffed half under the bed. He had nowhere to move. His efforts to force her arms away from his neck were too feeble to amount to anything.

More pressure on his windpipe. He was no longer sucking in air. He was underwater, groping desperately for the surface, flailing his arms, going nowhere.

He figured he had maybe ten, twenty seconds left, when his hand hit something just under the bed. The gun! He grabbed it, held it over his head, and fired.

The sound exploded into his ear, and his first thought was that he'd ruptured his eardrum. In his haze of semi-consciousness he heard a scream, and the pressure on his neck stopped.

He took several deep breaths, filling his lungs with precious air, rolled away from her grasp, and slid out from under her. He started to scramble to his feet, only to be yanked back to the floor.

Before he could move, she was again on top of him. Blood spewed from her left shoulder and dripped onto his face. The fucking woman is inhuman, he thought as she began pounding his face with her right fist, muttering words he couldn't decipher.

He felt the bridge of his nose crumble and remembered he still had the gun in his hand. With all the strength he could muster, he swung the gun into her wounded shoulder. She howled and rolled off him.

He staggered to his feet and backed away from the area, wet and slimy with blood from both of them. Carole managed to sit up and lean against the wall, looking dazed and confused.

He grabbed the handcuffs from the drawer and threw them to her. Keeping his distance and holding the gun on her, he sat on a chair and took several more deep breaths. His nose throbbed, but other than that, he began to feel like he would survive. "Put one of these on your wrist and the other on the bed post where it meets the crossbar," he said.

"Fuck you," she snarled. "Do it yourself."

There was no way he was going to get near her again. "Look, Carole, you're bleeding badly. I know something about bullet wounds and with the one you have, you'll bleed to death if I don't get some help for you."

Even with the blood pouring from her shoulder, she still wanted him. "You come over here and do it for me, honey."

"Forget it," he said, took out his cell phone, and called the police. And then he called Jennifer's office.

41

After the police arrived and took Carole and Sam's tape into custody, Sam prevailed upon them to give him an hour before going to the station to give his statement. He hopped into his car and headed for the Galt.

Jennifer's line was busy when he called. He knew why. She takes the goddamn phone off the hook when she works at night. And no answer at the house. He pounded his fist on the seat. The image of him trying to get in Jennifer's window flashed before him. "OK, take it easy," he said. "Don't get carried away again."

Still, he had bad vibes. Carole knowing nothing of Sarah's murder was a curve ball. The police were holding Jimbo only for Rossi's murder. Sarah's killer was still out there. Not necessarily. They have the size twelve sneaker prints, and only Jimbo's story that he went to see Jennifer during the day. That could be bullshit. He shook his head, not knowing what to believe now.

He pulled into the Galt parking lot, relieved that he'd made it without being stopped for speeding. The light was on in Jennifer's office, and her Jeep was parked outside. Time to go home, Jen.

He parked next to Jennifer's car, went to the front door, and opened it. Not too smart. She's out here this time of night alone and leaves the door unlocked.

The hall light was on and Jennifer's door was open. The woman's a workaholic. "Jen, it's me, Sam."

He walked into the empty office. The phone was off the hook. He hung it up and checked the ladies room. Dark and empty.

Back in the office, he tried calling her house and let it ring at least twenty times. Jen was a light sleeper. She'd have answered by now. Anyway, she wouldn't be there without her car.

And then he noticed her computer was gone and so were all the discs she kept next to it. Odd.

After checking Jennifer's Jeep and finding nothing out of the ordinary, he drove to her house and let himself in with the key she'd given him. He called the police and did the only thing he could do. He sat down and waited.

* * *

Thirty minutes earlier Jennifer got into the front seat of the man's car and they drove away. "Where are we going?" she asked.

The man gripped the steering wheel with one hand, the other held a revolver pointed at Jennifer. "Do you really want to know?"

She glanced at his face and shuddered. Even in the car's semi-darkness, his eyes glowed, as if reflecting madness behind them. At the very least he was unstable, and there was no denying the seriousness of her situation.

In spite of the air conditioning, bubbles of sweat lined his brow. She watched him take his hand from the steering wheel and wipe away the bubbles. They re-formed before he regained the wheel. He fidgeted in the driver's seat, and brushed his sleeve across his forehead.

"Yes, I want to know," she said with a calmness she didn't feel. She looked out the window and realized they were driving toward St. Armand's Circle. He would have to slow down going around the Circle, and she might be able to jump out.

As if reading her mind, he said, "We're going to a nice place. You'll like it. But don't get any funny ideas when we get to the Circle. I will shoot you right here in the car at the first sign of any foolishness. No one will even hear the shot."

She watched his constant motion, shifting his position in the seat, rubbing his eyes, looking out the window, back to her, gesturing wildly with the gun as he talked. She feared the cocked gun would go off any minute.

They were on the Circle now, and there was little traffic. He cruised past the few pedestrians still around, and headed toward the bridge and the mainland.

"You were about to tell me where we're going," she said.

"We're going to your final resting place, Jennifer."

"What do you mean, my final resting place?" She noticed the car had slowed as they encountered some traffic.

"I have selected the perfect spot to dispose of your body where no one will ever find you. You will have simply, he waved his hand, disappeared."

Her throat went dry and something twisted inside her stomach. She thought of Sarah and the ugly strangulation marks on her throat, and glanced again at the scary weapon pointed at her. "Does your job really mean that much to you to kill for it, Donald? You murdered an innocent young woman, and now you're going to kill me—all because of *donors*? How selfish and frivolous."

"It may sound frivolous to you, but you were bent on ruining my career, everything I've worked for. I know you never liked me and this was your way of punishing me, destroying me. You and your god-damn red tide." He spit the words out in a snake-like hiss.

Jennifer stared with disbelief at the man she thought she knew. His eyes bulged and a thick white saliva oozed from the corners of his mouth.

She had always thought of him as little more than an aggressive hustler, a bit of a creep, but certainly harmless. Somewhere along the way he had become a desperate, unbalanced killer. He's fucking crazy. "Of course I was the one you were after when you murdered Sarah. And now you're going to kill me. What a waste. Two murders and you will have nothing to show for it, Donald."

She flinched as he snapped his head toward her and jabbed her ribs with the gun. "What do you mean, 'Nothing to show for it', you stupid little fool? Do you think I haven't thought this through? Your computer and all your discs will be entombed with you, and I know what a loner you are with your work. Not even Cliff knows exactly where you stand. I think he'll be more than happy to let it lie for a while. Anyway, I happen to know that it will take months for someone else to get up to speed where you are. I can reassure our donors, particularly Conlin that they have nothing to fear." He began taking deep breaths as if the long speech had exhausted him.

In spite of her predicament, she allowed herself a smile. "Donald, Jimbo Conlin is in jail, charged with murdering Mike Rossi."

He turned to her again. His lips quivered as if trying to speak, but nothing came out.

She raised her eyebrows and nodded, as if to say, "Sorry, Donald."

He finally got the words out. "What are you talking about?"

"Just what I said. According to the detective in charge of the case, Conlin is going to be arraigned tomorrow. From what I hear, they have a strong case against him. So killing me will accomplish nothing for you. Even if you manage to salvage the other donors, without Conlin, you're toast."

She watched the expression drain from his face, and he seemed to shrink, the way a child might when being lectured. He went silent. What was he thinking? He had already admitted to her that he murdered Sarah and was going to kill her. He couldn't let her live now anyway.

"Oh, God," he said softly. "What have I done? Even if I wanted to spare you, I have no choice now. I'm sorry," he said in a whisper— more to himself than to her.

"Donald, listen to me. I—"

"Oh, goddamn it," he screamed and pounded the steering wheel.

She looked out the window and saw they had come to within three cars from the bridge, and the barriers were down, stopping traffic.

"The fucking bridge is going up," Donald shrieked.

She watched the two sections of the bridge separate and slowly rise, leaving a gaping hole over the water. Off to the right two large masted boats waited patiently for the signal to proceed. Through the side mirror Jennifer watched the cars lining up behind them, a solid phalanx of vehicles as far as her eyes could see.

They sat in silence. Donald stared straight ahead, his one hand squeezing the wheel until his knuckles were white and his face crimson. Jennifer kept her eyes on the traffic behind her. One car, three in back of them, moved slightly to the side, revealing a dome on the roof of a car behind it. Police car!

The sailboats cruised under the bridge and continued under motor until they were nearly out of sight. The bridge stayed put.

"Come on, open this fucking thing, you stupid bastard," Donald scolded the bridge tender. And still they sat.

A car's horn tooted. And then another. Donald leaned on his, joining the chorus of frustration. A man got out of the car in front of them and looked up at the tender. Another joined him, and soon the road was filled with people, milling about, gawking over the rails, and glaring at the hapless bridge man.

Jennifer alternated between watching the action outside and keeping an eye on Donald, who was now slumped in his seat, perspiration covering his face. He turned and stared at her. She met his gaze. Was it sweat or was that a tear she saw rolling from his eye? She watched his face distort into a child-like pucker, as if she was his mommy, and she would comfort him. Christ.

She glanced back at the police car and at the growing crowd outside. "Donald, the bridge is stuck. There is a large crowd of people outside, and a police vehicle three cars behind us. If you will excuse me, I'm getting out of the car and going home."

He raised the gun and held it with both hands. "Y-you try that and I'll kill you."

She looked at his hands, shaking as if he'd developed palsy, while she was looking out the window. "Don't be foolish, Donald." She slid her hand toward the door handle. "What you just told me is my word against yours. No one knows you killed Sarah. You kill me now and what have you gained? A sure trip to death row. I walk out of this car, and the worst that might happen to you is a kidnapping charge. Slide the gun off the bridge and who knows? You might even beat that."

She clicked the unlock and opened the door. "See you, Donald." She held her breath and stepped onto the road, bracing herself for a bullet in the back. When none came, she scurried along the road toward the police car. As she reached the cop, she turned and looked toward Donald. Through the rear window, she saw him, head down on the steering wheel, pounding his fists against the dashboard.

42

Sam opened his eyes for a second and closed them, trying to focus on where he was. He blinked several times until he remembered he was nestled in his own bed.

He rolled over and shrieked as the pain shot down his neck and into his ribs. Henry bounded into the room and hopped onto the bed. "Easy, boy," Sam whispered. "I'm a hurtin' dude."

Henry studied Sam's nose, moved in to get a closer look, and barked twice. Sam put a hand up and touched the large band-aids covering his nose, so swollen, he could see it. "It's OK, Henry, just a little temporary problem. It'll go away."

That seemed to mollify Henry, who leaped off the bed and disappeared into the kitchen. Sam lifted himself to a sitting position and reflected on last night's events.

It had been a long night, beginning with his visit to Carole's house, and ending when he finally left the police station at four a.m. In between he had watched Jennifer walk through her front door, accompanied by two police officers and listened to her bizarre escapade with Donald. She was exhausted, drained, and wanted only to go to bed.

Once again Sam insisted that she come home with him, but the police had orders to bring him to the station, where Detective Lewis awaited his statement. Anyway, Jen wanted to go to bed immediately.

He had agreed on the condition that one officer remain at Jennifer's until morning. Not that she was in any danger, but he simply refused to leave her alone. They agreed and he left with one of the officers.

On the way to the station he learned that Carole's wound turned out to be less severe than he thought. The bullet had only grazed her shoulder and ripped some cartilage.

When they reached the police station, Sam was ushered into a conference room, where Diane Lewis and another detective named Washington took a detailed statement from him. He also learned that Carole gave them a full confession and implicated Alexis. Donald was in custody on the kidnapping charge, and they were working on a plea bargain deal for a confession to Sarah's murder. When they finished, Lewis, who had said little during the proceedings, asked Sam to join her in her office. He smiled and followed her. Time for a little praise after all the shit he'd taken from her.

Instead of the praise he expected, he was stunned by a royal chewing out.

"Goddam it, Sam, what kind of asshole, stupid, maverick, loose cannon trick did you think you were pulling, breaking into a citizen's house like that. Not only could you have blown the whole case against them by breaking and entering without a search warrant, but do you realize you can also be prosecuted for burglary?" Through it all she waved her finger at him like he was a schoolboy.

That's probably what did it. He erupted. "Now you just wait one fucking minute. First of all, I happen to know and so do you, that as a private citizen I don't need a search warrant and without it I don't put your case in jeopardy. It's only if you, the police, break in without a warrant."

He was warming up to it now. "I also know that you as police officers need to get permission before you can tape someone and use the tape as admissible evidence. I, as a private citizen, do not need to have permission. My tape is a gift to you and the prosecutor. Even Carole knows that and that's why you got her confession.

"And finally, you're telling me I can be prosecuted for burglary is bullshit, and you know it. I could only be charged with 'malicious intent.' If you want to do that, be my guest."

He headed for the door and turned. "So, you can bust my chops all you want without even a thank you, but don't talk to me like I'm

some naive burglar who doesn't know his ass from the proverbial hole in the ground."

He had his hand on the doorknob when she finally spoke. "You can't leave now for two reasons."

He faced her, the smoke still steaming from him. "Oh?"

"Yes, first of all you need to sign your statement. Secondly," and here she broke into a broad grin. "I need to thank you for your help in solving this case and possibly saving an innocent man's life." She walked over to him and put her hand out. "I humbly apologize for 'busting your chops'."

He hesitated, ran his fingers across the bandage on his nose, then grinned, and offered his hand. "Apology accepted."

She pulled out a bottle of Jack Daniels from her desk drawer. "I keep this here for medicinal purposes and for celebrations. Will you join me?"

He nodded and she poured three fingers for each of them. He was not a Jack Daniels fan, but it never looked better than at that moment.

"This is a toast of thanks, Sam," she said, raising her glass.

He did the same and was about to drink when she added, "And a gentle reminder."

"OK, what now?" he said and set his glass down.

She smiled and shook her head. "Drink your whiskey, Sam and then we'll talk a little."

He shrugged and raised the glass again. The drink went down so smoothly, he took two more sips. Diane did the same, and neither said anything while they enjoyed the bourbon.

For the first time in the long night, he relaxed. And it was good to see Diane let her hair down, both figuratively and literally. Somewhere during the course of their conversation it had come unpinned and hung loosely at her shoulders.

It was late and she looked tired, but he also saw an earthy sultriness. Must be the whiskey.

She read his mind. "Sam, whether you know it or not, I like you. It's probably just as well that you appear to be involved with Ms. Belding, so we can keep our relationship strictly professional."

That one came right out of left field. He took another slug of his bourbon.

"I hear that you're thinking of staying around here for a while. Let me caution you that if you plan to continue playing detective, you'll have to get a license. Otherwise there can be no more cooperation from us. I'm sure you understand."

He was still digesting her comment about him and Jennifer when he noticed she had stopped and was awaiting his reply. "Uh, yes I do understand, Diane. Actually, I am thinking quite seriously about settling here, and if I do, I just might get a license."

"Good," she said and freshened their drinks.

43

As Sam started to get out of bed, his head throbbed with a pounding headache, along with everything else. "Where the hell did the headache come from?" he wondered aloud. And then he remembered the Jack Daniels.

He had to agree it was good that he was involved with Jennifer. A fella could get into some serious trouble with that detective lady.

But it was Jennifer that he wanted to see. He got out of bed, fed Henry, and carried the portable phone to the balcony. The fresh sea breeze washed away his headache, and the cloudless sky promised a beautiful day. His sliver of bay glistened with the color of the sky. He punched in the numbers and waited.

"Hello, this is Jennifer." He smiled when he heard the familiar melodious voice. He wasn't sure what to expect, but she sounded alert and upbeat. "Hi. How do you feel?"

"I took a sleeping pill and slept like a baby. I feel fine. I've been up for an hour—waiting for your call. How are you? You sound funny."

"Yeah, well it's probably my nose. It feels like there's a big clothespin on it."

"Oh, Sam. You—"

"Anyway," he interrupted her. "I have but one wish in life at the moment."

"Oh? You want to tell me what that is?"

Her chuckle was barely audible. But it was still good to hear her laugh again. "Yep. It's to spend the entire day with you. How 'bout if I drive over and we enjoy the day on Lido Beach?"

"No, I don't think so," she said.

His smile disappeared. "Why not?"

"Because my favorite beach is on Siesta Key. Why don't you put some coffee on, and I'll be there in a couple hours?"

Back came his smile, broader than the other. "Sounds good to me, but why two hours? Keep me waiting that long, and I might be out of control when you get here."

"Good, maybe I'll make you wait three hours. Seriously, Sam, I need to check the progress of the red tide for a while. It's changing directions. Tell you about it when I see you."

Henry appeared from inside and leaped onto Sam's lap. Sam scratched his ears and belly. Henry squeaked and sighed and burrowed in a little further. "Yeah, you're being nice to me again now that your new buddy's not around, huh?" Henry responded by licking his nose twice, being careful to avoid the band-aids.

After taking Henry for a walk, Sam made coffee and turned the television to the Sarasota News Network. He sat and listened as the announcer reported last night's events.

"Both Carole Durning and Alexis Helfrich are in custody and will be arraigned and charged with the two murders. Durning has reportedly signed a full confession implicating Helfrich. Details of what led police to Durning are sketchy at the moment.

"SNN has, however learned that a private citizen was instrumental in breaking this very high profile case. James Conlin, prominent developer and long time Sarasota resident, has been released and cleared of all charges. As more details emerge we will bring you up to date."

Sam sipped his coffee and smiled. "A private citizen who got his ass chewed for 'breaking this high profile case'."

The newscaster continued. "In other news, police arrested Donald Frazier, director of development at the Galt Marine Laboratory, for the armed kidnapping of Jennifer Belding, a marine biologist at the Galt. Police believe Frazier may have had something to do with the murder of Sarah Hanson, house guest of the same Ms. Belding. As more—"

Too early in the morning to absorb all this, Sam. He turned off the TV, and poured himself more coffee. So much happening, he'd almost forgot about Jimbo. He checked his answering machine. Nothing. Old Jimbo's probably sleeping it off. That's what he'd be doing if he'd been through what Jimbo has.

His nose ached, and his whole torso felt like he'd been rolled over by a truck. At the moment Jimbo had no corner on the misery market. In his wildest dreams, he never expected his nice little vacation in placid Sarasota to turn into this. He was reminded of why he was here in the first place, which in turn, reminded him how he had twice sidestepped Jennifer's curiosity over his dismissal from Whately. No big deal. He would simply tell her the whole story, including the skunk in Piro's office. Knowing Jennifer, she'll find the whole thing funny.

The breeze drifted in through the open doors. He closed his eyes and breathed deeply. He liked Sarasota, and the idea of moving back to Boston held very little appeal. The wild card, of course, was Jennifer. Take it slow, stick around, and see what happens.

The noise of heavy machinery shattered his reverie. He looked up and saw a huge girder being maneuvered into place on the condo rapidly rising next door. He closed the doors and thought of Miss Bunting and Henry's expanding waistline. Much as he'd come to like Sarasota, the prospect of long term residency in Paradise Towers made his stomach turn. It also reminded him he hadn't eaten.

After a breakfast of scrambled eggs, toast, and more coffee, he showered, shaved, and faced his first major decision of the day. Should he wear sandals or sneakers?

It was 11:30 when his buzzer rang. "Hi, it's me," she said. The two hours had stretched to three and a half, and he felt butterflies waiting for her to knock on the door.

When she did, Henry went into his routine, yapping at the door and waiting, tail straight out, to vanquish the intruder.

"Easy boy," Sam said. "It's your sweetie, Jennifer." He opened the door, and when she stepped into the room, he decided he was in love.

The sun filtering through the balcony doors found her red hair and radiated through it, weaving it into a lustrous lamé. Her eyes sparkled, and her complexion glowed with good health.

"You look," he paused, trying to find the right words. "Like a, like a morning sunrise," he finally blurted.

"Well, that's a new one," she said, fending off Henry's efforts to climb on her. "Sounds like a compliment, though." She reached over and caressed his cheek. "But look at your nose, Sam."

"I am. You want some coffee? I just made it."

She nodded. "Sam, I watched SNN just before coming over. They filled in a little bit of what you left out last night. I'm afraid I didn't absorb much anyway, after what I'd been through with that idiot, Donald. Tell me the whole story."

"Sit and I'll tell you," he said, handing her a cup of coffee. He joined her on the sofa and told her everything, beginning with his jail visit with Jimbo on through the encounter with Big Carole and her confession.

Through it all, she said nothing. Her mouth fell open and gaped wider with each twist of the story. "How did you know Carole wouldn't be home?"

"I called Alexis, disguised my voice with a German accent, and said I was a John looking for a date with Carole. She said Carole had appointments all evening, and wouldn't be available until ten. I said thanks, but I would try tomorrow. Jimbo had given me Carole's address, and I figured I had all evening, but she came home early."

When he finished, she remained silent, staring at him. She set her coffee down, leaned toward him, and spoke in a half whisper. "Sam, I think you're a little nutty."

He laughed uneasily, not sure if she meant it. "Yes, someone else has already pointed that out."

"Detective Lewis?"

He nodded. "Good guess. So you think I'm cuckoo too, huh?"

She covered his hand with hers and squeezed it. "Of course not. I just think you're—different."

He took his hand away and placed it over his nose again. "Hmm."

"Sam, that was a very brave and incredibly risky thing you did. And it could have turned out disastrously. It almost did. What made you think you would find anything at Carole's that would link her to any of the murders?"

"Well, one of the things Jimbo told me was that Carole was a born thief. Couldn't keep her hands off anything that looked to be of value. She had taken jewelry from him and when confronted, even laughed and said she was a kleptomaniac. After that he said he always took off his watch and rings and hid them whenever he knew he'd be with her." He got up and poured them more coffee and continued.

"I remember admiring Rossi's Cartier watch and diamond ring the two times I saw him. I asked Lewis if he was wearing them when they found the body. He wasn't."

"That's still a big leap you made," she said. "Anyone who killed him would have been tempted to take jewelry like that. If Jimbo did it, he probably would have taken them to make it look like a robbery."

"I know, but with everything else Jimbo told me, I just had this gut feeling that she did it and decided to try my luck. She was very clever. Once when she and Jimbo had a drink together at her place, she saved the glass with his fingerprints on it and put it on Rossi's table after she killed him. She then pressed Rossi's fingerprints on another glass to make it look like the two of them had a drink together before Jimbo killed him."

"What else?"

"Jimbo told me she liked to get physical. The last time he saw her, she got carried away, pulled his hair and hit him in the nose, giving him a nose bleed." His hand instinctively went up again. "She wiped the blood with a handkerchief and saved some of the hand full of hair she'd pulled out. Planted them at the scene of Rossi's murder. She actually dropped the bloody handkerchief in the driveway. Gotta hand it to her. She really knew how to put it to old Jimbo."

"Speaking of whom, have you heard from him?"

He got up, put the coffee mugs in the sink, and checked his watch. "No, I haven't. He's probably still sleeping. Hey, what's new on the red tide?"

She sighed and walked to the balcony doors, where she stood with her back to Sam. "The tide has definitely changed direction. I've been tracking it again all morning. It veered sharply west, and should hit somewhere between Galveston, Texas and Tampico, Mexico."

"That's good news, Jen. Why so glum?"

She turned and walked over to him. "I've caused a lot of trouble over nothing. If I hadn't cried wolf, Sarah would still be alive. And somehow, I pushed Donald over the edge. I had no idea how fragile — and dangerous he was. None of us did. It's just all so sad." She slumped against him and he held her in his arms.

"Jen, you can't beat up on yourself. You're a scientist, and you did what you're paid to do. You conducted your research and followed where it went. It's what you do. You had no way of knowing how unstable Frazier was. You said yourself that none of you did." He took her face in his hands.

When she turned the beautiful green eyes on him and slowly nodded, he brought her face up to his and kissed her.

She wrapped her arms around him and held on. He closed his eyes and lost himself into a world where only the two of them existed and nothing else mattered.

She lifted her lips from his and began gently rubbing him and whispering his name. The doorbell rang. And they quickly separated, as if having been caught. Sam grinned at her and eyed the door. Jennifer shrugged, like, "It's your call."

He kissed her again, but the buzzer refused to let up. Whoever was pushing it wasn't going to go away. He disengaged himself and Jennifer leaned against the wall, catching her breath.

"Yes, what is it," Sam asked the intercom.

Jimbo's voice filled the room. "Sam. I knew you were there. Saw your car. I gotta see you, Sam. Now. Won't wait. Beam me up."

He looked at Jennifer, who rolled her eyes, but nodded. "You should see him, Sam."

Sam rang him in and two minutes later he appeared. Sam opened the door and greeted a different Jimbo from the one he'd last seen in jail.

His eyes were bright and clear. He looked well rested and, most astonishing to Sam, he wore a neatly pressed pair of slacks and a stylish shirt with a little polo player logo. The only remnants of the old Jimbo were his high top sneakers. He burst through the door and grabbed Sam in a bear hug. "Sam, I love ya," he said softly and continued to hold on.

Sam extricated himself from the big man's grasp and rubbed his ribs. "Jimbo, this is Jennifer Belding."

Jimbo shook Jennifer's hand like he loved her, too, pumping it up and down. "A pleasure. It's a pleasure."

Sam and Jennifer stood by while Jimbo poured out emotional thank yous to Sam and hugged him several more times.

"Sam, you're the only person who would listen to me, and you believed me, didn't you?"

Sam watched the big fella vent a warmth and emotion that was very appealing. It was a side of Jimbo that was nice to see. "I did, Jimbo. Don't ask me why, but I did."

Jimbo glanced at Jennifer and remained standing. "Listen, I don't want to barge in on you two and interrupt whatever plans you had, but—what happened to your nose, Sam?"

"Cut myself shaving."

"It's OK, Jimbo," Jennifer spoke up. "We were just leaving to go to the beach."

Sam looked at her and wondered if they were really going to get to the beach before Jimbo called. He doubted it. The thought crossed his mind that he should have left him in jail.

"Hey, that's great," Jimbo said. "But first stop by my cottage. I bought some champagne to celebrate. Help me drink a bottle and celebrate with me. OK?"

Sam and Jennifer exchanged glances and grins. It was the right thing to do, and they both knew it. "OK," Sam said. "We'll follow you over."

44

"Jimbo, this place is adorable," Jennifer said as they walked onto the deck of the cottage. Sam was still in his car, spreading towels along the top of the dashboard to protect the expensive wood paneling from the sun. Eventually, he would have to find a better way, but for now the towels would have to do.

"Hell, you ain't even been inside yet, Jennifer. Come on in." He unlocked the door and Sam and Henry joined them.

Jennifer oohed and ahed as they stood in the sun dappled kitchen overlooking a living room furnished in wicker and glass. Tropical Andrea Beloff prints adorned the walls. Jimbo took them on a quick tour of the two bedrooms and two baths and provided a running commentary.

"You like all these pretty pastel colors, Jennifer? Had it all done in these blues and pinks and teals. Kinda like a Bermuda cottage."

"Oh yes," she said. "It all looks so cheerful and tropical. You have good taste, Jimbo."

Sam wandered around on his own, admiring the place. He took a whiff of the fresh flowers on the kitchen counter and smiled. Jimbo does have a touch.

Jimbo and Jennifer appeared. "Come on, you guys, let's have some champagne on the deck." He took a bottle from the refrigerator, uncorked it, and set it down with three glass flutes.

Sam held up the bottle. "Dom Perignon. You *are* up for a celebration."

Jimbo looked surprised and shrugged. "Dunno. I just asked the guy to give me the best in the store and that's what he gave me." He poured the champagne, grabbed the bottle, and led the way to the deck.

The tall oleander bushes were in full bloom, shielding the deck from the street. They sat in companionable silence, listening to the

291

sounds of the Gulf a block away. Henry sprawled next to Jennifer and was soon fast asleep.

Jimbo raised his glass. "Sam, I ain't much for speeches, but I gotta tell you I liked you the first time I saw you. Said to myself, there's a gentleman. Little did I know that from that chance meeting, you were going to save my life. You didn't have to do that, Sam, risking your life to help me."

Jennifer nodded and tilted her glass to Sam. Sam didn't say anything, just grinned and lifted his glass. After they drank their toast, Jimbo set his glass down and pulled Sam to his feet. He wrapped him in another of his bear hugs and barely choked out the words. "Thank you, Sam."

Sam felt the big man's body shake, literally feeling the emotion coming from him. "Hell, Jimbo, I probably did the county a favor. You'd have eaten that jailhouse broke in a week."

Jimbo released Sam and poured them all more champagne. "Sam, I got something for ya." He held up the key to the cottage and handed it to Sam.

"What's this for?"

"It's for you to use the cottage all you want. Enjoy."

Sam started to speak, but Jimbo talked over him. "And just to make sure you use it, I got somethin' else for you." He reached in his pocket and handed Sam a piece of paper.

Sam glanced at it and turned to Jennifer. "It's the deed to the cottage."

Jimbo squared his shoulders and beamed at them. "Yep, and it's got your name on it. The cottage is yours, Sam."

Sam looked at Jennifer for help, but all he got was a shit eating grin and a puzzled look. He shook his head. "Jimbo, I love the cottage, and it's very generous of you. But I can't accept it."

Jimbo's smile faded.

"But I will happily take it, if you let me pay you the fair market price," Sam added.

It was Jimbo's turn to shake his head. "Sam, you made me a very happy man by what you did. Now don't be a prick and deprive me of the chance to make you happy. Jennifer, tell him he's bein' a prick."

"You're being a prick, Sam."

"How much?" Sam asked.

Jimbo looked toward Jennifer. "You been around this town a long time, Jennifer. What do you think a dinky little cottage that's gotta be at least twenty-five, thirty years old is worth?"

Jennifer nodded and stroked her chin. "Needs a lot of work. It's probably going to need a new roof soon. Big bucks. An old building like this has to be loaded with termites. Mega bucks to get rid of them." She screwed up her face. "Hmm. Top dollar to take this old place off your hands would be, I'd say three, four thousand dollars."

Jimbo winked at her. "That's 'bout what I would figure." He snatched back the deed, scrawled something on it, and handed it back to Sam.

Sam read it aloud. "Sold to Sam Wallace for three thousand dollars. James Conlin."

"That's it, Sam," Jimbo said. "Ain't no room for negotiating. Take it or leave it."

Sam looked at Jennifer. She smiled and said, "Take it, Sam."

Sam eyed them both for a couple of beats and threw up his hands. "It's a deal."

"Good," Jimbo said. "Now, let's have some more champagne."

By the time they finished off the champagne at 6:30, dark thunder clouds had settled in and the air was thick with moisture.

"Gonna pour like hell any minute," Jimbo said. "I better head down the Key and get home."

They shook hands and promised to get together soon. Sam put up the top of his car manually, struggling and muttering again, closed the windows, and made it onto the deck a step ahead of the rain. Inside, he joined Jennifer and Henry. "So much for the beach," he said.

"Yes, but I'm glad we did this. He's much different from what I expected. He's really a good person."

"Yeah. Nothing like a stay in the slammer to humble a guy." He opened the refrigerator. "My God! It's full of champagne. All Dom Perignon."

"Open one," she said and hunkered onto the couch.

"Sounds good to me." Now that it was all over, he did feel like celebrating, but as he opened the champagne, a wave of sadness swept over him. Three people killed in such a short time, and the saddest of all was the innocent Sarah.

But now at least the police had the people responsible for it all, and he had something to do with not only that, but saving an innocent man from a possible death sentence. He poured the champagne and snuggled into the sofa next to Jennifer.

She flicked on the TV, and they recognized Cynthia Mayfair in her party finery, microphone in hand. "We are here tonight, celebrating the gala grand opening of the Ritz Hotel, for which all of Sarasota's party-goers have waited so long. It's a big night tonight as we Sarasotans celebrate our very own Ritz Hotel.

"Actually, tonight we celebrate two events. All the celebs are gathered for another important fundraiser, this one to benefit the *Save the Coral Snake Foundation*. Here with me are some of the movers and shakers, who, along with several hundred of their nearest and dearest, hope to raise over three hundred thousand dollars for this worthy cause."

"See what else is on," Sam said. "Oops, wait a minute." The camera panned the room and settled on a table filled with people in formal wear. "You see what I see?"

Jennifer nodded. "Yep. There he is."

Sam recognized several of the local "celebs" from the disastrous fundraiser at Mickey's on West, and there, craning his head toward the camera, in the thick of it all, sat Francis J. Wilson.

Cynthia Mayfair and her microphone strolled across the room to the table. "I'm here at the head table, where Sarasota's finest are gathered. I see Joshua Fishman and his lovely wife, Edna. Oh, and

294

there's Finley Spaulding and the Dexter Kingmans, and Sid and Selma Golden. Oh, this is a power table," Cynthia cooed.

Francis J. bobbed up and down and waved his arms. Cynthia walked over to him. "And of course Francis J. Wilson, who has rapidly become one of Sarasota's most ardent benefactors. Good evening, Francis. Splendid affair, isn't it?"

Francis nodded and reached for the microphone. Cynthia raised it out of his reach and continued. "I know how deeply you care about the cause which has brought us here tonight, Francis."

She lowered the microphone into Francis' waiting hands. He cleared his throat and gestured dramatically. "Yes, Cynthia, I have long been a supporter of the *Save the Coral Snake Foundation*, and I am pleased to be here this evening in this lovely atmosphere of Sarasota's Ritz Hotel. And furthermore—"

Cynthia raised her microphone and moved on.

Sam turned off the TV. "Well, Francis has finally made it. All's well with the world." The champagne was kicking in, and his earlier wave of sadness was replaced by a mellow contentment. "Jennifer, you've asked me about Whately and never got an answer."

"Hmm, hmm." She raised her head and kissed him. "You're a nice man, Sam Wallace."

"And you're a nice lady." He returned her kiss, and they let things follow their natural course.

When they surfaced for air, Jennifer whispered, "Seems like every time we're going to talk about Whately, we get sidetracked."

"Yes, I . . ."

She rolled onto him and covered his lips with hers. "We'll get around to it. But not right now."